The Last Post

by

Marcello Antonius Versace Tino

Thompson and Prince

The Last Post 2nd Edition
© Marcello Tino1998, 2016, 2019
Publisher: Thompson and Prince
Distributors: Amazon.com, Ingram Book Company, Baker & Taylor

ISBN - 13: 978-0-578-62171-5

Library of Congress Control Number: 2016911461
Thompson and Prince, Ithaca, NY

Key Words: American Literature, Fiction, Historical Novel, War Novel, World War Two, Korean War, Vietnam War.

Logo designed by William Benson

Acknowledgment

I've been a lucky man. The one person who I love the most loves my writing, my wife, Lorraine. For better or worse, I couldn't have written this book without her. I would also like to acknowledge my brother Joseph Tino, an award-winning poet, who was an excellent reader for me. Barbara Smith, who is a talented writer in her own right, was helpful in proofing the novel. Dan Weaver, who I knew when he was an editor at Random House, and who is now a teacher at Emerson College, was the first professional editor to recognize my writing, and his encouragement as both an editor and educator was very important to me. More recently, his feedback on the novel has been helpful. Finally, I would like to thank the veterans who I grew to know. They were the inspiration for the story, just by being who they are.

The Last Post

Prologue

The time is now. James Caleb Brown is at Arlington Cemetery amidst an army of white gravestones. He is standing in front of the graves of his two best friends, Charlie Tremaine and Bob Sumner.   In the background, he hears gun fire coming from the direction of the Capitol Building and the National Mall where supporters of the president have assembled. The president, whose supporters like to call him "The Boss", recently lost the election, but he has claimed that it was fixed, and he has called on his followers to march on Washington in protest. They have come, and they have come armed, thousands upon thousands of them, many of whom are veterans. Based on the news that James Caleb Brown was receiving from his cell phone, one hundred thousand people are laying siege to the Capital and the battle has begun.

How did we get to where we are now? It seemed to James Caleb Brown, who was called the Reverend by his friends because he was the post chaplain at the VFW, that with each war that we have fought, we have become madder and madder, and, now, in an ultimate act of madness, we have turned against each other, and we are at the threshold of a civil war. What have we done wrong? What is it that we have left unresolved? What have we lost or ignored? What is gnawing at our bones?

The ancients believed that everyone of us is a reflection of the universe, and the universe reflects us, that we are the microcosm of the macrocosm, and like the DNA in each individual cell, we can recreate the whole body of truth in our individual stories. That may be so, the Reverend thought, because, somehow, he believed that the answer is here, with Bob, with him, with Charlie, and with all the men buried here who sacrificed their lives for their country and haunted our history. Here, today, the past that has been buried in our forgotten memories has risen from the dead and is alive amongst us raging at the nexus of our being.

"Beware!" the Reverend shouted to no one and everyone.

Chapter One

It was 1996. Charlie Tremaine and his wife Daisy were attending a Memorial Day service at Dewitt Park in remembrance of the men and women who had fought and died in America's wars. Dewitt Park, located in the middle of downtown Ithaca, New York, had been the commons for the original settlers of Ithaca. Many of those settlers were soldiers in the Continental Army during the American Revolutionary War, and they had marched through this same piece of land when it was a burning Indian cornfield with stalks of corn taller than a man on horseback. They had set the fields on fire as part of a campaign to push the Iroquois out of what was their homeland and into Canada, a place from which they would never return. After the Revolutionary War, when the government offered the veterans land grants in payment for their service in the Continental Army, many of the veterans remembered the richness of the Finger Lakes region and settled in the area. Charlie's great-great-grandfather was one of those men, a beneficiary of the bounty that came from America's first war.

Present day Dewitt Park was a well-kept tree lined park with brick walkways, ornate wrought-iron and wood benches, antique street lanterns, and a splattering of lilacs, violets, and daffodils. Age old oak trees stood as sentinels along the pathways, and they all led to the center of the park and the monuments dedicated to the war dead. High above the monuments, an American flag fluttered in the wind.

At the far end of the park stood the Presbyterian Church, an old stone fortress structure with turrets to protect the believers from evil. Next to the Presbyterian Church stood another old church that had been converted into the city courthouse. In the courtroom, the city magistrate sat like a Puritan elder passing judgement day after day enthroned below a stained-glass window of God and his angels. Across the street, on the corner of Seneca and Cayuga Street, loomed Saint John's Episcopal Church with its needle point spire and its old quilted notions of body and soul. Charlie was married in that church. It was where Daisy and he prayed for peace and happiness and a good life for their children.

Across the street from Saint John's stood the old red brick schoolhouse that had been turned into a co-op apartment building and a mini mall. With its Gothic touches and factory style steel framed windows from the 50s, it gave the impression of being a cross between a warehouse for teenage testosterone and an ancient temple of learning haunted by the ghost of children's laughter.

4

Charlie looked up at one of the large multi-paned windows on the second floor, and he wondered in amusement why anyone would want to live in Mrs. Brewer's English classroom. He could imagine himself drunk, standing in front of door to his own apartment, afraid to go in because he didn't do his homework. Charlie smiled at the thought and the crazy quilt Ivy League college town he lived in surrounded by rural America. Some people joked that Ithaca was ten square miles surrounded by reality, but this was his hometown, and for better or worse this was where he was born, and this would probably be where he would die.

Charlie listening to the VFW post chaplain James Caleb Brown, who they called the Reverend say, "This is our story. This is our life. These are our brothers and sisters who died defending our country. Let us not forget."

Charlie wanted to believe this. He wanted to believe that this was "one country under God with freedom and justice for all." After all, that was what he believed he was fighting for, but Charlie could not help feeling depressed and disappointed. There were so few people at the park to honor the dead. In fact, some of the men in the honor guard looked like they had been resurrected from their graves to attend the ceremony. The rest of the men in the honor guard looked like what they were, just working-class guys who had fought for their country, been used up, and then discarded. In fact,

most of the vets who were there at the memorial service were working class men, except for Harry Woods who was an accountant and
Jeff Spence who owned a plumbing supply business and Harry
Travis who was a lawyer. At one time the mayor would have been
there, but this year they didn't even have enough people for a pa-
rade. Nobody seemed to care; most of the pedestrians who were
walking along the sidewalk at the edge of the park ignored the ceremony; and at the far end of the park, a group of college kids were
kicking a soccer ball around.

Whenever Charlie drove through the Cornell campus on a job
or to see his daughter who was a student at Cornell University, he
always was amazed at how many students were walking around
with cell phones to their ear or texting while they were walking or
crossing the street, totally oblivious of the world around. They
walked about like they were the center of the universe, and maybe
they are. Even his daughter who might as well be in China for as
much as he sees her anymore, said to him, "You're old and tired,
and we're fresh and new."

She's probably right. Charlie was tired just watching the students play. One of the students chased the soccer ball as it rolled
and bounced into the memorial service. Charlie envied him. He
was totally oblivious and innocent of the death that never dies.
Charlie wondered if even God cared. It was a beautiful sunny day,

and it should be raining. It should be raining an ocean of blood and tears for all the men, women, and children who have died and all the families that have grieved and are grieving. Charlie wondered if that is what the Biblical Apocalypse would be like, a collective scream of horror, or do we experience an apocalypse every time a newborn baby is born?

Charlie reminded himself that this is Memorial Day, and it was a time to remember, and so he did. He remembered another sunny day, when everywhere he looked, he could see B-17 Flying Fortresses, three hundred bombers spanning fifteen miles of blue sky. With their giant wings and aluminum skin they looked like 20th century mutations of prehistoric birds-of-prey flying 25,000 feet above sea level. It was twenty degrees below zero at that altitude, but things could get hot quick. The B-17 was filled with 20,000 gallons of high-octane gasoline, 150 gallons of oil, miles of pipes filled with extremely combustible hydraulic fluids, 14000 rounds of ammunition, and eight tons of bombs. One spark could turn the Flying Fortress into a flying inferno, but even though Charlie could get blown away at any moment, even though he was only a tail gunner, and even though he only got to see everything in retrospect or head on from the rear, Charlie loved it up here. Up here, he wasn't a nobody anymore. Up here, he was a somebody involved in a historical life and death struggle of good and evil.

"Hey, Ass End Charlie, are you awake back there?"

"Yes, sir, Cap."

"Keep alert, Charlie, we're in Kraut air space now. That goes for the rest of you jokers too. Let's hear it."

Everyone checked in. It was a ten-man crew. The Cap was Bob Stewart. He was a college boy before he enlisted. Bob wanted to be a lawyer, and he'd probably make a good lawyer too. He had the gift of gab, and he was cool under pressure. Sometime the crew called him Father Bob because he was the Flight Commander, and he was responsible for everyone, but they also called him Father Bob because they were more like a family than a crew. Cap was only twenty-three years old, and what was funny about him was that he always wore his Commander's flight cap wherever he went, even to bed when he was drunk. It was like he had to always re-mind himself that he was a grownup and the man in charge. Whenever the crew felt like The Cap had gone too far, they waited until he was drunk; and, then, when he had passed out, they hid his cap. When he woke up, he got really upset and looked all over for his cap until finally someone said, "Oh, look here, Cap. I found it," and they all laughed.

Cap, mad as hell, called them all, "Asshole," and then walked out, but he got the message. It was all in good fun. Sometimes they had to make a joke out of the situations they were in and make fun of how much their lives depended on each other, but when Bob Stewart got behind the controls of The Big Ass Bird, he was the Flight Commander, The Captain, Our Father, our spiritual leader, totally in command, no questions asked, and they were totally confident in him, if for no other reason than Father Bob had led them through Hell and back, not once but through eighteen missions.

The copilot was Bill O'Donnell, an Irish boy from Boston. Billy Boy had dropped out of Boston College during the depression, but he planned to go back to school and finish up. He didn't know what he wanted to be, except that he wanted to be somebody too. Billy Boy was okay, but he had a sharp tongue and a big mouth, and he was always cutting people up, especially when he was drunk. If there was a fight in a bar, you could bet that it was Billy Boy who started it, but he was a very good copilot and it took two very good pilots to efficiently fly The Big Ass Bird.

Steve Gilbert was the flight engineer and top gunner, and he was a career guy. Steve had been a crew chief before he was an engineer, and he knew the plane inside and out. Steve made sure that The Big Ass Bird was in tip top shape, and if anything went wrong, he fixed it. They called him Grandpa or just plain Pops because everyone else was in their teens or early twenties, and Grandpa Gilbert was twenty-six years old, and most of the time they saw him as having more experience, more sense because he was so old, was married, and had children too. Even Cap would listen to Steve.

Charlie and Frank Russo were the youngest members of the crew. They were both eighteen. Frank was the navigator. He was an Italian kid from New York City who they called Meatball. Charlie didn't know any Italians before the war, and he always thought that they were foreign, but Frank wasn't a foreigner. He was a regular guy and smart too. It wasn't easy to figure out the course they had to take. Charlie knew this because he had busted out of the navigation school. The math was too hard for him, but for Meatball it was easy, and even when they seemed to be lost, Meatball knew exactly where they were and which way to go. Meatball was their guide through the infinite wilderness of the sky.

Charlie thought it was funny that, like the hoboes, all the crew of the Big Ass Bird had nicknames and monikers. Maybe it was because, like the hoboes, they had to have new names to identify the nightmare that they were all a part of, and they had to do it with humor in order to survive the horror of it all. Billy Boy called it gallows humor, and when he was drunk, he called them "dead men laughing," but Charlie felt there was hope in their humor and their names united them, just like the hoboes. Charlie knew because he had been a hobo before the war.

Bob Chapman, the belly gunner, was called Hayseed. They called him Hayseed because he was a farm boy from Kansas, but behind that gee-wiz farm boy look, the freckles, and the blond hair there was a very sad story of a farm boy from Kansas whose family lost their farm during the Depression. According to Bob, the drought was so severe that all the soil had turned to dust, and during wind storms the sky went dark for days. It was like the sun was dying. His family like many other families in what they called the Dust Bowl States abandoned their farms after a long hard struggle and headed West in search of work as migrant workers. From his days as a hobo, Charlie remembered seeing these poor families on the road, their Model T Fords loaded down with all their belongings, some of them broken down on the road with their near starving children. He remembered one such family that somehow touched him the most. He could still see the young mother wearing what was once a pretty floral dress but was now filthy, faded, and torn. She was trying to start a bonfire to heat a can of beans for a family of five, and she was doing it with the torn-out pages from a Sears and Roebuck catalogue, all her once-upon-a-time-consumer-dreams going up in smoke.

Russ Zelko, the radio operator, was from the coal mine region of Pennsylvania, a place Charlie's dad told him about when he was a little boy. His dad told him that no matter where you walked in the coal mine region of Pennsylvania there were men underneath your feet digging holes, or there were abandoned mines that could cave in and take you and your house with it. Well, as a little boy it was bad enough that Charlie had to worry about who could be hiding underneath his bed without worrying about what was underneath his feet. It sounded like an awful place to live.

Russ was a third-generation coal miner. That was until he and his father and his two brothers got laid off, and they lost the home the company rented to them because they couldn't pay the rent. Russ was mad as hell, and at nineteen he became a union organizer for one of the radical unions. He handed out pamphlets, participated in sit-ins, and he was always at the front of the picket line protesting the injustice of it all.

Cap joked that Russ was so hardheaded that if you hit him over the head with a baseball bat it would simply bounce off. From the stories that Russ told, the cops gave it a try with their bully clubs at the picket lines. Repeatedly he was hit in the head and beaten up, but he kept coming back until at one of the strikes he finally hit back and broke a cop's jaw. He was dragged into court and charged with sedition. Charlie didn't know what that meant, but the judge gave Russ a choice. Go to jail or enlist. So, here he was.

Charlie was curious because when he was a hobo and on the road and faced with the threat of violence, he ran. He wondered why Russ stood and took all those beatings. Russ told Charlie that he didn't know much about what socialism and communism and

12

capitalism meant. As a union organizer he read all the pamphlets that he was handing out for the union, and some of it made sense, but he believed that there was something that made more sense and that something was called body genius. The body, Russ told him, was a lot smarter than the brain, meaning that when you hurt and your body tells you that you and yours are hurting, and it tells you who is hurting you, and even who is hiding behind the bully that is hurting you, you have two choices, you can run or fight. He chose to fight. Charlie and Russ both laughed because Charlie chose to run, and Russ chose to fight, and there they were - 25,000 feet up in the air ready to fight someone they never met. Life sure can get complicated.

Russ's nicknamed was Rock Head, and they would kid him about being Polish, dumb, and hardheaded. It was true. Rock Head could really be hard headed and slow to get the point, but up here, where they were, it was a blessing to have a guy like Rock Head on their crew because when the shit it's the fan, which it often did, Russ was the rock they stood on, the rock that won't move.

Their bombardier was Pete Lowe, a Jewish Boy from New York who they called Bagel Man because he always delivered the bread to the Krauts. Pete loved his job. Maybe because it was the first job he ever had. Like Charlie, Pete had been on the bum. Most of the guys on the crew had been on the bum or nearly on the bum before they joined up. Harry and Fred Nordlander, the side-gunners, who they called Number One and Number Two or Pee and Poop, were from Nebraska. Like Hayseed, the belly gunner, their family lost their farm during the Depression, and they were on the bum when they got drafted.

One night at the Stars and Stripes Bar & Grill in London, Billy Boy, who was drunk, made fun of them. He said, "If it wasn't for Adolph Hitler, none of you dumb-ass bastards would have ever got a job."

"Fuck you, Billy," Charlie said. Charlie didn't like to swear. His mom always said that swear words were for illiterate uneducated men. Charlie was illiterate and uneducated; but, still, he didn't like to be reminded of it. And besides, just because people were down and out didn't mean that they were dumb or bad. If nothing else, he'd learned that bad things happen to good people, and he didn't know why, but it seemed as if everything was getting better during The New Deal. Roosevelt promised them that America was going to be for the people and not just for the rich. People were beginning to get work. Everything was looking up, and then the Japs bombed Pearl Harbor, and America went to war. God, it seemed that every time things were beginning to look up for him, or he was happy, the floor would be taken out from underneath his feet, and now he was 25,000 feet up in the sky riding a bomb.

14

"OK, you Peckerwoods," Billy Boy said over the intercom. "It's time to fire off your penises, and I want a high sperm count, no blanks, please."

Charlie and the rest of the gunners fired a few rounds to see if their guns were operating properly. The Big Ass Bird had quite a bit of fire power-two fifty caliber "stinger" machine guns in the tail, a single fifty on each side, twin fifties in the belly turret, twin fifties in the top turret, a single machine gun for the radio operator, and two hand-operated machine guns in the Plexiglas nose that the navigator and the bombardier operated. They had their blind spots, but in formation, a division of Flying Fortresses put up one hell of a wall of fire.

Unfortunately for Charlie, one of the blind spots on the plane was in the rear, and the other blind spot was in the nose. As Billy Boy would say, "Gerry loved to give it to them in the ass or come on their face." Even worse, if they were wounded and broke formation, they were truly fucked, because the Gerry pilots would descend upon the wounded plane like a pack of wolves. Billy called it "a gang bang." Today, Charlie felt he was doubly fucked because not only was he in the ass end of his plane, but his group was in the ass end of the wing that was in the ass end of the 3rd Division.

"Hey Guys, listen up," Cap said. "I've got good news and bad news for you. Some of it you already know, but some of it you

15

don't. First off, our target is the Messerschmitt fighter factory at Regensburg in South Bavaria. However, what you don't know is that right behind us, they're sending out the 1st Division, and their target is the ball bearing plant at Schweinfurt. The plan is that we take the brunt of the German air attack. That will take some of the heat off the Schweinfurt mission."

Over the intercom, Charlie could hear a lot of complaints and swearing. Poop said it all when he moaned, "We're fucked again."

Triple fucked, Charlie thought.

"All right, I know," Cap said. "This isn't going to be a milk run, so everyone tighten everything up and be ready for the worst. The good news, however, is that after the mission, when the German's are regrouping to hit us on our way back to England, we'll be on our way to North Africa."

There were a lot of cheers and expressions of relief over the intercom. Charlie smiled. Maybe they could fool the Krauts, and the idea of going to North Africa was exciting to him. He's never been to North Africa. It was something to look forward to.

As Charlie checked all his gear, he could hear a lot of chatter over the radio. The navigators in the division were checking their course, the copilots were tightening up formations, and the commanders were giving orders. They were getting close, and when they made their turn to the target, Charlie began to scan the skies, moving his guns from right to left and up and down methodically covering the 45-degree scope of his guns. Most of the time, they ran into two types of fighters, the Messerschmitt 109 and the Focke-Wolf 190. Depending on the load, the Messerschmitt 109 and the Focke-Wolf 190 had speeds of about 400 mph, a range of approximately 500 miles, and a ceiling of 37,000 feet. Whereas the Big Ass Bird with the bomb load of 6000 pounds had a maximum speed of 220 mph and an approximate range of 2000 miles. If you didn't know better, you would think that the Big Ass Bird was a sitting duck, but in fact, the Fortresses flew in block formation, and that enabled all the guns on all the bombers to have a clear range of fire. In formation, the Flying Fortresses were well deserving of their name. The German fighter pilots, who Charlie admired for their courage, had to fly into a formidable shit storm, and the Flying Fortresses were built to take a beating. They were not easy to bring down. The Germans knew this, and they constantly came up with new strategies and weaponry to combat the bombers. Charlie was nervous. There was no way in hell that the Germans would not send up a shitload of fighters today. Not when they figured out where the Americans were heading.

"Hey, Guys." It was Bagel Man. "Did you hear the story about Miguel, the Mexican goat herder who marries Maria, a beautiful sixteen-year-old virgin from his village?

17

"On their wedding night, they're in the bedroom. She gets undressed, and she's gorgeous. Everything that Miguel could have ever wished for. She has beautiful little peaches for tits that are going to grow into great boobs with the proper care. She's got an ass like an apple, straight from the Garden of Eden. Miguel, he's got a hard-on that won't quit. So, he takes off his shirt, and then he takes off his pants.

'Oh, My God,' Marie says as she snatches up her night gown and covers her nakedness, 'What is that?'

"Miguel looks down at his hard-on and says, 'Maria, I have always been a very virtuous man, so I was given this gift of God, and now I'm going to give it to you.' So, Boom Bang Boom they fuck all night. Maria is overjoyed. They're very happy, but then Miguel has to go to the mountains to tend the goats. She smoothers him with kisses and begs him to hurry home with his gift of God.

"Miguel, he's up in the mountains for a long time. He's grown a beard, and he's as horny as his goats. When its' time to go home, he runs down the mountain in expectation. He flings open the kitchen door and shouts, 'Maria, I'm home!'

"Maria is furious. She throws pots and pans at him and tells him to 'Get out of the house!'

'Maria! Maria! What's the matter?'

'You lied to me! You lied to me! You said you had the only one.

And your friend, Jose, he has one too!'

"Miguel ducked another pot and says, 'But, Maria, you don't understand. I was so virtuous, that God gave me two, and, so, because Jose is my best friend, I give him one.'

"That's when she hit him over the head with the cast iron frying pan and said, 'You dumb son-of-a-bitch, you gave him the biggest one!'"

Amid the laughter, Charlie saw a lot of dark specks in the sky that became buzzing bees then screeching birds and then screaming fighter planes.

"Here they come!" Charlie shouted.

He heard Number One call out another batch of fighters to Hayseed. Everyone in the crew was talking, telling each other what was going on, calling out sightings and lines of flight, working together as a team. They were so tightly tied together that they were like the fingers on each other's hands, all ten of them grabbing on for dear life, swinging the twin 50s to fire at a 109 diving into the formation, spinning the ball turret around and firing in response to a warning from above. Cap firmly grasped the controls to keep them steady and in formation as all hell broke loose.

Charlie saw one of the Messerschmitt fighters crash head-on into a Flying Fortress. The explosion was tremendous. Plane parts and body parts were flying all over the place. He heard Billy Boy shout to Hayseed, "Down below, six o'clock," and Charlie saw a Focke-Wolf 190 swoop under the plane then burst into flames and spin out of sight.

Hayseed shouted, "I got him! I got him!"

Charlie heard something wiz by that wasn't cannon or machine gun fire. "What the hell was that?" he shouted.

"Rockets," Cap said, "It's a squadron of 88s. They're flying parallel to us. Two o'clock."

Charlie couldn't see them, but he could see one rocket go through a bomber leaving a huge gaping hole in its side where the waist gunners use to be, but the bomber kept on flying. What he saw next, he couldn't believe. He saw a bomb! Then he saw another one and another one. They were falling all around him. He thought that one of the bombers above them had been hit and the bombs had fallen out, but then he heard Pops say, "They got high altitude bombers flying over our heads dropping time bombs on us!"

One bomb hit the side of a Fortress below them, slid onto the wing, then fell off and exploded below. This was a horror Charlie never saw before, but amidst the dropping bombs, the roar of Flying Fortresses, the screams of fighter planes, and the raging fire fight, Charlie didn't have time to think or to be afraid. He was a part of the roar, an animal fighting for his life.

"You got one coming up your ass, Charlie!" Pops shouted.

Charlie swung his guns around and saw a Fouke-Wolf 190 nose on. They were firing point blank at each other. Charlie didn't have time to ask the German what his name was and where he came from. He just kept firing. He didn't have time to ask him if he had a family or children or believed in God. He heard bullets hitting the tail section above him, and then a bullet pierced the Plexiglas window, and all he could do was keep firing at the fuckin' Kraut until the fighter disintegrated and part of the fighter splattered against Charlie's plane. The Big Ass Bird rocked from the impact.

"What the fuck was that?" Cap shouted.

Pops responded, "Charlie just blew away a 190 up close, and it went splash all over our plane."

"Any damage," Cap asked.

"None that I can see, Cap," Pops said, "except there's a piece of the Kraut's wing embedded in our tail fin, but it doesn't look serious."

Over the intercom, Charlie heard Bagel Man say, "We got the wing from a Kraut plane stuck in our tail fin, and it ain't serious? What's fuckin serious around here anymore?"

Cap laughed and said, "Pops go back there and check it out. Everyone checked in. I need a damage report, now."

A few minutes later, Pop opened the door to Charlie's rear gunner position. He smiled, "You OK, Charlie?"

"Sure, Pops."

Pops pointed to one of the holes in the window, "Looks like one just missed you, Charlie."

Charlie looked at the hole. "Gee whiz, I guess so." Charlie hadn't noticed that one. He'd been too caught up in the moment.

"Is everything all right up front, Pops?"

"We're good, so far. We got a piece of that Jerry you killed in the tail fin, but nothing bad from what I can see. The Cap's got a scalp wound from a piece of flying Plexiglas, but he's good too."

Pops smiled again at Charlie like he was his little brother and said, "I have to go back, Charlie. Keep up the good work, boy."

Pops left and Charlie began to scan the sky again. As Billy Boy would say, "If you snooze, you lose." However, from what Charlie could see and hear from the crew, the German attack seemed to be petering out, but then Charlie saw a Flying Fortress below them in trouble. It had taken a lot of hits. Two engines were out. It was drifting out of formation, and the Krauts were swooping down on her for the kill when the Flying Fortress lowered her landing wheels and that, according to the code of air combat, was a signal that the crew was surrendering.

Seeing that the Flying Fortress had surrendered, two German fighters pulled up alongside the Fortress to escort it to a German air base. But then something strange happened. The wheels came back up, and the gunners on the Flying Fortress started firing at the two German fighters escorting it. They shot both fighters down. The remaining Germans, enraged by the violation of surrender protocol, threw everything they had left at the big plane, and it was torn apart within minutes. When one of the crew members managed to bail out, they shot him down too.

"Holy Cow, did you see that?" Hayseed said.

"Yeah, I saw it." Cap said. "Charlie, they were right below you. Did you see it?"

"Yes, Cap."

"What happened?"

"It looked like they surrendered then changed their minds."

"Yeah, that's what happened," Bagel Man said, "I saw it too."

"Maybe the hydraulic system failed, and the wheels came down on their own," Meatball said.

"Do you know whose plane it was?" Number Two asked.

"I think it was Captain Knox's plane," Pops said.

There was a moment of silence then Cap said, "OK, guys, this thing isn't over yet, not by a long shot, so let's keep alert. They may take one more pass at us before we hit the flak."

The Germans didn't come back again. They were heading home to fuel up so that they could take another shot at the bombers on their way home from Regensburg. That was where they were going to fool them.

Charlie could hear Meatball and Bagel Man talking to the Cap. They were going into the target zone now. The lead bombardier set the course, and the bombers were locked into the settings. From here on in there would be no evasive maneuvers, no changing of course until they dropped their bombs. Charlie put a metal plate under his ass, and he sat back and braced himself as the flak began to come in. This was the part that Charlie hated. He couldn't see a god-damned thing until it was all over, and all he could do was wait and hope that he didn't get his ass blown off while he watched with fascination the deadly black flowers of flak grow and explode into blossoms of death. He listened to a piece of shrapnel whiz by him. Jesus, the flak was so thick it looked like a black cloud ascending to cast a shroud around The Big Ass Bird.

He heard Bagel Man shout, "Bombs away," and he saw the trail of death that they had left behind, the smoke from the flames enveloping Regensburg. Charlie didn't know what it would be like to be down there. He had never been in an air raid at ground zero when the bombs fell, but he could guess. If it was hell up here, it must be an inferno down there. He was glad to be above it all, climbing up into the stratosphere beyond the range of the flak, beyond the range of the hurt, beyond the range of the guilt, and going to North Africa.

Now that the action was over, Charlie could feel the cold. It was below zero and getting colder as they ascended to 35,000 feet. Charlie stretched out for the first time since they took off for this mission. He had been kneeling in front of his twin 50s throughout the battle, and his knees were killing him. He took the two Army blankets that he had folded and used for cushions and wrapped them around his body for warmth, and he began to drift off into the constant throb of the Big Ass Bird's engines, its heartbeat, and the chatter over the intercom that connected him to the only family and friends that he had. He dreamt that he was a little boy again at home in Ithaca. He was in the bedroom of his childhood lying in his bed on a soft mattress with pure white cotton sheets. He was wrapped in a pure white down blanket, his head resting on a soft feathery pure white pillow. It was pleasantly warm, and he could hear the soothing sound of the waterfall in the gorge behind his house.

He was about to call his Mommy to come upstairs and tell him a bedtime story when he heard Billy Boy on the intercom, "Hey, I don't hear anything back there. Have all you pecker woods gone to sleep? You know, I feel asleep up here once, and when I woke up, I was looking up God's asshole. And do you know what I saw? I saw an image of myself in a mirror. I wasn't sure at first if it was me, so I waved, and the image waved back at me. I smiled, and the image smiled. Yep, it was me. That is when I heard God say,

25

'Behold, I made you in the image of my asshole."

Cap was laughing when he said, "Billy Boy's right. Everyone stay awake and alert. Let's hear it. Check in now."

As the Cap called off the role, Charlie knelt in front of his twin 50s again and forced himself to stay awake for the rest of the flight until they landed in a North African air base in the desert late that night. All the guys wanted to go into the small tent-town that had grown up around the air base, but Charlie was too tired, so he climbed up on the wing of the Big Ass Bird, and using his parachute for a pillow, he laid back on the wing and looked up at the stars and out at the desert that was starkly beautiful in a lonely way. He never saw so many stars in his life, and they seemed to be woven into the soft graceful lines of the desert that looked like a woman asleep in a blanket of sand that sparkled silver in the moonlight. Charlie closed his eyes and dreamt of Betty Grable, his favorite movie star, his pin-up girl. In the dream, she was waiting for him when he got home. The early colonial house was painted white, and Betty glowed with radiance as she waited at the door for him. She was wearing a light blue cashmere sweater, a white pleated skirt, bobby socks, and penny loafers; and when he touched her soft cashmere breast, Betty kissed him and said, "I missed you so much, Charlie."

The next day, the crew was back in the Big Ass Bird, and when they got back to their base in England, they took a train into London. London was old and looked grand and sad at the same time. The fact that everything was running on coal, even the cars and trucks, made the city look like a charcoal drawing with splotches of color here and there. The bombed-out buildings were a reminder that the war had been going on long before the Americans got there. But, even so, it was exciting. He, Charlie Tremaine, was in a foreign city thousands of miles away from home. Everything was old and strange yet new to him. Ever street and alley way, everywhere he turned, he found mystery.

The crew hit a few bars then went to the Stars and Stripes, a big hangout for service men. The pub was jammed with people, but they found a table and settled down to a long night of drinking.

"Could you believe those bombs?" Meatball said.

Charlie chugged down his beer, "I thought they were coming out of one of our planes."

"I'm not worried about the bombs. They weren't very effective," Cap said as he motioned to the waitress for more beer. "I'm more worried about those rockets they were firing from the Ju88s. They get that down, and we're in for some serious shit."

Meatball poured himself another beer, "I heard from a guy in the 1st Division that they got it worse than us on the Schweinfurt Mission. Because of the fog, they didn't take off when they should

27

have, so they were way behind us, and they and got it coming and going. They lost thirty-six bombers."

"How many did we lose?"

"Twenty-four," Number One said.

They all were silent. They knew the score. They had flown eighteen missions. They had ten more to go, and every day the brass was sending them deeper and deeper into Germany.

"Hey guys," Bagel Man said, "did you hear the one about the farmer's daughter?"

They all moaned, but the Bagel Man paid them no mind and went on with his story. "This traveling salesmen's car breaks down on the road in the middle of the night near this dilapidated old farmhouse. He knocks on the door of the farmhouse, and the farmer comes to the door. The traveling salesman asks the farmer if he will put him up for the night, but the farmer tells him he's got no room.

'Well, then, can I sleep in the barn?' says the traveling salesmen. "The farmer says, 'Sure,' and he gets a lantern and takes him to the barn, shows him a stall with some hay in it, and tells him he can sleep there.

'But whatever you do," the farmer says, 'don't put your dick in them there three holes in the wall.'

"Well, the traveling salesman gets really curious, so he sticks

28

his dick in the first hole, and it feels really good. He sticks his dick in the second hole, and it feels better. He sticks his dick in the third hole, and the farmer is woken up by this loud howling from the barn, so he goes to look.

'I told you not to put your dick in them there holes,' the farmer says. 'The first one was my wife. The second one was my daughter, and the third one is the milk machine, and it's set for thirty gallons.'"

There were a lot of moans and some laughter. Charlie laughed because it was so bad, and Number Two said, "Damn, Bagel Man, how many of those farmer's daughter jokes do you know? You got to have told us at least a hundred of them."

"It just seems like a hundred because they're so bad," Cap said.

Everyone laughed. They wanted to laugh. They even wanted to laugh at Bagel Man's bad jokes, anything to forget how frightened they were. Cap ordered another round of drinks, and Charlie noticed an English bomber crew walk in the door. They were all drunk too. As the English bomber crew walked past the table where Charlie and the crew were sitting, one of the English airmen stopped and said, "Are any of you Yanks from the 1st Division, 100th Group?"

"We all are," Rock Head said.

"I heard about the dumb ass stunt one of your guys pulled

29

dropping his landing gear then firing on the German fighters."

"So, what's it to you?" Billy Boy said, standing up.

"Well, Yank, the way I see it, you're all a bunch of bloody fools, and you shouldn't be up in the sky."

That did it. Billy Boy hit the Brit, and everyone started fighting. Tables were turned over, glasses broken. Charlie took a swing at one guy and caught him on the side of the head. They both were swinging away when he saw someone hit the Brit over the head with a chair. The Brit went down. Charlie turned around to swing at someone else, and he got hit by what looked like a pitcher of beer coming down on his head. The beer poured down his face as he slumped to the floor.

When Charlie came to, the pub was in bedlam. Everyone in the pub was fighting with no regard for whose side anyone was on. Charlie's head hurt like hell. The soldier he had been fighting was also rubbing his head. They both laughed. Then they heard whistles blowing. It was the military police.

The Brit helped Charlie up onto his feet and said, "Come on, Yank, we better get out of here."

The airman led Charlie through a door into the kitchen and out the back door into an alley. They heard more police whistles from the street. They sounded like they were coming nearer. The Brit climbed up a fire escape, and Charlie followed. From the top of the roof, they could see the MPs herding the servicemen out of the bar and into army trucks. Some of the servicemen had to be carried out.

The Brit extended his hand, "William Stewart, bombardier, 2nd Wing, 5th Bomber Group. Knowing how you Yanks like nicknames, you can call me Willy if you like, but don't call me Bill."

Charlie smiled. "Charlie Tremaine, rear gunner, 100th Group, 1st Division. They call me Ass End Charlie."

A big smile came across William Stewart's face. "They call you Ass End Charlie, and you're a rear gunner? That's bloody fuckin funny."

"Yeah, everyone thinks it's funny."

"Where are you from, Charlie?"

"Ithaca, New York. It's a small town in Upstate New York. It has a big university there, Cornell University. Ever heard of it?"

"No, can't say that I have. What's it like living in Ithaca, New York?"

"It was really nice before the depression. It's on a lake, and we have gorges and falls and creeks running through the town. It's real pretty, but the winters are long, and when the depression came, things got bad." Charlie took out a pack of cigarettes and offered a cigarette to the Brit.

"How about you? Where do you come from?" Charlie asked.

"Liverpool, it's a factory town. Lots of brick, lots of soot, lots of low paying jobs for blokes like me, but I love the old pile of bricks. I'll probably go back home after the war, find me a pretty girl with big headlights, have a good tumble or two, and then thirty years later, she'll be a shriveled up old hag, and I'll be a fat old sod sitting in my fat old chair counting the days to my pension and hoping that there will be another war, and a few bombs will drop on my head to break up the monotony. What are you going to do when you get out?"

"Golly, I don't know. Maybe I'll go back to school. I think I might want to go to college."

Willy stood up, "Jolly good, Charlie, but my advice to you is, if you want to get home, you should seriously think about transferring out of the 100th."

"Why?"

"Every pilot and serviceman in the British and American Air Force knows about what happened over Regensburg, and by now every pilot and serviceman in the Luftwaffe knows about it too. The bloody 100th is marked for extinction, and if I was you, I'd get my ass out of that group."

"You think so?"

"I know so."

Willy, seeing the worried expression on Charlie's face, slapped him on the back and said cheerfully, "Come on Charlie, I think the coast is clear. Let's go somewhere for a beer. Maybe we can start another fight. Get really bombed."

"Thanks Willy, but I think I'm going to stay here for a while. I got some thinking to do."

"Jolly good, me and my chaps hang out at the Post House mostly. Come on by and tip a few."

"I'll do that."

They vigorously shook hands and Charlie watched Willy climb down the fire escape. Charlie knew that the Brit might be right. The Germans probably will come after the 100th. It was always more satisfying to kill someone rather than something, and the 100th had become someone to the Luftwaffe, someone to hate, the enemy with a name and a number. Charlie thought about transferring out of the group, but he knew he couldn't do that. He couldn't leave his buddies. They were the only family he had. Charlie lit up another cigarette and looked out at London. It was a full moon, and he could clearly see Westminster Abby, Old Ben, and the Thames River. He thought London was strangely beautiful, exciting, and he wanted to come back here after the war, but then he realized that he wasn't going to be coming back here, and he wasn't going back home. He wasn't going to make it, not if they got hit again like they did on their last mission, not if the Germans targeted them. Like

Billy Boy said, "They are all dead men walking."

Jesus, Charlie thought, I'm eighteen years old, and I'm going to die, and I never had a life. Between the depression and the war my life for the most part has been a journey through hell, and it's about to get worse. He tried to remember the last time that he was happy, and he had to journey all the way back in time to his childhood when he had a real home. Compared to this, it seemed like Paradise.

He remembered being a child playing beside his mother in the flower garden, watching her tend her roses, blood red in the sun. Everything was floral about his mother. She smelled of flowers, the rugs in the house were floral swirls, the wallpaper was made up of garlands, and the dinner plates were rimed with daisies and violets. Nearly all her dresses had flowers on them, and flowers even seemed to pour out of her head when she put on her hats of flowers and feathers. Every day there were fresh cut flowers placed in vases all around the house, and in the summer when his windows were open, he could smell the flowers in the garden and hear the falls beyond flowing through Cascadilla Gorge.

Charlie lived halfway up the hill on Buffalo Street in a three-story red brick Victorian with chandeliers, big mahogany sliding doors, winding ornate hand carved stairways, and white marble fireplaces. On top of the hill was Cornell University where the rich kids lived, and below Charlie at the base of Cayuga Lake, near the marshes, the poor people lived in shacks. Back then, labor was so cheap that even a middle-class business owner like his father could afford a live-in housekeeper and a cook. Life was grand.

Charlie's father, Bill Tremaine, owned a hardware store. He took it over when his father retired, but he became successful when he went into the construction business and began to build houses around town. Because he owned a hardware store, and he knew all the carpenters, plumbers, and electricians in town, he could finance the jobs, subcontract out all the real work, and act as a general contractor whose role it was to supervise the jobs and make sure everyone did everything right and on time. Charlie loved to go to the construction sites with his dad. There was one carpenter that he especially liked, Dick Farris. Dick let Charlie hammer a nail and saw some boards from time to time, and it made him feel like he was a real working man, but his father didn't like him playing in the sawdust, cement, and dirt. According to his father, a gentleman never did manual labor or soiled his hands. To his father dirt was evil, and manual labor was for the poor people who lived near the marshes. He called them the Mud People. They were the un-redeemed by God, rural white trash, new immigrants from Southern Europe, Catholics of all kind and Jews. According to the preacher at his church, they were "the unclean children of the earth, wild and unruly, constantly tempted by the sins of darkness that came out of the wilderness of animal passions."

Charlie's father, on the other hand, always went to work looking like he was going to church. He looked like the minister of God's economy in his dark charcoal wool suit, his immaculately clean white dress shirt with its stiflingly starched white collar, his gold, coin-like cufflinks, and his solemn muted tie. From what Charlie could gather from the sermons at church and what his parents would say at home, his dad was amongst God's elect, and his financial success was proof of his moral superiority. To Charlie, his mother, on the other hand, was the spirit of love living amidst her flowers in the pure white light of God's grace, loving and merciful, forever forgiving and kind, a working member of many charities that helped the poor and suffering sinners who were what they were through no fault of their own.

But then something bad happened. Charlie's father became depressed, and he got more depressed every day, and his mother seemed to be trying to be sunny behind dark clouds that increasingly cast shadows over his life at home. At first, Charlie thought someone in the family had died, maybe grandpa or grandma, but they were still alive. Then he heard something about The Big Crash. He thought it was a big auto accident where a whole bunch of cars and trucks crashed into each other making a hell of a mess, but then he figured out that it had something to do with money. A whole lot of people had lost a whole lot of money, and now they didn't have money to buy the houses that his dad was building. In fact, people weren't building anything anymore and that wasn't so good for the hardware business either.

After school, Charlie began to work as a clerk at his father's hardware store. His father made him wear polished black shoes, well-ironed black dress pants, a white shirt, and a bow tie. Charlie hated the shoes. They hurt his feet. The pants were too tight when he had to bend over to pick something up or stack stuff on the shelves, and the white shirt showed up the slightest sins, but he got paid, "a fair wage for an honest day's work," his father said.

One day when he was walking home from the store, he saw a huge line of people in front of the Salvation Army headquarters, and he realized that the people were waiting in line for food, hundreds of them. One of the Soldiers of God dressed in the red and blue uniform of the Salvation Army was ladling out soup into tin bowls and a woman, also a uniformed member of God's Army, was handing each person a slice of bread.

Charlie saw a little girl clinging to her mother's dress. Her eyes were so big that he felt like they would swallow him up. Her face was dirty. Was she dirty because she was poor, or was she poor because she was dirty? Charlie didn't know, but he didn't think it was right for people to go without food or clean clothes or a job. He felt like he had to do something, so he ran back to the store.

Ned, who worked as a part-time clerk, was behind the counter. Charlie told Ned that he forgot one of his schoolbooks, and Ned, who was busy stocking some shelve behind the counter, just nodded and didn't pay much attention to Charlie. Charlie went into the back where his father stored his inventory and took what he could as quick as he could and ran out of the store. He was frightened to death. He knew he was doing wrong, but he couldn't stop himself. He also knew that if his dad found out, he would be furious.

Charlie ran all the way back to where the people were waiting in line for a bowl of soup and a piece of bread. He found the little girl who was wearing a blanket for a coat, and he handed her a bar of soap, a package of flower seeds, and a chocolate candy bar and said, "Here, this will make you feel better." He then ran off wondering if what he did was good or bad. Is he going to go to hell for stealing from his father, or is he going to go to heaven for helping the poor?

One night, several months after his encounter with the little girl, he heard his mother crying. He got out of bed, and from the darkness of the stairway, he could see that his mother and father were in the living room sitting on the couch. They didn't know he was there. There was a fire in the fireplace, and the shadows of the flames seemed to be dancing over the flowers on the wallpaper.

His father had his arm around his mother, and Charlie could hear his mother say, "But do we have to sell the house?"

"If we want to save the hardware store, we do. The bank is giving me one month to pay what I owe, or they'll take the store. Dad would die if I lost the store. I must do it. Mary, it's our only hope."

"Do you think we'll be able to buy a small house?"

"No, not now, I may even have to sell some of the furniture."

"Oh my God, Bill. What happened?"

"Jesus, Mary, I don't know. All of a sudden the floor just seemed to cave in on everything."

Mary wiped her eyes and managed a smile. "Well, dear, we will just have to make do and hope that God will provide."

Charlie's father got up and stared into the fire. "I think God is punishing us. The socialists and the godless communists are saying that it is capitalism and the free market system, but I firmly believe that capitalism and the free market system in the hands of godly men is a great tool for prosperity. But, in the hands of ungodly greedy men who only believe in science, materialism, and money, it can be a tool of disaster. Our sin is that we let the scum rise to the top and now saints and sinners alike have fallen."

A month later, they sold their home and rented a house down

in the mud flats. Soon after that, his dad lost the hardware store, and he went to work as a clerk working in a grocery store. His mom tried to keep a sunny face on things, and somehow, she managed to always have flowers in the apartment, wildflowers that she would find in the fields or along the gorge or near Fall Creek. One day she asked Charlie's father if they could get flowered wallpaper for their dingy kitchen, and he laughed at her and walked out of the house and came back home that night drunk.

Charlie had never seen his father drunk before, but he saw him that way more and more, night after night. Then one day some men came in a truck and began to take the furniture out of the house. His father did nothing. He just sat at the kitchen table with his head down. When they tried to take the kitchen table, he held on to it, and he wouldn't let go. One of the men looked at the other man and winked. He looked at a sheet of paper and said, "Look, Frank, it seems like the man is right. The kitchen table and chairs are not on our list."

The man then walked to Charlie's parent's bedroom and stood in the doorway. The bedroom was empty except for a mattress. His mother was sitting on the mattress crying. "Ma'am, it isn't our fault. It's our job. You know how it is. I got children too."

The other man came up to him and motioned that they should leave.

"It's a job," the man said weakly as they left.

The next day Charlie came home from school and found his father in the kitchen. There was a roll of flowered wallpaper on the floor, and his dad was sitting at the kitchen table in a pool of blood. He had shot himself in the head. He was dead, Charlie could see that, but all he could do was stare at his father, the flowered wallpaper, and the blood all over his father's pure white shirt and the floor. His head was a bloody mess. Charlie wanted to clean everything up. He didn't want anyone to see his father like this, but he didn't know where to start, and he couldn't move. He stayed that way through the screams of horror and sorrow when his mother discovered her husband's body. He remained that way when the police came, and the ambulance came to take his father away. He remembered his mother enveloping him in her arms and pleading with God to help them.

There were very few people at the funeral. Charlie thought that his father was popular and had a lot of friends, but it seems that being poor in the depression was like having the plague. Most people were afraid that they would catch it if they got too close to you. After the funeral his mom told him that they were going to go live with her parents, but Charlie had other plans. He had heard stories about how he could hitch a ride on a train and get away from where he was to somewhere new to start all over again, so the next day he

41

shoved some clothes, a bar of soap, and a toothbrush in a laundry bag and left a note for his mother.

Dear Mom

I'm going West to make my fortune.

Love

Charlie

Charlie heard gun shots, and it jolted him out of his remembrances and brought him back from his journey through time to where he started, standing in Dewitt Park at the Memorial Day service. The honor guard had just fired a volley in honor of the dead.

Daisy smiled at Charlie. He was the love of her life. "The service is over, dear. It's time to go."

"Yes, Daisy."

Chapter Two

After the memorial service, Charlie and Daisy drove ten blocks to the VFW, a cinder block building with a red brick façade. In front of the VFW was a rusted-out World War II anti-aircraft gun pointed at the sky waiting for the present to become the past and the past to become the future. A banner hung across the face of the building announcing Bingo every Tuesday and Thursday night. Charlie parked their pick-up truck and entered a side door of the VFW and walked downstairs to the bar. It was a large banquet size room with a spacious dance floor, an ample kitchen, and a four-sided bar that spanned the width of the room, but the lack of windows and the cinderblock walls dug deep into the earth gave it the feeling of being in a bunker safe from the external world surrounded by reminders of who they were and who they could be in the future if attacked. Death.

From the ceiling faded flags hung in honor of the different military services, each bearing the iconic symbols of American military power and glory. On the near wall was the bulletin board and a rare collection of military maps yellow with age that depicted major battles fought by the United States. Also hanging from the wall were pictures of many of the members who served their country, many in uniform, many in their youth, forever young. The Marne, Meuse-Argonne, Guadalcanal, The Battle of the Bulge, Normandy, Midway, The Chosen Reservoir, Khe San, Iraq, Afghanistan - battle after battle, war after war lined the faces of these common soldiers who forged an Empire.

Charlie looked at the bulletin board and saw that Jay Cohen was in the VFW hospital, and Jim Covar had died. There was a Fish Fry on Friday night, $6.95. On a long table underneath the bulletin board were platters of cold cuts, chicken wings, lake trout, venison, salads, and desserts that the veteran's wives had prepared. Performing on the stage was a country western band who was singing a Garth Brooks song, "I Got Friends in Low Places."

Charlie and Daisy sat down at the bar that was on the far side of the bandstand and the dance floor. Charlie always drank bottled Bud and Daisy always drank peppermint schnapps, and with the first sip of his beer, Charlie felt his spirits rising. A big, broad smile came across Charlie's face. This was better.

The Commandant of the VFW, Bob Sumner, slapped Charlie on the back and said, "Come on Charlie, Harry and Dick think

44

they can beat us in shuffleboard."

Charlie stood up and gestured as if he were a prize fighter warming up for a fight and said, "Sounds like they need a good ass whipping to me. Bring 'em on."

Daisy tugged on Charlie's sleeve, "Don't play all night, Charlie. I want to dance."

"Sure, Honey." As Charlie dug into his pocket for some quarters and sized up their opponents, he said to Bob, "Which one you got?"

"I'll take the small one."

Dick, who stood about five foot eight and was an auto mechanic at Prichard's, was still wearing his work clothes from the job. Dick laughed, "I'll show you who's small. Red or blue, you turkeys, what do you want?"

Charlie began to play. Both he and Bob were good at this game. As partners, they had won the post championship several times. Charlie was good at most games. He had excellent eye-to-hand coordination, and for a man his age, Charlie was in very good physical condition. He was slim, five feet ten inches tall, and well-proportioned. Charlie had his Dad's square jaw chiseled features and his mother's blue eyes. At one time, his hair had been blond, but now it was gray, and his body was beginning to fail him.

45

Charlie saw the Reverend enter the VFW. Charlie loved the Reverend. He loved to hear the Reverend talk. Half the time he couldn't understand what the Reverend was talking about, but there would be moments when it seemed like the Reverend had been touched by God or the Devil, Charlie wasn't quite sure. The Reverend was the post chaplain and the janitor at the VFW, and he was their spiritual leader. If you had a problem, you could go to the Reverend, and for the price of a drink he would rearrange reality so that no matter what, you felt better about yourself. For another drink, he would throw in a blessing or two and advise you to love the Lord Jesus, love one another, and re-member that you have seen a hell of a lot worse in your life.

Charlie smiled as he watched the Reverend graciously re-ceive compliments for his Memorial Day sermon. People shook his hand one after another, others patted him on the back, and Mildred Pace with tears in her eyes grasped the Reverend's hands in hers and brought them to her breast in gratitude. When she let go of his hands, the Reverend blessed them all with the sign of the cross and then turned to Jimmy Reeves, the bartender who was talking to a customer on the other side of the bar and shouted, "Can a man of God get a fuckin' drink in this bar?"

Jimmy rang the cow bell to let everyone know that there was a sinner at the bar. Many of the crowd at the bar laughed because

46

it was the Reverend who created the system where, if a member swore at the bar, he or she had to pay a dollar in penance. What was funny to everyone was that the Reverend was the worse penitent. Charlie laughed along with everyone else. He was happy. He was home amongst his friends. He belonged to all of this, to all the places on the war maps. His heart and soul were woven through the fabric of the American flag that hung over the shuffleboard next to the Miller High Life sign.

Charlie slid the metal puck down the board, knocked Harry's pock off the board, and his puck hung on the edge of the board for three points. "Yes!" he shouted.

He and Bob were winning. Charlie went to the bar to order another Bud, and Daisy was gone. She was on the other side of the bar playing her favorite game. He watched her manipulate the joystick, back and forth, up and down. A big metal claw at the end of a crane-like apparatus moved across the top of a glass case filled with stuffed animals and dolls. For a moment, the claw was suspended, and then it dropped onto a pink teddy bear that was wearing green boxing gloves and yellow boxing trunks. The claw picked the teddy bear up by one leg…

"Hey, Charlie, it's your turn," Bob said.

Charlie got back into the game. He played one game after another. Sometimes he would knock Dick and then Harry off the board, and sometimes he would pass them on the sly. Sometimes he would play it safe and block their shot, and other times he would just blast away. It was the American way, it was competition. He was about to play another game when Charlie felt someone touch his arm. It was Daisy.

"Come on Charlie, let's dance."

"All right, Honey."

Charlie liked dancing with Daisy, and he liked country western music because it told the story of ordinary guys like him and their everyday tragedies, so when he stepped out onto the dance floor with Daisy in his arms, he listened to how "you always lose the one you love." In the next song, the poor bastard loses his farm, and the bank came and took it all away. "All away, all away," the lyrics said it over and over again until there was nothing left. In the final song before the intermission, the poor bastard loses his wife, loses his truck, and gets arrested for DWI, but then he meets another woman in the bar who is wearing cowboy boots and a skirt that swirls to the country music. Later in the parking lot her soft lips tell him that this time "they will build a dream together that will last forever and ever."

When the band took a break, Charlie and Daisy walked back to where they were sitting at the bar. The Reverend was sitting next to them talking to Jake Stone.

"Oh, look," Daisy said. "Timmy is here."

Charlie turned around and saw Timmy, his retarded son. Timmy was forty years old, but he looked like a giant child. Timmy and his girlfriend Judy waved at them from across the room. Charlie waved back, and then he watched Timmy and Judy walk through the crowd. Timmy hugged everyone he could. He was so glad to see them all. His face radiated with good will.

Charlie also had a daughter, Rebecca. She graduated from Cornell, and then she went on to get a Ph.D. in English literature. Now she was a professor of English at the University of Virginia. She taught Feminist Literature and Deconstructionism. Charlie didn't know what "deconstructionism" meant. The Reverend said that it was what the schizophrenic, neurotic, dysfunctional, children of the rich called "literary criticism" to glorify their own spiritual fragmentation and disillusionment. Charlie didn't know what that meant either except that it was obvious to him that the Reverend thought it was a bunch of bullshit.

Charlie shrugged. It didn't matter to him. He was happy that his daughter was happy and that she was up there, successful beyond their dreams. At the same time, Charlie was sad because his daughter had left them behind.

Charlie only saw his daughter and his two grandchildren

49

once every other year at Christmas time, and then they would only stay for two or three days and be gone. Charlie knew how his daughter felt about him. He found that out one day when he drove to her sorority house to take her out to lunch. He was going to surprise her. The girl who met him at the door was very nice. She explained to him that Becky had gone to New York to see her parents who had just come back from Paris, France. It seems that Becky's father was a world-famous brain surgeon.

Charlie, stunned, began to walk away.

"Who should I say was calling?"

"Oh, Nobody," Charlie said and quickly got into his car and drove away. Driving home, he remembered carrying her on his shoulder upstairs to her crib, her laughing all the way. He also remembered her sitting on his knee. She said that he was the best daddy in the whole world, and she was going to love him forever. She promised. Charlie began to cry.

She also lied to them when she graduated. She said she wasn't going to the graduation ceremony. She made a big thing about it. "It's all a lot of nonsense," she said. But Charlie knew she was lying, so he went anyway, and there she was smiling and laughing with her friends. He wanted to go down there and say, "OK, maybe I'm dumb, and I didn't give you everything you wanted in life, but your mother worked thirty years as a secretary at Cornell so that you could get free tuition, and I spent most of my life on my knees putting in floors for other people to walk on. You are an ungrateful little brat." But he didn't do it. He loved her, so he slipped away and went down to the VFW and got drunk.

Charlie took a sip from his drink then felt someone come up from behind him and gently put his hand on his shoulder. Charlie turned to see who it was. It was Timmy, his son. Timmy, put his arms around his dad and gave him a big hug then kissed him on the cheek. Judy kissed him too. Charlie smiled, "How you doing, son?"

"Wonderful, Dad."

Timmy embraced the Reverend and said, "I love you, Reverend."

The Reverend laughed and said, "Oh, Timmy, you love everyone, even bad people."

"Bad people are bad because they don't get enough love. And you know what else I figured out?"

"What's that?" the Reverend asked.

"That if everyone loved each other, no one would ever die."

Judy tugged at Timmy, "Come on Timmy. I want to dance to this song." She pulled him towards the dance floor. Timmy stopped at the big glass box with all the stuffed animals and dolls in it. He was about to reach into his pocket for a quarter when Judy pulled him onto the dance floor. They danced barely moving, just touching, and staring into space.

The Reverend wondered what they saw. Was it angels with halos that never ate?

Charlie turned to the Reverend and said, "That boy's the biggest tragedy of my life."

"You shouldn't feel that way Charlie. You've been blessed. Timmy's a pure soul. That's why he seems so retarded. In a corrupt distorted world like this, even the Lord Jesus Christ would look like a moron."

Daisy hugged the Reverend. She had tears in her eyes.

Bob came up to Charlie and whispered in his ear, "We have two more suckers on the line, Charlie."

Charlie got up from his stool. He was getting too depressed and happy at the same time. The Reverend often had that effect on him. "Mother, can you buy me another beer?"

Daisy nodded and reached into her purse.

While Charlie was waiting for his beer, Bob said to him, "I have a job for you."

"What's that?"

The Commandant pointed to the floor.

"You want me to redo it?"

"Yes," Bob said, "it's a mess."

"I've been tellin' you that for a while, Bob," Charlie said.

The Reverend who was listening in said, "Yes, it's a mess. That's because you did it the last time." The Reverend looked at Bob, his face a caricature of disbelief as he said, "And now you're going to let him do it again?"

"What are you guys talking about?" Charlie said. "I did that job ten years ago, and I did it for free."

The Commandant winked at the Reverend and Daisy, "You think if we paid you this time you might do a better job?"

Charlie laughed, "That depends, how much you going to pay me?"

"Ten dollars an hour," Bob said. "With all the money I've been stealing from this place, that's all we can afford."

Ten dollars an hour, Charlie thought. He and Daisy have been living off her meager pension from Cornell and her social security for the last two years. Charlie had worked for himself all his life, so he didn't have any social security, and his savings were gone. It would be great to have some money in his pocket again.

"Sure, I'll do it. When do I start?"

"How about tomorrow," Bob asked.

"I'll be here."

"Then it's settled," Bob said. "Now let's go pull in some fish."

Charlie played some more shuffleboard, and, at the same time, he thought about the thousands of people he killed with his bombs, faceless people except for the German pilot who he had splattered all over his Flying Fortress. Damn Memorial Day, all he did was remember. Charlie had a few more beers, played a few more games, danced with Daisy again, and then they went home.

Charlie and Daisy lived in the Town of Ithaca on Sapsucker Woods Road. There was nothing special about their house. It was like every other house on the road, a single story three-bedroom ranch style house on a half-acre of land that was made on the cheap to be affordable to working class families. Charlie bought it after the war with a GI Home Loan, and over the years, he made a few changes to the house. He put on aluminum siding, painted the house bright yellow with orange trim to please Daisy, replaced the cheap carpet and plywood floors with oak floors that he installed himself, and built an enclosed porch and flagstone patio that looked out into the Sapsucker Woods and the bird sanctuary. Daisy planted flowers everywhere which pleased Charlie because it reminded him of his childhood. Charlie planted a cherry tree and an apple tree in their backyard, and now, after all these years, they were full grown and in bloom.

When the trees bear fruit later in the summer his backyard will become a feasting place for deer, squirrels, and all sorts of birds. Charlie liked that. He even liked the sapsucker woodpecker that visited the woods behind his house every summer and pecked away in the morning, making a hell of a racket looking for grubs and bugs when Charlie had a hangover. To some people his home probably seemed like nothing, but not to him. It was the home he dreamt of when he was homeless. It was the home that he dreamt of when he was in the ass end of the Flying Fortress, and it was a dream that he made come true.

Charlie parked the car in the driveway, and they entered the house through the kitchen door. The kitchen cabinets were made of knotty pine, and there was a 50s era green Formica kitchen table with chrome trim and matching chairs in the center of room. All the appliances and almost everything else in the kitchen had been bought at Montgomery Wards or Sears. Charlie had painted the kitchen sky blue last year, and Daisy made dark blue curtains with yellow flowers for the windows. On one of the walls there was a painting of a white colonial farmhouse with a red barn and cows grazing in the foreground. It was one of those paintings that you did by the numbers. Daisy had worked on it for a month, and it looked like a real painting to Charlie.

When they went upstairs, Daisy went into what had been Becky's bedroom, and she put the stuffed animals and dolls that she had won at the VFW on the bed. Becky's and Timmy's beds were full of the stuffed animals and dolls Daisy had collected over time. They were also here and there all over the house, like sentinels of the family dream.

Daisy went into the bathroom to get ready for bed, but Charlie wasn't sleepy. He went back downstairs, took a beer out of the refrigerator, and went out onto the patio and sat down at the picnic table. Charlie lit a cigarette and looked up at the stars then looked out into the woods. The crickets and the fireflies were out tonight, and it was quite beautiful in a modest way. It was all that he wanted, but he feared that it was all beginning to fall apart. The house sorely needed to be repainted, and the refrigerator and the stove were antiques from the 50s when they were modern and new. The dish washer was broken, and the living room furniture was becoming thread bare. Daisy put a happy face on it and said that it didn't matter. They had each other, but he knew it bothered her. She didn't invite anyone over for dinner anymore. She was ashamed.

Charlie would have like to work more, but he was in his seventies, and he had an irregular heartbeat, high blood pressure, and he peed a lot. Bob and the Reverend thought that they were

56

doing him a favor by giving him a job redoing the floors at the VFW, but all those years on his knees putting in floors had nearly crippled him. God, he felt so broke, and it was sad to think that he would never be new again.

"Count your blessings, Charlie," he said to himself. The Reverend was right. He'd gone through a hell of a lot worse than this. Charlie thought back to a time when he was sixteen, and he didn't have a home. It was right after his father com-mitted suicide, and they were about to be evicted from the apartment that they were living in. He remembered walking to the railway crossing near Stewart Park. He knew that the train slowed down for the crossing, so he hid in the bushes, and when the train came by, he looked for an open boxcar, spotted one, and began to run. He ran alongside the boxcar, but he couldn't quite figure out how he was going to jump on. He was holding his bag of clothes, and he only had one hand free. He began to slip on the loose gravel, and out of desperation, he threw his bag of clothes into the box car and reached for the edge of the open door, but he missed it. He tried to run faster, and he was about to fall on his face when a hand reached out to him.

He grabbed it, and he was yanked up and into the boxcar. He was on the train. He was about to thank the man who helped him when he realized that it was Dick Farris, the carpenter who had worked for his father. The one he liked.

"How ya doin, Charlie?"

"Hello, Mr. Farris. Thank you for helping me."

Charlie looked around and saw that the car was empty of cargo except for some loose straw, some bales of hay, and several men who, like him, were hitching a free ride to somewhere. Charlie's dad would have disapproved of Charlie being in the company of men like this. They were dirty, and they smelled. Their clothes were ragged, and they had holes in their shoes, but they weren't dead with a bullet hole in their head, and they didn't seem to mind him being there.

Dick Farris sat down and propped his back against the side wall of the boxcar, "Where yah going, son?"

"I'm going west, sir."

Dick Farris smiled, "Did ya bring your six guns, Charlie?"

"No, sir, but I'm willing to work."

Everyone burst out laughing, but Charlie couldn't figure out what was so funny.

Dick pointed at Charlie's laundry bag filled with his things and said, "Let's see what you got there, Charlie. See if you came prepared for your long journey west."

Charlie handed Dick the bag, and he dumped it out revealing an extra pair of jeans, two pairs of socks, a couple pair of underwear, two white t-shirts, a dark blue wool sweater, a bar of soap, a tooth brush, tooth paste, and a dark brown light-weight wool blanket.

"Not bad as far as it goes, but, here, let me show you something."

Dick Farris motioned to one of the men and said, "Cactus Jack, throw me some of that twine over there."

Cactus Jack, who was a big bearded man, the kind of man you might see on a construction site, reached over and grabbed some bailing twine that was lying on the floor of the car amidst the straw and threw it over to Dick.

Dick took Charlie's things and carefully bundled them up together. He then rolled them in Charlie's blanket, tied the blanket at both ends, and made loops so that Charlie could put his arms through the strap-like-loops and carry his bundle like a knapsack. Charlie tried it out, and Dick adjusted it some and said, "There, now you got yourself a bindle."

Charlie could immediately see the advantage of what Mr. Farris called a "bindle," and thanked him for it.

"Now he needs a moniker," another man said.

Dick Farris smiled at the thought and said, "You're right, Sneaky Pete."

With what Charlie's mother would call a "smirk" on his face,

Sneaky Pete said, "You can call him Angelina, and you can be his joker."

Dick Farris looked mad, "I'll have none of that, Jack. This boy's father was good to me when I worked for him, and he helped out my family and me when we were in need. I'm just payin off a debt to his dad. Gonna make sure Charlie starts off on the right track."

Dick Farris turned to Charlie and smiled kindly and said, "But Sneaky Pete's right, Charlie, you do need a moniker. Nobody who is on the rails and knows the code calls themselves by their Christian name, at least not in public." Dick thought for a moment then said, "You say you want to go west, so how about the name, West? Yeah, I got it, Beau West, how about that?"

Charlie thought about it for a moment and said, "You mean like a bow and arrow?"

"Yeah, sure something like that or short for "hobo," but with some class, spelled B-E-A-U."

Dick turned to another man who was in the boxcar with them and asked, "What do you think, Weary Willie?

Weary Willie had big wide eyes and a bulbous nose, and he looked like the saddest man Charlie ever saw. A very small hand came out of cuff of a very large black wool overcoat, and he waved almost as if he were cleaning the windshield of a car for a dime and said, "Hey Beau."

"Well, that's settled then," Dick Farris said. "Your moniker is Beau West, and your sign will be a bow and arrow."

"Do you have a moniker, Mr. Farris?" Charlie asked.

"They call me Cat Walker, Charlie."

"What's that mean?"

Dick Farris smiled and said, "I'll be showing you soon enough, Beau."

Dick leaned back on a bale of hay and stared out the door of the boxcar at the passing landscape. Charlie was very tired, and soon he drifted off to the sound of the thumping heartbeat of the train...

He woke up when Dick Farris grabbing a hold of his shoulder and said, "Come on, Charlie, we get off here."

"But, Dick, the train is still moving."

"I know, son, but you don't want to wait until it stops, and you have to deal with the yard-bulls. Just do what I do. The train will slow down soon, and when it does, we'll jump. Just keep relaxed and don't try to stay on your feet, roll with it, like you did in high school when you tumbled on the gym mats. Remember?"

"Yes."

Charlie waited. He was frightened but excited at the same

time. When the train slowed down, Dick said, "Now," and Dick jumped, and Charlie followed.

"Oh, my God!" he shouted as his heels hit the incline of the gravel bank, and he slid for a distance like a drunk on his heels flailing his arms before he tumbled over and over again and rolled into a big bush face first.

"Wow!" Charlie got up. He had some scratches on his face, but he was in one piece. "Wow!" he shouted again. This was exciting. He was on an adventure.

Dick came up to him. "You okay?"

"Yep."

"Good, let's go."

Dick led him away from the railroad station. From a distance, Charlie saw men with clubs appear as the train neared the station. They were chasing the hoboes and swinging wildly at the fleeing men. One man got hit in the head so hard Charlie heard the sound from where he was standing. Charlie stood there in shock and watched the yard bull hit the man again and again. He was mesmerized by a level of violence that he had never seen before.

Dick grabbed Charlie and pushed him along. "Rule number one - Don't get on or off a train unless it's moving. Don't try to get in a boxcar in a railroad yard at night thinking you're going to sleep in it. The bulls inspect them at night. Don't try to get on the train in the morning, before it gets moving. They inspect them again then. And don't get caught on the train alone with a bull. He'll hit you over the head and throw you off the train while it's going full speed. And before you jump into an open box car, look inside, there may be a bull in there waiting for you. He'll smack you right in the face with his bully club as you're getting on."

"But why do they do that?"

"There's no free ride in America, Charlie."

They avoided the railway station and walked to what looked like the prosperous part of town. The street they were walking on was lined with big old trees, and the houses were mostly Victorian with well-keep lawns. They were the kind of houses that Charlie's father built before the crash.

They were walking by a large gray house trimmed with black and gold when Dick stopped and said, "We'll get food here."

"How do you know?"

Dick pointed to the walkway leading up to the front door of the house. "See those chalk marks, the square and the circle?"

At first Charlie didn't see what Dick was pointing at, but then he saw the small chalk marks on the edge of the walkway near one of the rose bushes. "I see it," Charlie said. "What does it mean?"

"It means that other hoboes have been through here before us, and they've marked the street for us. That sign there on the walkway means, food here."

As they walked up the walkway to the front door of the house, Dick explained all the signs to Charlie and what they meant. "Wow," Charlie said, "it's like Morse code."

Dick laughed, "Yeah, I guess you could say that."

"Is that why we didn't stop at any of the other houses we passed by?"

"You got it, Charlie. What we got here is a marked trail. You ready?"

Charlie was a little confused, "So what do we do? Do we just go up to the door and beg for food or money?"

"No, Charlie, we don't beg. We're not beggars. We're hoboes. We offer to work for whatever people will give us. Then it's up to them."

By the time Dick finished telling Charlie about who they were and what they do and how they do it, they were standing on the front porch. There were flowering plants hanging from the porch and lace curtains in the windows. It was a pretty nice house, Charlie thought, and he wished he lived there.

Dick knocked on the door and an old woman appeared. She

looked like she was in her late sixties or early seventies. She had on a yellow dress, and she was wearing a faded green apron with pink frills. Charlie noticed that she had flour on her hand and apron, and her nylon stockings were rolled down to her swollen ankles. He could smell a pie baking, apple.

"Excuse me, ma'am, but me and my son here have fallen on bad times. Could you spare some food? We're willing to work for it. Maybe you have some chores that need to be done. We are willing to work for whatever you give us."

The old woman looked past Dick at Charlie and said, "You poor thing. You wait right here. I'll be right back."

The woman left, and ten minutes later she was back. She handed them each a sandwich wrapped in wax paper and then handed them each a quarter and said, "I hope you like peanut butter and jelly sandwiches."

"Yes ma'am," Charlie said.

"Thank you, ma'am," Dick said. "Now is there something you would like us to do for you?"

"Oh, my goodness, no, I just hope things get better for you and your son. God bless you both," she said as she closed the door before Charlie could even say, thank you.

Dick smiled, "Food and money, not bad. This is going to be an easy day, Charlie. All we got to do is read the signs."

Sure enough, they read the signs and things went pretty easy. They were given food and some money too. They offered to work, but everyone seemed to be glad to get rid of them as soon as possible, and it didn't seem much different than bumming to Charlie.

It was getting late in the day, and they were getting hungry, so they stopped at a grocery store and bought two bottles of Coca Cola and sat down on a park bench and ate the two bologna sandwiches that they were given, a couple of carrots, and a stalk of limp celery. They split a stale sugar doughnut, and then Dick held up the two cans of beans that they got from one of the houses and said, "This is what we really want, canned goods. It's money in the bank. We'll save this for when we need it." Dick put the two cans of beans back in his pack and took out the two apples that they had panhandled.

As Charlie was eating his apple, he realized that some of the people who were passing by were looking at him, or they were consciously trying not to look at him at all. He looked at his clothes and his hands, and he realized that he was one of the dirty people. Charlie reached into his sack and pulled out the bar of soap and showed it to Dick as if it were the last remaining fragment of Paradise Lost.

"Will I ever be able to wash again?" Charlie asked.

Dick laughed, "Sure you will, Charlie. It's not quite that bad." For a moment he studied Charlie. Then he said, "I have to be honest with you, Charlie. I never did like your dad much. But he helped me when I was in need and what happened to you and your Mom shouldn't happen to anyone, so if you want to travel with me for a while until you get the feel of the thing... well, that's just fine with me."

"I'd like that a lot, Dick."

"OK, then it's settled."

Dick smiled at Charlie. "Charlie, you ever been camping?"

"No sir."

Dick laughed, "Well, son, you're in for a treat."

When they finished eating, they walked along the railroad tracks until they were out of the city and into the countryside. When they got to a railroad crossing, Dick headed for the forest that was nearby. They walked into the woods, and Dick took a round brass case out of his pocket. The top snapped open, and there was a compass inside.

"You have to always know where you're going, Charlie."

Dick showed him how to use it, and when they came to a stream, Dick stopped. "We'll camp here." Dick took off his backpack, and he pulled out a neatly folded sheet of dark green canvas. He strung it over a rope between two trees and staked the corners of the sheet to the ground, and it made a tent. Dick had a whole lot of things in his backpack. He had a small dented tin coffee pot and a cooking pot too, and he had matches and a little hand saw for cutting limbs off dead trees. He even had a can opener for the cans of beans they had panhandled and utensils to eat with. When Dick took out his pocketknife with the carved bone handle, Charlie realized that Dick had everything.

They ate their beans and drank from the spring, and Dick sang his favorite song, a song that Dick would sing repeatedly in their travels.

Life is just a bowl of cherries.
Don't make it serious,
Life's too mysterious.
You work, you save; you worry so,
But you can't take your dough when you go-go-go,
So keep repeating it's the berries,
The strongest oak must fall.
The sweet things in life,
To you were just a loan,
So how can you lose what you've never owned.
Life is just a bowl of cherries,
So live and laugh at it all.

Charlie fell asleep under the stars, and the next day they were on the move again, and they kept on the move, jumping trains from one town to the next. Dick and Charlie worked out their father and son routine, and sometimes Charlie would fantasize that Dick was his real father. Sometime Charlie would go to the door of a house without Dick because some people felt sorry for a boy who was only sixteen years old, alone, and without a home. Sometimes they put him to work mowing their lawn or raking leaves or cleaning out the garage or taking out the garbage. Sometimes there was real work, like bringing in a farmer's crop. It was seasonal work, and Charlie was lucky that he started bumming in the fall because there was a lot of that. Sometimes, when they went to a house, Dick would see something that needed repair. He would go with Charlie to the door and tell the person who answered the door that he was a carpenter, and he could fix it just fine. Charlie loved those moments. He worked as Dick's apprentice, and he was learning a trade.

Sometimes they had quite a bit of money. Charlie re-membered one time when they went to a diner and had a real steak. It was great! They had mashed potatoes, and string beans and biscuits and apple pie. Charlie wolfed it down, and he never felt so good. After dinner, they went to the movies, and he saw Betty Grable for the first time. He fell in love instantly. Afterwards Charlie rolled his first cigarette and smoked it, and he felt like a man. It was his seventeenth birthday.

A week later, Charlie and Dick were walking through a poor

neighborhood in a small suburban town in Michigan when Charlie saw two men carrying furniture out of an apartment building and placing it on the street. Standing next to the furniture was a woman holding a child in her arms. She was crying. The woman and child were being evicted from their home. When Charlie saw the two men reappear carrying the kitchen table, something snapped in Charlie. He was enraged. He ran over to where the men were and grabbed the table.

"You can't do this," he shouted, "This isn't right."

"Get the fuck out of here," one of the men said, and he pushed Charlie to the ground. He was about to kick Charlie when Dick hit the man so hard that he knocked him on his ass. The other man jumped Dick, and they began to wrestle around. The man who Dick had knocked down got up and tried to grab Dick from behind and pin his arms back. Charlie jumped on the man's back. He had one arm around the man's neck and was trying to hit him with his free hand, but he didn't seem to be having any effect, the man was twice his size. The man swung Charlie around wildly. Charlie lost his grip, and he went flying and slammed into the wall of the apartment building. The man kicked him once and was about to kick him again when two of the woman's neighbors joined in the fight. They grabbed the man and threw him aside. More of the woman's neighbors joined in, and they roughed up the two men plenty.

Charlie heard someone growl, "Now get the hell out of here and don't come back. We see you around here again, and we're going to break your fuckin' legs."

The women's neighbors, there must have been five or six of them now, took the furniture the men had taken from the woman and her children off the truck. The two men who had attempted to evict the woman drove away, and Charlie thought that it was over, but as the two men were driving away, the man who was seated on the passenger's side of the truck stuck his head out the window and shouted, "Next time we will be back with the cops."

Someone picked up a rock and threw it at the truck and shouted, "Fuck you."

Charlie got up from the ground and brushed himself off. He had a bump on his head and his ribs hurt, but he was all right. He was more than all right. He felt like a hero. He picked up a chair and went up to the woman. "Where's this go, ma'am?"

The woman smiled at him like Betty Grable and said, "Up on the second floor, apartment number five."

Charlie picked up a chair, walked into the building, climbed the stairs, and found apartment number five. It was nearly empty. It was sad. It brought back memories of the sadist days of his life. Charlie put the chairs in the kitchen and turned around to go back downstairs to get something else when two tough looking men, who you would never imagine could be so kind, entered the apartment carrying the living room sofa. Everyone was helping. In a short time, everything was back where it belonged, and Charlie felt like he had done something meaningful for the first time in his life.

That night Dick and he camped at a Hooverville. There were thousands of Hooverville's all over the country. Dick told him that this one was typical. There were hundreds of people in the camp living in packing boxes or shipping crates, tents or makeshift shacks made of tar paper, odd pieces of wood, and sheet metal roofing. He saw a family of five living in an abandoned delivery truck.

As soon as they entered the hobo camp, Charlie and Dick's identities changed. They were no longer who they were. They were who they are in hobo society. Charlie and Dick became Beau West and Cat Walker. For dinner, Beau West and Cat Walker pooled their food with the hoboes in the camp. They all contributed to a potluck stew that the Crumb Boss cooked and keep stewing throughout the day and night. Beau West was surprised. The stew was very good. He asked Cat Walker what was in it, and the Cat smiled and said, "You don't want to know."

After they ate, Beau sat at a big campfire with a lot of the other men. He smoked, drank moonshine that tasted like turpentine, and listened to the men tell stories. The flames of the fire flickered from face to face, many of the men were just shadows talking, ghost, whisperers fading into the night.

A farm boy, not much older than Beau, who they called Cabbage Head said, "Things are so bad where I come from that we nearly lynched a judge who was foreclosing on the farms in the area."

"Shit," Cat Walker said, "Beau West and I saw that in Indiana. The farmers there are damned mad too. About a week ago, Beau and I were walking down an old dirt country road looking for a place to camp, and we walked right into twenty or thirty farmers carrying shotguns. They had blockaded the road, and they were waiting for the sheriff to come. Beau and I took to the woods, and we found more armed farmers hiding there. One farmer told us 'to git', and we got, as fast as we could because those farmers meant business."

"I bet them farmers were all vets too," one man said.

"Nothin' scarier than a red neck vet with a shotgun and shit on his boots to scare the hell out of you," Sneaky Pete said and, all the men laughed.

"It ain't only the farmers that are getting' a screwin'," Detroit Joe said. "I worked in a factory where you clocked in at seven, and you were locked into that damned sweat box until seven at night, and if there was a fire...well... you all know what happened in Boston. Most of those workers couldn't get out because the doors were chained up like ours, and, except for a few, they all died in the fire. Anyhow, at my factory, if you were one minute late, you were docked one hour. If you were late two times you were fired. It was so bad that you had to get permission to take a pee, just like in school. I made five dollars a day, and when we doubled production, they fired me. That was my reward for being a hard worker."

Beau decided to tell his story. He told them about how they saved the woman and her little baby from being evicted from their apartment.

"You did right, Beau West," one man said.

Beau heard many more voices of approval, but then a man appeared out of the shadows and said, "They probably came back the next day with the police and threw them out on their asses, into the street for good."

The man began to pass leaflets around. In the fire light he looked like the Devil. "If you want to do something real about the way things are, come to Chicago." As he vanished into the

74

darkness, Charlie heard him say, "Unite Brothers and Sisters, you have nothing to lose but your chains."

"Who was that guy?" Someone asked.

"He's a Red," another man said.

Beau looked at the leaflet. It was about a mass demonstration that was going to happen in Chicago to protest unemployment and homelessness.

"What's a Red?" Beau asked.

One of the voices out of the darkness said, "They're a bunch of radicals that say the working class should run the country. It's a lot of bullshit."

"It may be a lot of bullshit, but anything's got to be better than this," another voice said. "I'm going."

"Me too," another voice said.

In the flickering light of the flames from the campfire and contrasting darkness one man said, "I'm not a Russian lover, and I'm not going. I don't care how bad it is. I'm no traitor."

"I'm not a Commie either," Detroit Joe said, "but the Commies are right. This country is being run by the rich. We got to come together like an army. Let them know that we're serious. This is our country too. We all helped to build it."

"You're damn right," said another man on the other side of the campfire, his face ablaze. "For and by the people, that's what it supposed to be all about, not for and by the rich. If sayin that makes me a commie or a socialist, well, so be it."

An old man that was sitting near Beau said, "So you boys want to be an army, do you? You better think twice about that one. In 1924 us veterans from the First World War marched on Washington. There were thousands of us. We petitioned Hoover to give us the bonus that we were promised. We camped out in abandoned buildings and built a Hooverville across the Potomac at Anacostia Flats. We told them that we weren't going to move until we got our money. We surrounded the White House. They ordered us to move, but we wouldn't budge. The Police Chief refused to move us, and some Marine Commander refused to remove us too. We thought we might win, but then George Fuckin' MacArthur, that son-of-a-bitch, came in riding a white horse, and he turned regular army troops loose on us bunch of veterans. We were beaten out of the abandoned buildings and beaten and shot and burned out of Hooverville. So, boys, be forewarned. If you want to go to that demonstration, you better be ready to fight because they're not going to let a bunch of bums like you tell them what to do."

"Who you callin' a bum."

Who's they? Beau wondered. He was just about to ask when Cat said to him, "Come on, Charlie. Let's get out of here. There's going to be a fight." He grabbed Charlie and pulled him to his feet.

"Dick, let's go to the demonstration."

"No way, the old man is right, you don't beat the system; the system beats you."

"What about our right to vote? I learned in school we're a democracy."

"Democracy, my ass, you have to have a home to vote. Homeless people don't have the right to vote. We don't matter."

Dick was mad, and there was no talking to him when he got like that, so Charlie just went along, and Dick was right about the fight. He could hear the men shouting now. They were fighting amongst themselves.

The next day they hopped a train. Weeks later, while Charlie and Dick were riding a boxcar, Charlie noticed a sign indicating that they were near Chicago. He reached into his coat pocket and pulled out the leaflet that the old man had passed around at the campfire. He had saved the leaflet, and he read it repeatedly. There was something about it that fascinated him, so he read it again.

30% of America is out of Work
Soon
There will be more of Us than there are of Them

Face the Enemy
Join
Us
In
Chicago
At a Mass Demonstration
Against
Unemployment and Homelessness

When Charlie finished reading the leaflet, and he thought about how close they were to Chicago and the date of the demonstration, he realized that he could go there. He could be part of something important. There was something wrong here. Things shouldn't be like this.

He showed the leaflet to Dick and said, "Dick, I want to go to Chicago."

"No."

Dick and Charlie were the only ones in the box car. Dick was sitting next to the open door looking out at the countryside as it passed by.

"If you don't want to go, I'm goin' without you," Charlie said.

"Feelin' your oats, are you?"

"No, sir, but that man was right. The cops did probably come the next day and throw that woman and child out onto the street. I have to go. I have to do something."

"It means that we'll have to break up. But maybe it's time

78

that you were on your own."

"No, no, I don't mean that. I could meet you somewhere else."

"It don't work like that, Charlie. When you're on the road, you go where you can go, not where you want to go. If you try to go against the flow, you're going to be drowned by all the sewage you left behind."

Charlie was heartbroken. He didn't want to leave Dick, but he didn't understand him. How could he be so indifferent about doing something? "Dick, don't you believe in anything?"

"Sure, I do, Charlie. I believe in the moment. For example, right now, you're not here. You're in Chicago someplace, and I'm here right now enjoying the scenery. I don't know whether you noticed it or not, but it's a pretty nice day out there."

Charlie looked out the open door of the boxcar. Dick was right. It was a beautiful fall day. The leaves of the trees were orange, red, purple and green, and they looked like a beautiful bouquet of rolling hills. Dick put his arm around Charlie and sang his favorite song, and Charlie sang along.

Life is just a bowl of cherries
Don't make it serious,
Life's too mysterious.
You work, you save, you worry so,
But you can't take your dough when you go-go-go,

So keep repeating it's the berries,
The strongest oak must fall.
The sweet things in life,
To you were just a loan,
So how can you lose what you've never owned.
Life is just a bowl of cherries,
So live and laugh at it all.

They both laughed when the song was over, and for a while, they sat staring out at the passing countryside, then Dick said, "You still want to go to Chicago?"

"Yes."

"OK. I'll go with you, but not because I want to. I think it's a damn fool thing, but I better go with you to make sure you don't get yourself in trouble, but after that I think we should go west, all the way to the end, just like you wanted to do."

"Oh boy, that would be great, Dick!"

"But remember, we have to get over the Rockies before winter sets in. "Right, Beau West?"

Charlie smiled, Right, Cat Walker."

Charlie was very happy. He didn't want to leave Dick, ever. He was also excited. He'd never been to a big city like Chicago.

"You ever been to Chicago, Dick?"

"Nope."

"Isn't it exciting?"

"Nope, it's just a bunch of boxes piled up on top of each other with a lot of people livin' in them. Ain't much different than a Hooverville except it's a lot more fancy and a lot more crowded."

The next day, they hopped a train to Chicago, but Dick made Charlie get off the train way out of town. They were twenty miles outside of Chicago when they hitched a ride on the back of a pickup truck, and it was a good thing too because the yard-bulls and the cops must have been reading the same leaflet that Charlie had been reading. They were pulling trains over way out of town and beating up hoboes, but the hoboes kept on coming, joining other homeless and jobless people who had come to protest the injustice of it all. There were other people there too, even men in suits and ladies in nice dresses. It was a strange and new experience for Charlie, and as more and more people came together, Charlie felt stronger and stronger. He felt a part of something massive that was growing. It was like each of these people was an extension of his body. He felt a part of everyone.

Charlie turned to Dick and said, "Dick, don't you feel a part of something big?"

Dick laughed and said, "Yeah, a big bed bug that's about to be squished."

Charlie listened to the speeches. He especially liked the last speaker who was a tall bony man with large knobby hands, high cheekbones, sunken eyes, and a shock of blond hair that he had to constantly brush away from his eyes. He looked like a farmer or maybe a cowboy wearing his going-to-church-suit, and he had a deep rich voice that carried through the crowd. From this man he learned that everyone had the right to life, liberty, and the pursuit of happiness. It was in the Constitution. Charlie learned that in grade school, but he had forgotten. The man talked about a thing called "capitalism", but Charlie didn't understand that. It had something to do with a lot of people who didn't work, who were bums like him but made lots of money. At the end of the speech the man said that all the workers in the world should unite.

After the speech, Charlie wanted to talk to the man. He wanted to ask him if he was a Red. He wanted to ask the man if he could help him find a job. He had a whole lot of questions to ask, but that's when the cops came, and they came in mass. Many of them were on horseback.

Dick grabbed Charlie and tried to pull him away, "Come on, Charlie. Let's get out of here."

"No!" Charlie said.

As Charlie broke loose of Dick's grip on his arm, he saw the mounted police charge the crowd. They were clubbing everyone in their way. The horses were trampling over men, women, and children, but then someone in the crowd threw marbles all over the street, and the horses began to slip and fall. The demonstrators surged forward, and Charlie ran forward with them. That's when the police started firing into the crowd, and Charlie saw several people hit. He saw a bullet blow away a woman's breast. It was horrible. The blood poured all over her flowery dress.

A man right next to him got hit and fell to the pavement like a sack of potatoes. Charlie went to the man's aid, but when he knelt and stared into the man's lifeless eyes, he knew he was dead. The man had a brick in his hand. Charlie picked up the brick and threw it. He didn't know where he was throwing it, but he just threw it as hard and far as he could. He saw a policeman on horseback bearing down on him at full gallop. He raised his hands up to protect himself and then everything went blank.

He woke up in an alleyway. Dick was wiping blood from his head.

"Am I all right, Dick?"

"You're OK, Charlie. Scalp wounds bleed a lot. It just looks bad."

Dick held up his handkerchief. It was full of blood. "This is why they call them Reds, Charlie. They bleed a lot."

They both laughed, and Dick helped Charlie up.

"There's a Hooverville outside town," Dick said. "We'll go there. I don't know if it's safe or not, but we'll probably find a horse doctor or a vet or at least someone who knows more about patching you up than I do. I think that cut is going need stitches."

They made their way out of town. The cops were picking up anyone who looked like a vagrant, so it was tough going, but they made it to the campsite by nightfall, and they did find someone to look at Charlie. The guy had worked in a hospital, and he seemed to know what he was doing. He put three stitches in Charlie's head and said that Charlie was going to be all right. He just needed some rest.

Dick strung their tent in the dark. Charlie took the aspirins that the man had given him and then he laid down on his brown blanket. Dick covered him with another blanket and soon he was fast asleep. Later that night Charlie woke up, and he had to take a pee. He walked into the woods. His head ached like hell. When he was peeing, he heard voices. He looked around and saw the shadows of men walking through the woods. There were lots of them. He ducked down behind a bush. They came by him, and he saw guns and clubs. He wanted to shout a warning, but he was too afraid. He had already taken a beating, and he didn't want to get beaten again. He didn't want to die.

Minutes later, he heard screams and shouts, and then he saw the flames. They were burning down Hooverville. The shadows came and went and left behind them the wails and moans of men, women, and children. He saw a woman bleeding from her head. She was holding her young boy in her arms, and he had been beaten badly too. There were flames all around them. He saw a man face down in the campfire burning. He tried to pull him out of the campfire, but he realized it was Detroit Joe and that he was dead with a bullet hole in his head. Charlie was terrified. Charlie had to find Dick.

Charlie grabbed one of the logs in the fire and raised it up as a torch. He ran through the camp, and the shadows looked like devils dancing in a blood red hell. When he reached their camp site, he found Dick. Dick looked like he was asleep, all curled up like a little baby in the womb, but his head had been bashed in, and he was dead.

"Oh, my God, Oh, my God," Charlie wailed and moaned as he rocked Dick in his arms. "Oh, God, help us. Oh, God, no. Dick never hurt anyone. Oh Dick, I'm sorry. I'm so sorry. It's my fault. I should have shouted out, when I saw them." Charlie cried and cried.

Two days later Dick was buried in a pauper's field. He was buried in a mass grave, boxes upon boxes of poor people stacked one upon the other. There was a special pile of little wood coffins for dead children and babies. There was no service, no prayers, and no eulogies for the poor and homeless. There was only a bulldozer that plowed dirt over the graves like they were so much garbage to be buried and forgotten without a marker. Charlie felt then what it was like to truly be nothing, to be dirt.

Charlie now possessed Dick's backpack, his coffee pot, cooking pan, a fork and a knife, the canvas sheet and rope that Dick used for a tent, and his compass and pocketknife. That was all that was left of the man Charlie loved. Charlie went to the police station to see if they had caught the men who had murdered his friend. The sergeant behind the desk motioned to two other policemen who came over and grabbed Charlie by the arms and ushered him out of the police station. They drove him out of town, threw him out of the car, and told him to get the hell out of town and never come back.

As the cops were driving away, he shouted, "And what am I guilty off, being poor? You sons-of-a-bitches, is that what you murder people for? I'm never going to forget this, and I'm never going to forgive you."

The cops paid him no mind. They just drove away leaving him on the road.

"I'm an American!" Charlie shouted, but there was no one

there to hear him.

Charlie took out Dick's compass to get his bearing and then headed west. He remembered what Dick had said about getting over the Rockies before winter set in, but Charlie didn't quite make it. It was getting colder and colder as he made his way across the country. He stuffed newspapers in his clothes to keep warm and stuffed newspaper in his shoes when the holes appeared. The headline on one of the newspapers read, **Germany Invades Austria,** but Charlie didn't notice it. When the soles on his shoes began to fall off, he taped them back on, and the headline to the newspaper he was using to stuff in his shoe read, **Germany Attacks Poland**, but he didn't notice that either because he was more concerned about freezing to death. Charlie didn't know nothing about a country called, Poland, except that it was somewhere in Europe, and Europe was just a name to him.

One day, on his way over the Rockies, Charlie was on a flatbed car trying to get to a box car where he might find more shelter. Charlie was overwhelmed by the vastness of the mountains and the power of nature, the deadly magnificent beauty of the ice and snow, the frozen jagged edges of the escarpments, the frozen falls, and the evergreens that looked like spears piercing the gray sky looking for light. He was wearing two layers of clothes, an old raggedy wool overcoat, a scarf around his face, and a knit cap and gloves with holes in them, but it wasn't enough. The cold was like icy knives piercing every hole in his clothes and every crack in his defenses. There was a warm spot deep inside of him where he wanted to curl up in and go to sleep, but he was afraid of that amber burning out, and he would never wake up. Charlie felt like things just couldn't get worse until he saw the cinder-dick, Blackjack Fenner, cat walking the box car above him. He was called Blackjack because he carried a leather wrapped lead weight attached to the end of a coil spring and a handle. He carried the blackjack from a lanyard around his neck. This allowed him to catwalk and chase hoboes without the hindrance of carrying a bully club. Blackjack was a legendary cinder-dick noted for his violence. Hoboes told stories about his brutality and how, when he caught a hobo on his train, he would beat them senseless with the lead weighted blackjack and then throw them off the train leaving them dead on the side of the tracks or crippled for life.

Charlie bolted from the flatbed car, and he climbed up onto the next box car. He began to cat-walk across the car just like Dick had taught him. He was frightened to death, both of slipping and falling or having Blackjack catch up to him from behind and knocking him off the train with a blow to the head.

Charlie tried to remember everything that Dick had taught him about cat walking. He crouched with his weight on the balls of his feet, and rather than fighting the swaying back and forth of the shaking train, he tried to go with it.

"There's a rhythm to every train, Charlie," Dick said. "Go with it. It's like dancing on top of a steel snake. Listen to the beat of its heart. When you're doing it right, you'll know what I mean, boy."

Dick said he heard a blues guitar playing when he cat-walked. Charlie couldn't hear a blues guitar, but he could hear the jingling of the steel symbols, the banging of the steel couplings that held the cars together, and the thump, thump, thump of the beat, so he did what Dick said, and when he felt like he was losing his balance, he stopped, took a deep breath, listened, gathered himself, and went on again. When he got to the end of the box car, he did what Dick said again. He didn't hesitate. He jumped to the next car. This must be where you hear the soaring blues guitar he thought, but he didn't, and when he hit on the other side, he slipped. He frantically reached out, and he grabbed hold of a handrail. For a moment he was dangling between the cars, the steel couplings banging together ready to crush a hand or an arm or leg caught between its steel joints. Below that was the cinder bed, the almost hypnotic whirling of the steel wheels over steel rails, and the thumping and the beat beckoning him to be crushed under the wheels of the train and end it all, all his suffering.

He climbed back up onto the top of the box car, and he looked back to see Blackjack Fenner one car behind him. Blackjack was smiling, and Charlie realized that this was a sadistic game of chicken that the cinder-dick was playing with him.

Fuck him, Charlie said. I'm the Cat Walker now. I was taught by the best, and I will walk on top of this metal snake from Hell all the way up the mountain and down until the Devil gives up. Charlie picked up his pace, and when he jumped to the next car, he landed square and balanced. He swayed and stepped to the rhythm of the snake, and he began to hear that blues guitar that Dick was talking about. It was a steel bottle neck slid guitar playing. Charlie smiled, spread his arms like he was flying, and began to sing as he leaped forward.

Justice ain't no lady
She's a twisted, battered whore
She's laying bruised and naked
On a blood-stained wooden floor.

Our days are over
Times have changed around these parts
There ain't no more cowboys
Only men with violent hearts.

Redemption Blues

My time is drawing thinner
I'm just a tired sinner
No chips left on this shoulder
No pride in growing older
But when my borrowed time is through
I'll be with you.

Redemption Blues

It was then that he saw the tunnel ahead, and he realized that he was about to be "Baptized in Hades," as the hoboes called it. Charlie looked to see where Blackjack was, and he was nowhere to be seen. He had given up and for good reason. Dick had told him that when you went into a long tunnel like this under the Rockies it was like being in Hell. The locomotive's steam engine driven by coal became a fiery mass that turned the tunnel into an oven. The hoboes told stories of people being cooked in tunnels like this and coming out smoked pork.

Charlie laid down spread eagle, covered his face and mouth with his scarf, and began to pray as the heat turned into smoke and the smoke turned into fire, and he began to see red and black shadows dancing along the brick walls of the tunnel like devils. The smoke filled his lungs and he could barely breathe. It was so hot that the newspapers he was wearing underneath his coat and shirt for insulation were burning his skin. He tore open his coat and shirt and began to throw the newspapers away, and as he was doing so, he saw two headlines. **Japan Attacks Pearl Harbor! America Declares War on Japan!**

The headlines barely registered with Charlie, but just as he felt he was done for, and he began to wonder what it was all about, he saw the end of the tunnel, and he was through to the other side. He made it.

The train began to descend the mountain, and as it did, it got warmer and warmer and the snow began to melt. Charlie had crossed the country, and he was in California, but he realized that he was not out of danger. Blackjack Fenner seemed to have given up on Charlie, but to be safe he crawled through the broken boards in one of the box cars and hid behind bales of hay and the cows that were being transported for slaughter.

Charlie fell asleep and dreamt that he was a child again playing with his toy soldiers in his mother's garden amidst the flowers, tomatoes, cucumbers, lettuce, radishes, and corn. He was defending Paradise, but then he heard a thumping noise like the footsteps of a giant. The Japs and Germans were invading the garden! He had to hide so that the invaders couldn't find him, but then he heard the boxcar door fly open!

Oh my God, Blackjack Fenner, Charlie thought. He was full of terror, but it turned out to be California state troopers, and by the time Charlie figured out what was happening, it was too late. He was trapped in the box car with no way out. He thought the state troopers were going to beat him, but they herded him together with about thirty other men, women, and children, and they took them to a government camp where he took a shower, and they gave him clean clothes. That night he slept on clean sheets in a real bed, and the next day he had bacon and eggs for breakfast. He was interviewed by a man from something called the Works Project Administration. A giant picture of Franklin Delano Roosevelt was hanging from the wall, and when the man asked Charlie what kind of work he did, Charlie told him that he had been a carpenter's apprentice, so he got a job working on the construction crew at an Army Air Force base. Charlie was happy. He had gone through a trial of fire and ice, but he had made it to the west coast, and now he had a job. God Bless the New Deal and God Bless President Roosevelt. Finally, there was someone who cared, and he was going to get a chance to prove his worth.

They housed the workers in tents while they built the barracks, hangers, and administrative buildings. When the airstrip was finally finished, Charlie saw the first Flying Fortress come in, and he knew what he wanted to do. He wanted to be in one of them. He wanted to be way up there in the sky as far away from where he had been as he could get. He wanted to feel powerful, so he joined the Air Force.

They first sent him to navigation school, but he didn't do too well there, so they sent him to gunner's school. It was great. He had escaped the depression. He wore clean clothes, got three squares a day, and up in the sky he was part of something big. The depression seemed to be disappearing like magic. Everyone had a goal now, and Charlie had a target for all the frustration and anger that had built up over the years. He knew who "they" were now. They were the Germans and the Japs, and Charlie's job was to destroy the enemy.

Once Charlie was in the war, he forgot about the bumming, the starving, and the dirt. He forgot about the Reds and the beatings he took, and he forgot about nearly freezing to death, but he never forgot about Dick. Dick was a casualty of the war on poverty, but Charlie never discovered who the other "they" were, the men who beat his best friend to death. One thing he knew. It wasn't the Germans or the Japs, and it wasn't the Reds or the Blacks.

Charlie's journey into his past ended when he reached into his pocket and pulled out Dick's compass. He had held on to

Dick's compass now for almost fifty years. He stroked the polished brass with his finger then put it back in his pocket, got up, and walked back into the house from the patio. He walked upstairs to the bedroom, undressed, and got into bed.

Daisy turned over and said, "Is anything wrong, Charlie?"

"No, Daisy." Charlie smiled through his tears, "Life is just a bowl of cherries."

Chapter Three

Back at the VFW, the Reverend got tired of waiting for everyone to leave. The band had quit and gone home, even the bartender was gone, but there were some stragglers trying to hold onto that feeling of omnipotence that only comes from booze or sucking on your mother's tit. Finally, the Reverend lost patience and he picked up his broom and began to sweep the suckers out of the bar.

"Jesus, Reverend," Bill Fusco said. "Can we finish our drinks?"

"Finish your drinks? My ass, you've been suckling on that bottle for the last half hour. Get the hell out of here, all of you. I have work to do."

The Reverend swept Bill Fusco and his party out the door. He then began to place the bar stools on top of the front bar. As he worked his way down the bar, he came to Bud Schooley.

"Stand up for a minute, will you, Bud."

Bud stood up, and the Reverend put Bud's bar stool on the bar.

"You got no heart, Reverend."

"Out."

Without a word of protest, Pete, who was sitting next to Bud, got up from his seat and headed for the door with Bud. At the door, Bud turned and said, "Reverend, this is not a Christian thing to do."

The Reverend held the door open and said, "You'll thank me tomorrow when you wake up feeling like shit. You'll remember how I saved you from yourself, and if you're wise, you'll glory in the pain of revelation, for verily I say unto you Brothers, the only proof of God is a hangover."

The Reverend closed the door and locked it for the night. He wasn't going anywhere. The Reverend lived at the VFW. He slept on the couch in the back room, and he seldom left the bunker-like-building except for funerals and special occasions like Memorial Day.

The Reverend swept the plastic cups and cigarette butts off the floor then cleaned the tables. He cleaned the back bar and the kitchen, and then he mopped the floors. When he was done, the kitchen and barroom were spotless and ready for military inspection, and the tables and chairs were in straight rows like little soldiers. He used a heavy disinfectant and detergent to rid the place of the smell of dying men and dying dreams, frustration, disappointment, and rotten old farts. He left the bathrooms for last. It was in the shithouse, the temple of death, that he could inhale the pure essence of reality and recall the biggest shit hole of all,

Vietnam.

The sun was setting in South Vietnam, and the Reverend's re-connaissance unit was in a Huey helicopter flying over the border from South Vietnam into Laos. The Reverend was called Doc when he was in Vietnam, and he was a part of a six man unit that included Doc, Rocker, and four Montagnard tribesmen from the central highlands of Vietnam who they nicknamed Happy, Grumpy, Sleepy, and Sneezy after the dwarfs in the fairy tale, *Snow White*. Rocker's real name was James Graves, and Lieutenant Graves was the leader of the unit. The team was part of a special SOG unit involved in covert missions that took them "over the fence" into Laos to find and track the movement of the enemy on the Ho Chi Minh Trail. SOG stood for Studies and Observation Group, a very innocuous name for a top-secret recon and strike force that worked behind enemy lines and in "neutral" territory. Nobody knew they existed except the President of the United States and his immediate advisors, the Joint Chiefs of Staff, General Westmoreland, and the CIA.

Doc was observing the Huey helicopter trailing behind them and listening to the racket they were making and smiled to himself and thought, the American eagle sure makes a hell of a lot of noise for a stealth operation. He then looked down at their target zone, a steaming jungle where a whole world of plants struggled against one another for sunlight, the losers rotting on the jungle floor, food for the winners.

Doc heard Rocker shout over the sound of the helicopter, "Doc, tell the Dwarfs that there's seven hundred bucks a piece in it for them if they can capture a North Vietnamese soldier and bring him back alive on this trip."

Doc turned to the Dwarfs, and in Vietnamese he translated what Rocker had said. Sleepy held up two fingers and said, "Maybe we can get two."

"One's good enough," Doc said.

Happy pointed to the 22 pistol that Doc was carrying. The main purpose of the pistol was to wound a soldier and disable him. Happy laughed and said to the other Dwarfs, "Remember the last time that Doc tried to shoot a VC in the leg, and he shot him in the head? We'll never snatch anyone with Doc doing the shooting. He can't hit shit with that thing."

The Dwarfs all laughed at Happy's joke.

"What the hell are you spear-chuckers laughing at?" Doc said. "I was shooting a gun when you assholes were still shooting bows and arrows." That wasn't that long ago, Doc thought to himself. When he and Rocker first came to the central highlands to pacify and train the mountain tribe people, the only weapons they had were bows and arrows, spears, and a few front-loading antique

99

rifles.

Grumpy pointed at the pistol and said, "I can shoot a bow and arrow better than you can shoot that."

"I can shoot a stone better than Doc can shoot that," Sleepy said.

Sneezy laughed and said, "I can piss better than Doc can shoot."

"My wife can piss better than Doc can shoot," Grumpy said, and they all laughed as one.

"Fuck you guys."

Rocker leaned towards Doc so that he could heard, "What's going on?"

"They're busting my balls."

The pilot rapped on the sidewall of the helicopter to get their attention and pointed down below, and Doc could see the landing sight up ahead, a clearing of elephant grass.

As they neared the landing sight and began to drop down, the wash of the helicopter blades matted down the elephant grass. Doc and Rocker looked for any signs of booby traps, mines, or bamboo stakes tempered in fire and planted by the enemy to pierce them like skewered meat when they jumped from the helicopter. The site looked clean, so Rocker motioned to the pilot to touch down. As the helicopter came down to land, the trailing helicopter passed overhead to hide the sound of the landing. To anyone nearby who heard the helicopters, it would sound as if they were just passing overhead.

Doc and his team hit the ground running, and when they got to the edge of the clearing, they merged with the jungle and listened for gunshots. Laotian tribesmen were paid by the enemy to work as sentinels. They were armed with obsolete weapons, so they didn't pursue the recon and strike teams or engage them in battle. Their function was to be lookouts and warn the enemy that the Americans were coming by firing their rifles in the air in pre-arranged patterns that would not only tell the Viet Cong that the Americans were coming but also from where, what sector.

Doc heard no warning shots. For twenty minutes they crouched at the edge of the clearing, motionless. Doc, like the rest of the unit, carried no identification, and they wore nothing that would identify them as members of the American or South Vietnamese armed forces. Doc wore gray jungle fatigues and carried a M45 9mm "Swedish K" submachine gun and an HD.22 caliber pistol with a silencer. His Vietnamese rucksack contained a poncho, extra socks, foot powder, a plastic bottle filled with salt tablets, Tabasco sauce, a hammock, black duck-tape, two claymore mines, and twelve magazines of ammunition. Two canteens of water were packed in pockets on his rucksack and two more hung from a pistol belt. Also hanging from the pistol belt were four M26 fragmentation grenades and two ammunition pouches holding four magazines of ammunition each.

A sheathed bayonet and first aid kit were attached to one shoulder strap and a container of battle dressing was fastened to the other. Doc tied bandages together to make a sweat band and wove more bandages through his belt loops. His pockets were stuffed with medical supplies, and GI socks packed with cooked rice tied end to end hung around his neck. He also wore a Stabo rig, a chest harness that enabled him to be plucked out of the jungle by a hovering helicopter. Every potential noisemaker was taped.

They were all equipped similarly, except three of the Montagnards wore black pajamas and carried AK-47 machine guns to look like the VC. Sleepy, who hauled the "Puck 25" radio on his back, wore a tiger suit and was armed with a 5.56mm Colt Command submachine gun, and Rocker, who wore gray fatigues like Doc, was armed with a M76 grenade launcher and a 9mm Beretta in a shoulder holster.

They were only the tip of the eagle's claws. The modern version of the American eagle was a bio/mechanical monster that through an electronic nerve network of communications connected the attack unit to a recon plane flying high up and out of sight that dogged them night and day, and it was connected to the command post that, with a word, could unleash back-up attack units on the border and the Super Sabers, Sky Raiders, F-4 Phantoms jets, and

B-52s nesting in Vietnam, on carriers, in Thailand, and Japan. The wings of the American eagle cast a vast dark shadow of terror, but in the end, Doc thought, it was boots on the ground that won a war.

Rocker motioned for them to move out. They moved slowly and quietly, and at staggered intervals, they stopped, listened, and scanned the jungle for the enemy. They meticulously repeated this procedure again and again using all their senses to determine if danger was near. It was nearly dark, and the objective was to get far enough into the jungle so they could hide for the night and become part of the darkness.

Rocker signaled for them to halt their movement. For twenty minutes they waited and searched the night. They were in no hurry to get killed. Sometimes, they would take a day to travel a mile.

Doc just squatted there and listened. The air was electric with a symphony of insects gnawing and rubbing their stick legs together like violins. Doc heard the jungle devour itself, the silent screams of plants and trees strangling each other, but he couldn't hear the enemy. He couldn't hear their footsteps or smell their scent. He couldn't hear anything human, only the sound of his own breathing and his heart beating like a single drum, calling out for help, again and again.

Rocker called in their location to the recon plane. He would communicate their location to the recon plane every thirty minutes.

When he was finished, they moved out again. Doc was sweating profusely. His shirt was buttoned tight, and he wore a bush hat pushed down over his head to keep the ticks and blood suckers off his face and skin. One blood sucker that dropped from the trees attached itself to the barrel of his machine gun and another latched onto his boot. Doc imagined ticks crawling all over his shirt searching for access to his flesh. From time to time Doc tried to brush them off, but most of the time Doc suffered silently the agony and fear of being eaten alive piece by little piece.

Rocker pointed to a spot on a knoll. Doc saw it, and he pointed it out to the Dwarfs who nodded in recognition. They walked on until Rocker stopped at a clearing surrounded by needle trees and dwarf bamboo, and he motioned for them to make camp there. They took out their ponchos and tied them together to make a shelter from the rain. Doc mixed cooked rice with some water from a canteen and poured some Tabasco sauce over it, and he began to eat.

Sneezy nudged Doc and held up some dried fish that the Dwarfs had prepared. Doc took the fish and mixed it in with the rice and water. Rocker took some too.

In sign language, Grumpy said, "Doc, can you explain the meaning of our name again. Who is Thor?"

Doc had been with the four Dwarfs and the mountain people for over two years. He first encountered them when his Special Forces unit was sent to the central highlands to pacify the Rhade tribesmen and train them to defend themselves. As part of the educational program he taught them how to read and write in their own language. He also developed a sign language based on the sign language for the deaf and dumb. This was the language they communicated in when they were on a mission. It was a silent language, but it was a language nevertheless, and to the Montegnard tribesmen words were very important. Words were powerful. With words the shaman cast spells. For weeks now they had been worrying over the new name of their unit, Thor's Hammer.

Doc, in sign language, began his story again. "Thor is a Norse God that lives in the land of snow and ice where everything is cold."

Happy pointed to Doc and Rocker, "Like you and him."

Doc shrugged and said, "Yes."

"What's snow?" asked Sleepy.

"I told you before, Sleepy. It's white rain. Remember when we went to Saigon, the shaved icy in the glass, frozen water?"

Sleepy nodded.

"Snow," Doc said, and he went on with the story of Thor. "Thor lives in the land of snow, and he carries a big hammer. All our lives, from the day we are born, he bangs down on us with his hammer.

The more we try to grow, the more he pounds us down. Every time we get uppity, he bangs us down again and again until he finally bangs us down into a grave. Then he puts a rock over our head that we call a "gravestone" so that we can't get uppity again. Thor is the God of Gravity."

Doc smiled. He liked making up stories for the Dwarfs. He especially liked this story. It made a lot of sense.

All the Dwarfs nodded, and then Grumpy said, "But what happens to the spirit?"

"It's trapped under the rock," Doc said.

Sleepy asked Grumpy, "Is Doc saying that they trap the spirit of their ancestors underground forever?"

"Yes, it's like when we cut off the head of our enemy," Grumpy said.

Sleepy looked at Doc and Rocker and said, "Cold."

It was getting very dark now, and Doc could barely see their hands, but he saw one hand say, "Maybe we should change our name."

Another hand said, "We should call ourselves, Snow Ghosts."

There was instantaneous approval by all the Dwarfs. Their hands worked as one now as they told Doc that this was what they wanted.

"Oh, I don't know," Doc said. "Major Shaman says we have to

name our units after an animal or a tool." Major Shaman was the nickname that Doc had given the CIA intelligence officer who ran the SOG operations.

"You try. We are uneasy."

"I will, but…"

Rocker, who was keeping watch, nudged Doc, and Doc signaled to the Dwarfs that it was time to break camp and move out.

They quietly took apart the shelter that they had made with their ponchos and silently crept away. They moved by inches through the darkness until they had reached the first spot that Rocker had pointed out to them. This would be their real campsite for the night. Setting up a false campsite and then moving to another one was a precaution that they always took in case they'd been spotted at the landing sight, and someone was following them. Normally, the enemy would not take on a fully armed SOG unit in daylight. They'd rather wait until the SOG unit bedded down at their over-night camping site and then attack them when they were most vulnerable.

The new campsite was on top of a knoll with good cover. They silently set up their shelter again and bunched together so that they were within arm's reach of each other. Everyone went to sleep except Happy and Sneezy who had the first watch. Four hours later, Doc was woken by Happy. He and Grumpy had the next watch.

Starring out into the darkness, Doc remembered his first encounter with death. He was a little boy, eight years old. His family lived on the edge of a deep gorge, a two-hundred -foot drop to the falls below, certain death, but his parents seemed totally oblivious to the danger. Maybe it was the frontier mentality of his parents who came from old American stock. His father's family went west in a covered wagon in search of a homestead, and they settled in Ohio. His mother claimed that she was a Daughter of the American Revolution, a descendant of Arthur Middleton, one of the original signers of the Declaration of Independence. Whatever the source, the pioneering spirit or utter neglect, Willie and his two sisters ran wild in the forests and along the edges of the gorge.

One day Willie slipped and fell into the gorge, but as he fell over the edge, he became entangled in the limbs of a tree that was growing out of the fissures on the side of the cliff. As he dangled from the limbs of a tree like it was his crib, he looked down into the gaping maw that had been gorged out in the last Ice Age ready to swallow him up. He heard the falls, the water that would flush him away over jagged stone steps, and he screamed for help. Suspended in air, he saw his parents in the living room. His dad was probably telling his mother about his latest book, and his mother was probably telling his dad about her latest real estate deal. They were both drinking martinis, and they were totally oblivious to his screams. It was his sisters who heard his cries and saved him by climbing out onto the limbs of the tree. Katie held Susan by her ankles as Susie pulled him to safety. When Doc looked over at the house, he saw his father in the window vaguely wave at him then turn away. He said something to his mother that made her laugh, and then left the living room for his study.

Doc's father was a sociology professor at Cornell University, and he was totally caught up in his work and spent most of his time in his study writing and researching books or going off to give lectures here and there. He had no time for James Caleb Brown the III, or "Jimmy" as his parents liked to call him. His mother was in many ways worse than his father because he expected more from her. He expected love, but his mother had very little time for her children. She had other interests. His mother was obsessed with social status, and despite her claims of an illustrious family past, his mother's immediate family was at best middle class, and her father was a low-level supervisor at a food processing plant. To her credit she climbed out of those poor beginnings and a small town in South Carolina to go on to achieve a degree from Harvard University in English Literature. It was at Harvard that she met his father, and they got married soon after graduation. Now many years later she lived on the top of the hill in Ithaca, New York where she could play the professor's wife at cocktail parties, organize charity campaigns to get her name in the paper, and buy real estate all over the county so that she could become the queen of the plantation once again. Doc's mother was incapable of true love. She was the kind of woman who would embrace you and push you away at the same time. Doc disliked them both. She was vain and self-absorbed, and he was pompous and bubbling over with self-importance. His father's eyes sparkled with the knowledge of his own intelligence.

Nothing Doc did seemed to please them. The fact that he got all A's, and he was considered gifted and talented was taken for granted. After all, he was their child. He tried to get their attention by being bad. He got B's and C's which to his parents were worse than F's. They were average, or as his father would say, "normative," which made him just another statistic. He began to smoke. No response. He hung out with the wrong boys, nothing. He did drugs. Nothing seemed to phase their tranquility. Oh sure, he would get the perfunctory lectures on responsibility and maturity. Coming from them, it was a joke. Somehow, they had managed to never grow up. His mother played monopoly and the southern belle, and his father played the wizard with cap and gown.

His sisters couldn't get their parent's attention either. Katie married a junkie, and Susan went off to live in a sod hut somewhere out west. Nothing his sisters did seemed to affect his parents. They would send them money when they needed it, and his father would then go back to his study, and his mother would go back to her charities and saving some poor unfortunate children halfway across the world. At the same time, she would be evicting some poor unfortunate family halfway across town because they couldn't pay their rent.

When Doc graduated from high school, his grades were less than normative, they were downright deviant, but his father pulled some strings to get him into Cornell. He was classified as an under-achiever with one special and unique talent. He had an extraordinary ability to pick up languages. When he graduated from high school, he could speak French, Spanish, and German fluently. He had even invented his own language. After one year at Cornell he spoke Russian and Mandarin Chinese fluently, and he was well on his way to mastering two African tribal languages. However, no matter what language he thought in, except Mandarin Chinese, Cornell seemed like bullshit to him, so he decided to drop out of school and join the Army. It was one of the most satisfying moments in his life. His father was a dedicated pacifist, and when Doc told him that he was joining the Army, his father's face registered total disgust, total disapproval, and, more important, his father's face registered pain. Doc was so pleased with his father's reaction that he signed up for the Special Forces.

As Doc stared out into the jungle, he had to stop himself from laughing into the darkness, but only God gets to do that, laugh at death in the face of folly.

Grumpy tapped Doc on the shoulder. His fingers played in front of Doc's face so that he could see them. "Listen," Grumpy said, "they're out there."

Doc listened. At first, he thought he was hearing the wind and the usual buzz of insects, but then he realized that he was listening to the sound of men creeping through the jungle and whispering to each other. The recon team must have been spotted by the enemy when they hit the landing zone, and the North Vietnamese soldiers or the Laotian tribesmen who acted as lookouts must have followed them to the original camp sight. Now the enemy was slowly encircling that spot believing that the SOG team was still there. All night, they would slowly tighten the circle. Then when daylight came, they would toss grenades into the tightly bunched SOG team and blow then into bits and pieces of dead meat to be swallowed up by the jungle and all the carnivores out there ready to join in the feast of flesh and body parts.

Grumpy had awakened Rocker and the three Dwarfs, and they all stared into the darkness and listened. It was weird watching their shadows being stalked as prey. Maybe the Dwarfs were right. Maybe they were the Snow Ghosts.

Just before dawn they moved out. They moved by inches, then

112

feet, and when first light came, they moved out more quickly. They heard the grenades go off, and they quickened their pace to distance themselves from the enemy.

Doc, Rocker, and the Dwarfs marked the trail that the enemy would take. Their plan was to turn things around and ambush the NVA unit that had just tried to ambush them. They needed to be careful because the enemy had many trails, and often you found the one that they wanted you to find. What you found sometimes was a pit covered over with dirt and leaves, and at the bottom of the pit, you found bamboo spears to impale you with, or in a shallow stream you found a board studded with iron barbs. Sometimes you found a crossbow primed and attached to a trip wire or a mine made from coconut shells filled with gunpowder.

The inventiveness of the human mind when conjuring up death never ceased to amaze Doc, but when they came to one clearing, Happy uncovered something that they had never seen before and only heard about. They discovered a Malay Whip, a fifteen-meter - long thick log attached to two trees by a taunt vine rope ready to be triggered by a trip wire. Doc figured that when it was tripped it would whip through in a ninety-degree arc one foot off the ground. It was like a giant baseball bat that could kneecap a whole patrol.

Rocker whispered to Doc, "Why not here? We can re-rig the "Whip" so that they will trigger it. We can make the snatch from the rear and wipe out everyone else. There can't be more than ten NVA in that squad, maybe less. We can also rig claymore mines back of the clearing and rig some more up front, so if the tree doesn't get them the mines will."

Doc nodded approval then looked around. There were some beautiful purple and blue orchids growing near some rhododendrons, and in the tree where the Malay Whip was nestled was a parrot-like bird with a long golden beak and black feathers with beautiful blue and red markings on its wings.

"God," Doc said, "this is the most beautiful restaurant in the world. That is, if you don't mind being on the menu."

He turned to the Dwarfs and explained to them what he wanted them to do. They liked it. Happy and Sleepy would hang back in the rear and make the snatch. Grumpy and Sneezy would handle the claymore mines on the backside of the trail and take out the NVA from there. Doc and Rocker would spring the Whip and the claymore mines on the front side of the trail. Doc gave his twenty-two pistol with the silencer to Sleepy who smiled in triumph. Doc and Rocker quickly set the mines, and then they arranged the new trip wire for the trap.

The Malay Whip was suspended high above the trail, and the trip wire was strung between two small trees. Rocker and Doc suspended a new trip wire five feet beyond the original wire, and they hoped the NVA wouldn't see it. Doc and Rocker then camouflaged themselves and became a part of the jungle. As Doc was waiting and wondering if the NVA would come down the trail that they had chosen for the ambush, he heard something strange behind him. He listened more carefully then signaled to Rocker to listen.

"What?" Rocker whispered.

"Don't you hear it?"

"What?"

"It sounds like a truck."

Rocker listened more carefully, "You're right. It does sound like a fuckin truck, more than one, maybe a mile or less away."

Doc put his finger to his lips and pointed.

The first NVA soldier appeared on the pathway. The rest followed. They were moving slowly in single file, and they were following the trail that he and Rocker anticipated that they would follow. When the NVA got to the trip wire that they themselves had set for the Malay Whip they simply stepped over it, warning each other of its presence, but then one of the North Vietnamese soldiers tripped the second trip wire that Doc and Rocker had set, and the log whipped across the clearing.

The NVA soldiers were knocked over like bowling pins. Mangled bodies flew in the air. One soldier was minus a leg and spraying blood like a red jungle flower in bloom. The six NVA who had avoided the trap ran forward across the clearing. Rocker fired his grenade launcher, and Doc set off the Claymore mines that fired 700 steel pellets each. The blasts from the grenades and the Claymore mines, the thousands of flying steel pellets, and the grenade fragments cut the NVA soldiers into shreds. Doc should have been horrified, but over time he had become anesthetized to the blood and gore. He had become a butcher.

The silence was deadening after the explosions. There were no screams from the wounded. They were all dead except for the two handcuffed North Vietnamese soldiers that Sleepy, Sneezy, and Happy led into the clearing. Doc noticed that Sleepy, Sneezy, and Happy had tears in their eyes. Doc became alarmed, "Where's Grumpy?"

"He's dead," Sleepy said. "He was shot in the head during the fire fight."

Doc felt a deep sorrow. He had grown to love the Dwarfs.

Rocker felt bad too. The Reverend could see it in his face, but there was no time for sorrow in the middle of a battle. Rocker picked up the phone from the radio that Sleepy was carrying, and he contacted the high-flying reconnaissance plane that was trailing them. He told him the situation.

A few minutes later the recon pilot got back to him. "Charlie-Charlie has an extraction team on the way, Hammer. They will meet you at the alternative landing zone at 0200 hours, over."

"Roger, Bird Dog," Rocker said then turned to the Dwarfs, "You take Grumpy and the two prisoners back to the landing zone now. Make certain it is clear. Doc and I are going to check out something. I think we may have found the main trail."

"Wait a minute, Rocker," Doc said. "The NVA had to hear this fire fight. They're going to be checking this shit out."

"We got time, Doc. Come on. This is what we are here for." Rocker headed for the other end of the clearing, and Doc took the radio from Sleepy and hurried to catch up to him.

They picked up the trail and followed it up the side of a mountain. When they neared the top of the mountain, they heard the truck engines again, and when they reached the top of the mountain and looked down below, they saw trucks through the canopy of trees. Doc and Rocker slowly and carefully descended the slope. When Doc saw steps built into the mountain to make ascending and descending the slope easier, he knew that they were on the Ho Chi Minh Trail, and below the NVA had built a road wide enough for trucks to drive on. That was what all the noise was about. The trucks were driving up to this point, unloading, and then turning around to go back home. They had hit the jackpot. This was the main trail, and there had to be a major depot nearby.

Rocker motioned to Doc for the radio, and seconds later he

contacted the recon plane. In a coded message Rocker informed the pilot of their sighting and gave him the coordinates. A few minutes later the recon pilot was back to him.

"The birds are on the way."

"Let's get the hell out of here, Doc."

"That's a fuckin understatement."

They climbed back up the mountain. Near the top they looked back down and could see North Vietnamese soldiers climbing up the trail after them. Rocker and Doc dropped their packs and ran like hell. When they broke into the clearing where they had ambushed the NVA, Doc stopped dead.

On top of the log that had done so much of the killing were the heads of the NVA soldiers that they had killed in the ambush, all lined up in a one neat row. On top of each head was a rock.

"Jesus Christ!" Doc said, and then he started running for his life again. When he came to the landing zone, the chopper and the Dwarfs were waiting for him in the clearing. There was a gun ship overhead. With a final burst of energy, he and Rocker raced to the chopper, jumped in, and they were airborne in seconds. As the helicopter gained altitude, they saw the recon plane swoop low and drop smoke bombs to mark the spot for the three F-4 Phantoms that appeared minutes later. They roared in low over the jungle and dropped cluster bombs on the coordinates that Rocker had given them. There were a series of flash explosions then a large secondary explosion that ignited the jungle into a barbeque.

The helicopter made a long sweep out of the flight path of the jets. Doc saw three more F-4s armed with napalm bombs coming in, but they wouldn't be seeing the rest of the cookout. They were on their way home.

On the way back to their base camp, Doc stared into Grumpy's dead face. Grumpy's real name was Da Ko Ho. He was twenty-eight years old when he died. He had been a hunter all his life, yet he dreamed of being a farmer. He dreamt of his tribe being literate and healthy and prosperous and independent of both the North and South Vietnamese. At one time, Doc and Da Ko Ho had dreamed those dreams together, but many broken promises later, all that Grumpy had was a life insurance policy gratis the US. This was why he joined SOG. His death would be worth something to his family.

Sleepy, Sneezy, and Happy were grief stricken. In a tribal society, the loss of a member of that tribe was like losing a body part. The pain was deep and organic. They looked at the two NVA prisoners with utter hatred. The prisoners' hands were handcuffed behind their back, and their legs were tied. They had duct tape across their mouths, but their eyes expressed total terror as they stared back at the Dwarfs. God knows what they were told would happen to them if they were captured. Most of it was true. Cutting your enemy's head off in this war was not unusual. The Vietnamese believed that if you cut a man's head off, he couldn't join his ancestors, and he would be condemned to wander as a ghost. If the NVA had killed the Montagnards, they would have probably done the same thing and stuck the heads up on poles as a warning to others.

Doc noticed that Happy had a gash on his forehead. He told Doc that he had been creased by a bullet. Doc dressed the wound and then observed that one of the prisoners had a bullet hole in his leg. He examined the wound. It was from the twenty-two pistol that Doc had given Happy. Not bad, the bullet had gone clean through the leg, and it didn't hit an artery. Doc was about to dress the wound when Sleepy stuck his finger in the wound. The prisoner jumped so high he hit his head on the roof of the helicopter.

"Cut it out, Sleepy," Doc snapped.

When the helicopter landed, Doc first went to his tent to clean up and change his clothes, and then he went to the group's headquarters. When he got there, one of the prisoners was waiting for him in the interrogation room. Rocker was in the office typing a report, and Sneezy was at the door guarding the prisoner.

Doc had been interrogating prisoners for a long time now. It was one of his main jobs, and he was good at it, primarily because he had a genuine sympathy for the prisoners.

Doc offered the prisoner a cigarette. The prisoner took the cigarette; Doc lit it for him and asked in Vietnamese, "What is your name?"

"Le Tang," the prisoner said.

"Well, Le Tang, let's get right to the point. It's useless to withhold information from me because if you don't talk to me, I will have to turn you over to the Montagnards."

The young man was terrified. He heard his comrade being tortured somewhere outside. He heard the screams, and he could see the hatred in Sneezy's eyes.

"How old are you, and where do you come from?"

The young man glanced over at Sneezy and then said, "I'm twenty-two years old. I come from a farm cooperative outside of Hanoi."

Le Tang was about average height and weight for a Vietnamese his age. Doc estimated that he was about five foot two and weighed about a hundred and fifty pounds. "Are you a party member?" Doc asked.

"No, I'm a Buddhist." He hesitated, then defiantly said, "but I believe in the revolution."

"So, you were eager to come down south and fight."

"I didn't want to leave home. I don't like being away from my family, but it was my duty to fight the Americans."

"Why do you think we're here?"

"To take what the French lost."

"And what is that?"

"The plantations, the rice, the land, and when you have that, you'll invade the North."

"This is what your leaders told you?"

"Yes."

"And you believe them?"

"Yes."

"You hate us?"

Le Tang looked Doc straight in the eyes and said, "Yes, you have bombed our country and destroyed what took years of sacrifice to build. I myself have worked on two public works projects, but now everything is gone, and I have lost friends, and they have lost family in the bombing raids. I think the communists are right. Nothing will satisfy you. The more you consume, the more you want."

"So then, you volunteered for the army."

"Yes."

"Tell me about your trip down south. After your training where did you go from there?"

Le Tang hesitated, but Doc could see that despite his defiance and show of bravery, Le Tang was desperately afraid. Doc needed a convincer, a visual and audio aid. He picked up Le Teng's rucksack and began to sort through it, and he was not surprised when he found an NVA uniform in Le Tang's pack, it only confirm-ed that Le Tang was North Vietnamese Army. Doc dug through Le Tang's clothes, his bivouac equipment and his mess kit. Under his mosquito net and some AK-47 clips, he found what he was looking for. He untied two pieces of carboard and in-between the two pieces of cardboard, folded carefully inside rice paper was a picture of a couple who looked in their late forties. They were standing in a rice field; the sky was blue; and they were smiling broadly. Doc showed the pictures to the prisoner and asked, "Who?"

"My mother and father."

In another picture were two girls and a boy in their early teens. They were standing in front of a statue of Ho Chi Minh. Judging by the traffic and the buildings in the background, they were in Hanoi. The teenagers were smiling broadly as if to say, look where I am. Doc showed Le Tang the picture.

"My sisters and brother."

The last picture was a picture of a single girl in her teens. It was a coming of age picture of a girl in love. She had a beautiful smile. Doc held up her picture as if she was Kuan Yin, the Vietnamese Goddess of Love and Compassion.

There were tears in the young man's eyes, "My girlfriend. We are engaged to be married."

123

Doc stood up and opened the door to the interrogation room so that the young man could hear the screams more clearly. Then he squatted down in front of him, eye to eye. He put his hand on Le Tang's shoulder to comfort him. The young man was shaking. As he showed Le Tang the pictures again, one by one, he said, "Trust me. I don't want to turn you over to them. Answer my questions truthfully and accurately, and I promise you, at the end of this fuckin war, you will be able to go back to them, to her. Don't be a fool. There are no heroes here."

Le Tang began to cry. Doc paused long enough for the young man to compose himself and then he said, "Now, where were we? Oh, yes, tell me about your trip south. After your training, where did you go from there?

Le Tang seemed to have accepted the reality of his situation. He wanted to survive, so he began to tell his story. According to Le Tang they were shipped by train to Dong Hoe in southern North Vietnam where they received a week's supply of dry field rations, sugar, salt, tea, cans of condensed milk, salted meat, and rice. More rice was available to them along the way. To escape detection by American aircraft, they marched at night to the southwest corner of the DMZ where they rested for several days in a place called, "Ho Village", several days walk from the Laotian border. There they exchanged army uniforms for the black pajamas of the VC, and they began their journey down the Ho Chi Minh Trail.

Doc pressed the prisoner further, "How did you leave, in what numbers? Did you all leave together, or did you spread it out?"

"They broke us up into companies or battalions, and we left at two-or-three-day intervals. We weren't told where we were or where we were going. All we knew was that we were going south."

"Who guided you?"

"We picked up different guides at different parts of the trail, and the guides only knew their section of the trail. I guess that was for security reasons."

"I guess so. Tell me about your average day on the trail."

Le Tang shrugged and said, "We marched. We got up at three-thirty in the morning and marched from four in the morning to eleven o'clock. After breaking for lunch, we marched out again until six in the evening. We rested ten minutes for each hour we walked and took one day off out of every five. We covered some fifteen to twenty-five kilometers per day, depending on the terrain. It was very difficult. Many men died."

Doc saw Le Tang looking at his cigarettes, and he offered him another one. Le Tang's hands were still shaking. The screams from outside were even unnerving. Doc, but he continued the inter-ro-gation. "So, how did you end up where we captured you? What were you doing there?"

"When we came to the depot, my company was detached from the main body of the column. Our job was to patrol the area and protect the weapons and ammunition that were being stored there. We were warned of your presence, and we picked up your trail."

"And shit happened."

The young man shrugged.

Doc handed Le Tang a map and a pencil. "Trace the trail for me. From Dong Hoe to where you were stationed."

Doc watched Le Tang struggle with the task, but finally he was able to draw a snake-like line down the map to where Doc and his unit had snatched him.

"Where is the storage facility?"

Le Tang pointed out the location of the storage facility. It was about half a mile off the road.

"What about the road?"

"They have been working on the road for the last six months," Le Tang smiled, "I was told that soon we would be driving tanks down the road on the way to Saigon."

Doc had heard most of this before. What Le Tang was saying was generally true. The turning of the trail into a road, however, was new, and the storage facility was a stroke of luck.

"Continue," Doc said.

Le Tang shrugged. "I don't know anymore."

Doc knew that the prisoner knew a lot more. but he was losing him because he was unwilling to give the inevitable command. Sneezy, who had been listening to the interrogation, knew too, and he did not hesitate. He came over to the young man, grabbed him by the hair, and dragged him out of the room so he could see what needed to be seen. Doc heard a blood curdling scream and then a thud, the sound of the prisoner's decapitated head hitting the ground. Then there was silence.

Sneezy dragged the prisoner back into the interrogation room. He was squirming like a worm on a hook. Sneezy threw him down in from of Doc and said, "Now, you tell the Snow Ghost what he wants to fuckin know, or you are next."

Le Tang had shit his pants. The stench was awful, and Doc felt ashamed, but he took advantage of the moment. "Show me every god damned trail along the area you patrol, every trap," Doc snapped. "And if I find out that you lied about anything, I'm going to turn you over to the Rhades out there."

Le Tang was gone. He was broken. He began to point out the trails to Doc. Doc gave him another map that was a much more detailed map of that sector. Le Tang was diligent. He was desperately trying to convince Doc of his truthfulness. Doc was an interrogator and a member of SOG, so he had access to most intelligence reports, and he knew more about the war in Vietnam than most anyone. He

knew more than this young man. He knew that if Le Tang had continued his journey he would have been guided by Montagnards
working for the Vietcong on a month long back breaking march
through the highlands of Laos to the Vietnamese border of Kontum
Province where he would join forces with VC units operating in the
province. Doc knew that there were now three regiments of NVA
totaling fifty-eight hundred men fighting in the south and more
were on the way.

Doc studied the prisoner. There was nothing left. Doc took a
pair of socks, underwear, a pair of khaki pants, a sweater, and Le
Tang's khaki hat from the young man's rucksack. He put the
clothes in front of Le Tang, unlocked the handcuffs, and said,
"Clean yourself up and change your clothes." He handed him the
pictures. "Put these in your pocket, and don't worry. Nothing is
going to happen to you."

Doc helped Le Tang up. Rocker was standing in the doorway of
his office watching. There was a knock on the door. It was Happy,
Sleepy, and another Dwarf who Doc did not recognize. They had
blood all over them. They looked horrible.

Happy pointed to the prisoner. "We want him."

Behind him, Doc could hear Rocker say, "This is getting a little
too fuckin' rare for me." He stepped forward and pointed at the
Dwarfs. "You listen to me you little sons-of-a bitches. Because we

snatched this guy alive, Doc and I are getting four days R&R in Saigon, and you're getting seven hundred bucks a piece. Seven-hundred dollars is going to Grumpy's family. If you touch a fuckin' hair on this guy's head, there's going to be more heads rolling around here!"

Rocker turned to Doc, "You tell them that, Doc."

Doc translated for the Dwarfs. They thought about it for a moment, then they saluted Doc and Rocker. Happy pointed to the Montagnard that they had with them, someone Doc had never seen before. "This is the new Grumpy," Happy said.

Doc shook the man's hand and said, "Nice to have you back, Grumpy."

Rocker shook hands with him too then ordered Sneezy to watch the prisoner.

Doc and Rocker walked out of the building. Sleepy, Happy, and the new Grumpy followed behind them. A helicopter was ready to take Doc and Rocker to Saigon. Doc couldn't wait. He was desperately in need of a drink. Alcohol was his only escape.

On his way to the helicopter, Doc saw the body of the other prisoner. He had been gutted and beheaded.

The Montagnards were not monsters. They were an incredibly generous people who shared everything with one another. They believed that whatever was taken in this life had to be given back.

It was sort of an eternal cycle of life theory of energy. By killing their friend, the enemy took vital life energy away from the tribe and that energy had to be restored. Grumpy's life force had been lost, now it was replaced by the life force of the dead NVA soldier. It was more than an eye for an eye. It was a spiritual transplant.

When Doc looked more closely at the severed head, he noticed that there was a rock on this head too. He turned to the Dwarfs and said, "When I get back, we need to have another talk about the God of Gravity."

Chapter Four

The Reverend woke up the day after Memorial Day on the couch in the card room at the VFW. Every night after he closed the VFW, he drank himself into oblivion and then travelled through the black hole of his mind where his life was compressed into one word and everything else was forgiven, and he came out the other side, reborn.

The Reverend got up from the beat-up thread worn couch that Jim Stanton's wife had donated to the VFW ten years ago, and he went into the bathroom. On the bathroom wall, every night, he wrote his story, and every morning he would clear it away with white paint in hopes of starting anew in the pure white light of Jesus. The story he had scribbled on the wall last night was written in French, German, English, and Vietnamese. At points in the story, he changed languages from paragraph to paragraph or from word to word, and at other points in his story he used the language that he invented. Intermingled with the words that conjured up his past were sketches of the severed heads of the NVA with rocks like gravestones on their heads and sketches of Rocker and the Dwarfs,

131

all dead. The jungle was a huge gaping mouth that was swallowing them all up and transforming them back into itself, the leaves, and the trees. A beautiful golden orchid that looked like a woman's vagina peeked out at him from behind a spray of palm leaves.

The Reverend opened a can of white paint and poured it into the paint pan. He then began to roll the white paint over his story, his sins, leaving the walls, in the end, a blank tabula rosa, his soul purified. He then cleaned the bathroom until it was spotless, put a statue of Jesus on the Cross on top of the toilet tank and then knelt in front of his altar and began to pray. "Oh, Jesus, help us. We are all lost souls. Deliver us from this shithole and show us the way. Oh, Jesus, my Redeemer and Savior, give me the strength to follow in your path. I am so afraid."

He got up and took an artist's brush and a can of black paint, and he began to meticulously write his sermon for the day above the toilet. When he finally finished, he stepped back and said, "Amen" and left his chapel and the sermon for the day for all to read who entered the temple of God amidst the lepers of turds.

When the Son of Man comes in his glory, escorted by all the angels of heaven, he will sit upon his royal throne, and all the nations will be assembled before him. Then he will separate them into groups, as a shepherd separates sheep from goats. The sheep he will place on his right hand, the goats on his left. The king will say to those on his right: 'Come. You have my Father's blessing! Inherit the kingdom prepared for you from the creation of the world, for I was hungry, and you gave me food. I was thirsty and you gave me drink. I was a stranger and you welcomed me, naked and you clothed me. I was ill and you comforted me, I was in prison and you came to visit me.'

Then the just will ask him: 'Lord, when did we see you hungry and feed you or see you thirsty and give you drink? When did we welcome you away from home or clothe you in your nakedness? When did we visit you when you were ill or in prison?'

The king will answer them: 'I assure you, as often as you did it for one of my least brothers, you did it for me.'" - Matthew 25:31-40

The Reverend took a shower and dressed, and when he came out of the bathroom, Charlie was on his knees ripping up the floor. "What the hell are you doing here?" the Reverend asked.

"Putting in the new floor, what the hell do you think I'm doing?"

"Oh, yes, I forgot. Carry on, soldier."

The Reverend went behind the bar and opened one of the doors to the beer cooler. "You want a beer, Charlie?"

Charlie hesitated for a moment then said, "No thanks, Reverend. I'll have one later."

The Reverend took out a bottle of Bud and then turned on the four TVs in the VFW barroom to four different channels. He sat down at the bar in such a way that he could see all the screens and view and hear them simultaneously. The post had a state-of-the-art satellite dish on the rooftop, and they received two thousand TV channels from almost everywhere in the world. Charlie was certain that Bob got it for the Reverend. Nobody else cared.

After a while, Charlie stopped working and said, "Reverend, why the hell do you watch four different channels at the same time? Why do you keep changing the channels? What are you looking for? What do you hear?"

"They're speaking in tongues, Charlie."

"Do you know what they are saying?"

The Reverend waves his hand at the TVs. "They're all saying the same thing to me, Charlie. Every story, every ad, every word, image, and symbol all revolve around a single word, a single metaphor. It is a word that spawns millions of words and images in order to create a labyrinth of lies to hide us from the truth, the

Minotaur that will gore us in the end. The truth is that Money is God in America, and money is blood, our blood, our work, our hopes and dreams, and our children's futures. If that is so, the question then becomes, how is the blood circulated through the body politic? Does it nurture everybody part, every cell, every self, and every one of us? Or, are the blood banks on Wall Street the modern version of the ancient Aztec temples where our lives are sacrificed by the temple priests to the God of Money, a beast that can never be satisfied and that has to continually grow or it will die? I think the latter is quite obviously true and that this cancerous growth has turned our most sacred values into commodities to be bought and sold, and when we can't buy and sell enough to feed the beast anymore, it cashes us all in, liquidates us in a bloodbath of profit where everyone pays to die, winners and losers alike. War, Charlie, it's the God of Money's version of the Resurrection."

"I didn't fight for money, Reverend. I fought to save my country."

"I know Charlie. We all did. That is the tragedy of it all. Unwilling to face the truth of who we are and what we have become, we have gone further and further away from the dream that was America, and we have become lost in a deadly labyrinth of lies, growing madder and madder with each war that we fight. Now, I fear, the Minotaur is near, and Jesus Christ is over there in the shithouse making his last stand.

Charlie wanted to ask the Reverend what a Minotaur was, but he could see that the Reverend had gone back to watching the TVs, changing channels. He seemed to be at peace with the chaos, but it was too much for Charlie, so he put his ear plugs in his ears, and just as he was about to go back to work tearing up the floor, the side door opened, and the Commandant, Bob Sumner, walked in.

"What the hell is this," the Reverend said, "a fuckin' party?"

"Shut the fuck up, Reverend, and give me a drink."

The Reverend grabbed a bottle of Jameson's Irish whiskey, and he poured Bob a shot. Bob's hand was shaking, but he managed to get the shot glass to his lips without spilling a drop, and he downed it in one gulp. Bob owned two suits, a blue one and a gray one. Sometimes he would mix and match the two suits, but no matter what he did nothing quite fit. Today he was wearing the gray suit, and the coat didn't quite fit over his potbelly, so he left it unbuttoned. His dark blue tie was loose, and the top button of his white shirt was unbuttoned, but his black cordovan shoes were polished like he was still in the army, and in many ways, he was still in the service, a member of the force and a homicide detective in the Ithaca Police Department.

Bob walked over to a picture frame that contained a World War II vintage poster of Uncle Sam pointing his finger at Bob.

136

The caption said, We Want You. In the glass that covered the poster Bob could see his reflection, the silver-gray military brush cut, his cold pale blue eyes, and the puffy cheeks and heavy bags under his eyes from too much alcohol and not enough sleep. Using the glass as a mirror, he buttoned the top button of his shirt and adjusted his tie. He straightened up as if he was coming to attention, and for a moment he could see beyond the dissipation to what was once a handsome man with strong features.

Bob looked over at Charlie working on the floor and turned to the Reverend and winked.

The Reverend smiled.

Bob headed for the door, "I have to go."

"What's the hurry?" the Reverend said.

"We have a homicide out on Turkey Hill Road."

Bob left the VFW and got into a white Ford unmarked police car. He drove up to College Town passed the new apartment buildings and the old homes. Many of the houses were beautiful Victorian and Federalist homes from the turn of the century. Most of them had been converted into apartment buildings for students, many of them in disrepair; sad reminders of a more caring era before Ithaca become one big rental property for students.

Bob turned onto College Avenue and drove out Dryden Road

and then onto Turkey Hill Road into what was once the rural countryside of Ithaca but was now becoming gentrified with new
expensive homes discretely and tastefully situated around and
about posted woodlands and unplowed fields. Some of the old
farmhouses had been renovated to look like new houses, and some
new houses were built to look like old farmhouses from an ideal-
ized past.

The house that Bob was approaching was a new house that was
built to look like an old colonial farmhouse except it did not squat
down against the pending winter like the old colonial homes did,
nor was it concerned about losing precious heat. It was more up-
right and more vertical to make room for taller ambitions, larger
vistas, and higher ceilings. Well planned flower beds bordered the
house, and Bob wondered if they hired someone to maintain the
landscape, someone who would know the house. The large maple
tree on the front lawn that shaded the house looked well-trimmed,
and it was a fall bouquet of color as were the woods in the background. The house would have looked quite pretty in its pastoral
setting if it weren't for the yellow crime tape, the fire trucks, and
the patrol cars parked in the driveway.

Bob pulled into the driveway and parked next to Ned Hickey's
patrol car. Getting out of his car, the first thing he noticed was that
the door to the two-car garage was open and there was only one

vehicle there, a light green late-model Honda, a soccer-mom's-van. Ned was on the porch, and Bob could tell from the look on everyone's face that this was a bad one.

He walked up to Ned. "You were the first one here?"

"Yes, a neighbor heard the smoke alarms and called in a possible fire. I was nearby."

"Tell me what you did."

"I parked where I am now, walked up the driveway, saw that the garage door was open, and I took a look. I called out, but no one answered."

"There's only one car in the garage," Bob said.

Yes, I know. One car seems to be missing. Keith Van Gorder, the dead man in the house owed a 1996 blue Volvo station wagon registered to his name. I put out an APB on it."

"Good, go on."

"Then I saw the smoke coming from the house. I walked to the front door, knocked on the door and shouted to see if anyone was there, but there was no answer. I walked around to the back of the house, and the kitchen door was unlocked, so I shouted again, no reply, so I walked in. There was a lot of smoke. I walked through the first floor, saw the gas can, smelled the gasoline, and knew something was wrong, so I ran upstairs, gun drawn. That's when I found them. They were all shot dead."

"Don't tell me anymore. Did you touch anything?"

"No, I called the station then the fire department. Bob..." Ned was visibly shaken.

"Don't tell me. I want to see for myself. Call the state troopers and tell them we're going to need a forensic team here. Then call the coroner."

Bob walked to the back of the house following the route that Ned had taken. With the firemen coming and going there were footprints all over the place, most of them mashed together, but it couldn't be helped. He opened the back door and walked into the kitchen. It was a modern kitchen painted in pastels to look light and cheerful. He noticed that the cord to the phone was cut, and next to the phone was a security box, state of the art. He looked carefully at it. It was unarmed. On the floor, near the phone, was an empty red and yellow gasoline can. He smelled the vapors and guessed that it had been used in the fire.

On the wall next to the phone was a Junior League Hockey schedule. Some games had been marked red with a magic marker, and the team highlighted was called The Little Devils. Above the schedule was a picture of what Bob guessed to be the father and son. The boy, when the picture was taken, looked to be about eleven or twelve years old. He was wearing a red and white hockey uniform and holding a hockey stick. Bob guessed that the man that had his arm around the boy in the picture was his father. They both had blond hair, blue eyes, and similar features. They were smiling broadly for the camera.

Bob walked out of the kitchen into the living room. It was furnished with antique and handcrafted replica furniture meant to give an authentic impression of colonial America. On the wall was a large hand-sawn-patchwork quilted blanket that was probably valued as a work of art. There were pictures on the wall of rural settings, several oils, abstracts in splashes of color, and several prints, all money left behind by the perpetrators. This was not the work of professionals.

What a waste, Bob thought. The living room was probably quite nice at one time, but now the ceiling was charred and stained with claw-like burn marks, and the couch and one of the chairs were charred remains drenched in water.

He walked into the family room. It was a large spacious room with comfortable chairs and a cushy couch. There was a thick carpet for the children to lie on and wires and cables where Bob guessed the big screen TV was located before it was stolen. On the coffee table and on the floor were gift boxes and wrapping paper strewn all around.

He looked at one of the tags and it said, "Happy Birthday Bobby - Mom and Dad." It was a box for a Rawling's baseball glove. It

141

was the kind of glove that Bob had wanted all his childhood but never got. It was the kind of glove his father would have gotten him if he had lived. There was nothing there. The box was empty.

He walked back into the living room and walked up the open stairway that led to a balcony and the rooms upstairs. Just as Bob was about to walk up to the second floor, three firemen came out of a room and descended the stairs. One of the firemen rushed outside, and Bob could hear him vomiting. Another fireman stopped and said to him, "It's fuckin' terrible, Bob. It's the worst thing I've ever seen. I hope you get the son-of-a-bitch who did this."

As he was walking up the stairs into the smoke and fire, Bob could feel himself getting colder and colder. He always got this way in situations like this. By the time he walked into the master bedroom, he felt nothing except ice cold rage as he looked at the body of a naked girl, about sixteen years old, dead on the floor. Her hands had been tied with pieces of panty hose, and her mouth had been stuffed with an athletic sock. She had probably been raped and then shot in the back of the head. She had soiled herself when she died. Bob had always found this to be a disgusting phenomenon of nature, the final humiliation, but there was another smell in the air, and he walked out of the master bedroom and followed the smell of cooked human flesh.

In the bedroom, down the hall, he found the mother and father tied together to the bedpost with duct tape. They were badly burned and seemed melted together. The boy had been shot in the head and the impact of the shoots had thrown him against the wall, the back of his head blown away. The smell of burnt flesh, feces, and rotting flesh was overwhelming, and Bob reached into his jacket pocket and pulled out a small bottle of camphor oil and coated his nose with it to block the smell.

Once he did that, he noted that the man's wallet was missing, and the woman's wedding ring was gone. It was the boy's bedroom. It had been all bright red, white, and blue. On the wall, was a partially burned poster of Martin Brodeur, the star goalie the New Jersey Devils.

Bob remembered that the little boy played for The Little Devils. Of course, this is who the little boy would like to be. There were also sport posters on the wall of Bret Favre and Mark McGuire, burned remnants of a little boy's dream of becoming a star. The department will need to be very careful how they handle this case because the media is going to love this, the American Dream turned into a nightmare.

Bob left the room and walked into the room adjoining the bedroom. The room looked like it was used as an office or a study or both. There were bookshelves and a workstation for what probably was a computer and a printer-scanner, but there were only cables and cable hookups there now. Bob looked through some letters and bills on the desktop of the workstation. They were addressed to Keith Van Gorder and Elizabeth Van Gorder. One of the letters to Keith Van Gorder was addressed to the Director of Software Development, Skyline Software Corporation. On the desk was a picture of Keith's wife, a woman in her thirties with light brown hair and eyes. She looked like one of those women who smiled too much, tried too hard, the kind he couldn't stand. Next to the picture of the wife was a picture of the daughter in tennis clothes. She had light brown hair like her mother and blue eyes like her father. Cute, he thought, nice body, pretty legs. What a waste. He had seen enough for now.

When he walked out of the room, He could hear a car pulling into the driveway. It was probably the forensic team from the state trooper's station or the coroner. He walked down the stairs and out the kitchen door then sat on the steps and lit a cigarette. Around the corner of the house appeared Al Cohen, the coroner.

"What do we have, Bob?"

"We got a quadruple homicide, mother, father, teenage daughter and a twelve-year -old boy. The person or persons unknown probably raped the girl, killed the family, and then tried to burn down the house to destroy the evidence. They have a Stanley security-and-fire alarm-system in there. The security system was

144

unarmed but the fire alarm went off and scared the perps off. They probably took one of the family cars. The father's name is Keith Van Gorder. He's the Director of Software Development at Skyline Software Corporation. The boy's name is Bobby. Today was his birthday."

Bob lit up a cigarette, and he handed the coroner his bottle of camphor oil.

"That bad?"

Bob nodded.

"Any clues to who did it?"

"Too early for that, but I'll tell you one thing, it's not a simple burglary gone bad. It's a hate crime. Go see for yourself."

After Al Cohen left, Bob continued to stare into the field and smoke his cigarette. A shiver of ice-cold rage passed through him. It was an icy trail that led him back forty-seven years to the Korean War and the cold that never left him. It was thirty degrees below zero, and he was walking up the road to Yadam-ni.

The bitter Manchurian winds howled down from the Taebek Mountains into the valleys cutting like a knife through layers upon layers of clothing until the icy cold penetrated Bob's skin and caused him to clench his fist and grit his teeth. Amidst the howling winds and the bitter cold, he trudged on to the sound of thousands upon thousands of boots crunching through the dry snow like a monster chewing on a bone.

Bob had to take a piss. He didn't want to, but he couldn't hold it in anymore. He stepped out of line and unzipped his parka, unbuttoned his fleece lined jacket, unzipped his waterproof outer trousers, and then unbuttoned his woolen trousers and dungarees. He groped through his wool shirt into his woolen long johns looking for his penis, looking for the hole in his cotton underwear.

He heard his buddy Jeff Slade say, "Hey Bob, it ain't easy getting two inches of dick out of six inches of clothing, is it?"

Bob turned and saw Jeff standing next to him. Jeff's beard was frozen and caked with snow, and the icicles hanging down from his beard and mustache looked like teeth. He looked like Bob looked. He looked like a snow monster.

"Shut the fuck up and hold my god damned rifle for me."

Bob handed Jeff his M-1 rifle and dropped his backpack. Jeff had been kidding him about taking a piss ever since Bob got frostbite pissing down his leg. It seemed to be the easiest thing to do at the time. At first there was a wonderful feeling of warmth, but then the piss froze to his leg, and he had to be hospitalized for frostbite for a day. Being hospitalized on the road with no base camp meant that he was thrown into a truck with the seriously wounded and frozen dead bodies that were stacked like logs.

Finally, Bob found his penis, and while he was relieving himself

Jeff said, "Look, Bob." He pointed to a deer up on a ridge about a hundred yards away. It looked nervous. "That's the eighth deer I've seen today. Something is out there is spooking them and driving them towards us."

Bob buttoned up his fly and zipped up his outer waterproof trousers. Jeff was from Kentucky and an avid deer hunter, and Bob thought that Jeff was right about the deer. Bob had seen the same thing and wondered. Another curious thing, he hadn't seen any refugees lately. Usually they came up to the Marines and tried to bum some food or cigarettes. The children would beg for a chocolate bar or the cans of fruit cocktail that they loved to eat. There was something out there scaring the game out of the woods and scaring the refugees away from the road, away from the Marines. Bob buttoned his jacket and zipped up his parka. He then put his backpack on and grabbed his rifle.

Jeff shouted into the wind. "I talked to the guys in one of the recon units, and they told me that there are a lot of footprints out there in the snow."

"It's probably just some stray North Korean units."

"They think it's a lot more, maybe a battalion or bigger."

"Bullshit, they're just nervous."

"I don't know, Bob. I got a feeling."

Bob had that feeling too. It was a gut feeling that something was wrong. But what could be wrong? They had broken the back of the North Koreans at Inchon, and then they had driven across North Korean to the west coast. Now the First Division Marines were heading north along the western shoreline of the Chosen Reservoir. Tomorrow, one regiment would head northwest to hook up with the Eight Army and Bob's Regiment would sweep northeast and hook up with the Seventh Army that was on the eastern side of the reservoir. Once the Army was complete, they would march north to the Yalu River, the border between Korea and The Republic of China.

There was nothing to stop them. The North Korean Army had been defeated. North Korean soldiers were surrendering in mass or taking off their uniforms and disappearing into the countryside. Bob was sure that some of the North Koreans who had bummed food off him on the road or smiled and waved at him as he passed by had been the enemy only days before, but now they were happy with a can of Spam or a can of fruit cocktail or a cigarette and a chocolate bar. They were out of it, the lucky bastards. They were heading home to their villages. Bob wanted to go home too. There was talk that they would be home by Christmas, but for now, he would be happy to get to Yudam-ni. Once they were in Yudam-ni they would dig in for the night. There would be warming tents and food, and he could crawl into his sleeping bag and go to sleep.

Bob did what all grunts do. He trudged on, and an hour later they entered Yudam-ni. Yudam-ni was situated about halfway up the rugged shore of the Chosen Reservoir in a long narrow north-south valley. The valley of Yudam-ni branched off into five smaller valleys, each separated from the next by a high and hilly ridge complex. The road they were following ran through the main valley, and there was a road junction north of town where one fork of the road continued north to skirt the western shore of the Chosen Reservoir, while the other fork in the road turned abruptly west to snake through the formidable Taebek Mountains.

Bob was half asleep when he heard Lieutenant Green, their company commander, shout, "Snap to, assholes. Be alert. It's time to go to work." They had reached Yadam-ni.

"I want you boys to search the village," the Lieutenant said. "You know the drill. Be careful. Keep a sharp eye out for booby traps, and if you find anybody, bring them to me. OK, move out."

Bob, Jeff, and the rest of the company walked down into the village. Bob guessed that the people who dwelled in this village were loggers. Their cabins were something like cabins at home, made of pine from the surrounding forest. They were simple shelters to keep out the cold and they looked like that had been built by hand. House after house they searched only to find that it was a petrified ghost town. After the search was completed, they were ordered up a nearby hill where they dug in for the night. The ground was so hard, they used hand grenades and dynamite to soften it up, and when they were done digging their holes and building up their lines of defense, they took turns going to the warming tents.

When Bob and Jeff got to the warming tent, it was full of Marines that were trying to get out of the wind. Bob took off his pack, parka, helmet, and shoe packs and felt a hundred pounds lighter. The room stank of men who hadn't taken a bath in months, men who had lived, fought, slept, ate, shit, and pissed in their clothes. There was another smell too. It smelled like someone had just opened a tomb. It was the smell of death, and it followed them everywhere. The only way to be safe from it was to be part of it and roll up in it like a dog rolls up into the carcass of a dead animal.

Bob asked the Marines hanging out around him if they knew what was going on. Nobody seemed to know anything except that X Corp was strung out from Koto-ri to the Chosen Reservoir. The Eighth Army was somewhere to the west, and they were a long way from the sea and their lines of supply.

Jeff and Bob changed their socks and underwear, and for a moment Bob was nearly naked, vulnerable, and weak, but he quickly put his clothes back on layer after layer until he was a snow monster again. He took out the can of Spam that he had buried deep within his clothing so that it wouldn't freeze and began to eat. He also took out a can of peaches. It was gooey but good.

When they finished eating, Bob was relieved to get out of the tent into the clean cold air where he was clear of the human stench. They walked back to their foxhole and bundled up in their sleeping bags and felt warm and refreshed for the first time in a while. Bob lit a cigarette, and he and Jeff just stared down at the valley, the hills, and the mountains beyond.

Jeff finally said, "This is some nasty country, Bob. It ain't gonna be no cake walk to the Yalu River."

"Someone told me that MacArthur said that when we get to the Yalu, we're going to piss in it and go home," Bob said.

Jeff laughed, "I don't think MacArthur ever tried to take a piss in thirty degree below zero weather, Bob. If he did, he wouldn't be so cocky. Maybe you ought to write him a letter and tell him what it's like. Personally, I don't want to whip it out just to keep that old bastard happy."

"Don't be disrespectful, Jeff. The old man got us this far, and he's going to get us home."

"I sure hope so, but we got one hell of a walk ahead of us."

Jeff was right. It was very rugged country, one hill after another rose up into a formidable mountain range that they would have to cross to get to the Yalu. The forest was mostly pine with some dwarfed oak trees twisted by the wind. Large patches of the forest had been lumbered out and soil erosion had cut deep gashes into the side of the mountain causing it to look like the frozen carcass of a dead animal.

"You know, Bob, now that this war is nearly over, I been thinkin'."

"What have you been thinking about?"

"I've been thinkin' that we've done a lot of killin' since we've been here. Do you think we'll ever get over it?"

"Don't be a pussy, Jeff. When you get home, you'll forget all about it and get on with your life. You did your duty, and you fought with honor. Be proud."

"I don't know, Bob. They're men like us."

"They're not like us. They're Communists, Reds. They're not even fuckin' human. They're zombies who follow their leaders mindlessly and believe that everyone is equal, and we're not. The hard truth is that there are only winners and losers in life, and the winners define what is right and what is wrong. That is the nature of things. Darwin knew this. It's scientific, Jeff. It's how we evolve into a higher life form, and it is called natural selection and the survival of the fittest. Everything else is fuckin' bullshit, fairytales for children."

Bob laughed and said, "You don't think America became great because we are more moral, or more intelligent, or more hard-working than other people? America is great because we kicked fuckin' ass from the very beginning. We've kicked ass all the way across the American continent, first the English, then the Indians, then the French, Spanish, and Mexicans, and then the whole of Latin America until we claimed two continents. Then we fought the world in Europe, North Africa, the Middle East, and Asia. We kicked the ass of the Germans and the Japanese, and as a result of that, Europe, Japan, and most of Southeast Asia, and the Pacific is ours. Now we are kicking the ass of the North Koreans, and we'll eventually kick the ass of the Chinese and the Russians. Why? Because this is what we do, and this is what we have always done. We are the greatest conquerors in history, and all the fruit cakes want us to feel guilty about it. They wouldn't have a fuckin' thing in their lives if it wasn't for us, Jeff."

"Jesus, Bob," Jeff said. "That sounds so glorious, but honestly I don't see myself as much of a warrior. I'm just doing my duty the best I can, and most of the time I'm scared as hell."

Jeff paused for a moment, deep in thought, then said, "You know, when I was a little boy, I was deathly afraid of blood. It was the damnedest thing. My dad was a farmer and a fundamentalist minister, and it just didn't make any sense to me how he could shoot a deer or rabbits for dinner, slaughter pigs and chickens, and then preach the love of Jesus. One of my earliest memories was of

153

my father casually walking up to my pet pig, Porky, and hitting the old boar right between the eyes with a sledgehammer. Poor Porky was dead on the spot, and I watched my father chain the hind legs of the poor dead Porky to the rear end of his tractor and drag it to the back of the barn where he strung it up and gutted it. I watched that pig's inners pour out of him into a big pool of blood, and I was so scared that I ran like hell and hid under my mother's skirt. She wore these long skirts that came down to her ankles. I was all smeared with blood. My mother just let me stay there until I calmed down." Jeff laughed. "God, I wish I was there right now."

They both laughed and then Jeff said, "Bob, you never talk about your dad. Is he alive? What was he like?"

"My dad got fried in a tank in North Africa, and I only have vague childhood memories of him, but I remember that we were happy. I also remember his funeral and an Army officer handing my mother a very neatly folded American flag. Well, that was the end of it for her.

"After my father's death, I got a job hawking newspapers in downtown Chicago. I would shout,

"China Turns Red

McCarthy Warns Us, Beware of the Enemy Within

The Reds are Coming

Babe Ruth is Dead."

Bob laughed. "I was pretty good at it, and I was proud of the money I was making to help my mom make ends meet. During the war, my mother worked in a munition's factory, but after the war, the men who came home took their jobs back, and my mother had to take work where she could find it.

"Anyway, one day when I got home from work, and I entered the house from the front door, I heard my mother moaning and screaming. The first thought that came to my mind was a headline, Home Invasion! My mother was being attacked. I grabbed my baseball bat that I always left near the front door and ran upstairs to my mother's bedroom. My mother was on the bed naked, and there was a naked man on top of her pumping away. She was being raped. I attacked the rapist with my baseball bat hitting the man again and again with my mother shouting and pleading for me to stop.

"I didn't understand, but then I realized that she wanted it.

Later that night, she came into my bedroom and tried to explain. Life was hard on her. She had to work two jobs, and she was lonely. She needed love too."

"But what about Dad," I asked.

"Dad is dead, Bobby, and we have to go on with our lives."

After that night, I watched the family pictures disappear in a box that went into the attic, the pictures of my dad, the pictures of my dad and his mom together, the pictures of the three of us together smiling happily. After that it was one man after another. My mother became what she probably always was, what all women are, a whore. She worked as a waitress and a store clerk, but her main job, like most women, was spreading her legs for any man who told her that she was beautiful and paid the fuckin bills. I hated them all, but most of all I hated her. She betrayed the memory of my father and all that he died for."

Bob was getting angry when he said, "The last one was the worse. He moved in with us just before I left home, just before I joined the Marines, and watched everything that was my father's become someone else's. He even ended up wearing my father's clothes. It was like he was wearing his skin. How could she let him do that? The man was a total scumbag. He claimed he wasn't a communist. He claimed he was a socialist who believed in democracy, but that was bullshit. They're all the same. They want to turn America upside down and turn losers into winners and winners into losers. They want to turn men into women and women into men so that they all can go fuck themselves and live happily ever after."

Bob laughed, "But I got even with him. One night I went to one of their labor meetings to spy on him. He was a radical labor organizer, and they were planning a strike, so I called the cops and told them that this group was a bunch of commie radicals who were planning to burn down that factory.

The cops seemed to believe me because they showed up at the meeting that night, and when the workers protested and became abusive, the cops started swinging away with their bully clubs and beating the hell out of all of them.

One cop came up onto the podium and grabbed Jack, my mother's boyfriend. He gave him the one, two, three with his bully club and shouted, 'Come with me you god-damned commie.'

Jack shouted back, 'What the hell are you talking about. I'm no communist. I'm a Democrat!'

The cop hit him again and said, 'I don't give a damned what kind of commie you are. You're under arrest.'"

Bob laughed, "I think I decided right then and there that I was going to be a cop someday."

Jeff laughed too, "You got a hell of a sense of humor, Bob."

"I'm serious."

"I know. That's why you're so god-damned funny."

Bob was about to protest but he heard the Sergeant say, "Shut up you two." He was talking to them.

Bob buried himself in his sleeping bag, and amidst the freezing cold, Bob tried to cuddle up to the warmth of loving memories, but there was nothing there but the bitterness of a wounded child

157

drifting off into oblivion where he was becoming the snow, a single crystal of light, lighter than air. During his dream it occurred to him that he was freezing to death, but curiously he found that as he got smaller, he was finding warmth in the cold. When he was about to become a single amber and disappear into a galaxy of particles in space, he felt Jeff nudge him and say, "There's something out there."

Bob crawled out of his sleeping bag and into the coldest depths of hell. He grabbed his M-1 rifle and listened.

At first, he couldn't hear anything, but then he heard it, the crunching of snow, here, there. Christ, they seemed to be every-where. He heard the Sergeant and the Lieutenant whispering in the foxhole next to them, and he saw their silhouettes crouching down behind a machine gun emplacement. They heard it too, and they were passing the word along the front line when one of the warning flares that they had attached to the trip wires around the perimeter burst into the night sky. More and more flares were triggered, and the sky began to rain ghostly bursts of silver white light that re-vealed thousands upon thousands of Chinese soldiers nearing their lines. There were Chinese as far as Bob could see.

"Jesus Christ!" someone shouted.

Everyone opened fire almost instantaneously and then came a barrage of mortar fire from the enemy's side. One Marine got blown up as he came out of his foxhole yawning, wondering what the hell was going on. The Chinese were screaming like crazy men as they charged. Amidst the screaming Bob heard a shepherd's horns and bugles and whistles. It was madness. Bob keep firing, and the Chinese keep coming. Bob didn't even have to aim. It was a wave of bodies that the Chinese were throwing at them. The machine guns were mowing them down by the dozens in one sweep after another until the Chinese had to crawl over the dead bodies of their own men to get to the Marines, but they kept coming. A barrage of mortar shells was exploding in their midst, and, yet, they kept coming. An artillery battery had zeroed in on the Chinese and was firing at almost point-blank range. More and more ammo was dropped into Bob's foxhole, and he kept firing. The barrel of his M-1 rifle was getting so hot that from time to time he had to dip it into the snow and ice to cool it off.

From his vantage point up on the hill Bob observed that there was a battle raging all through the valley. He followed the in-coming and outgoing tracers in a 360-degree arc. They were surrounded.

A Chinese soldier appeared above the trench, and Jeff stuck his bayonet into his gut and fired at the same time. Fortunately, very few Chinese soldiers were breaking through. Once of the reasons was that their own dead had created a wall of bodies as a barrier between them and the Americans. Bob was ankle deep in spent shells when he heard the Chinese buglers call for retreat. A roar of triumph came from the American lines, and it echoed through the valley as something inhuman.

The snow monster speaks.

As Bob watched the Chinese retreat, he noticed something strange. There was a cabin down in the valley that had been hit by a mortar shell, and it was on fire. The Chinese soldiers were gathering around the fire to get warm, but the American mortar crews had the sight zeroed in, and they kept pouring shells down on the Chinese. The Chinese were getting massacred down there next to the burning cabin, but they kept coming back to it like moths to light.

"Look how stupid they are," Bob said.

"They're not stupid, Bob," Jeff said. "They're just freezing to death."

Bob looked up and saw that the first rays of sunlight were appearing as blood red splotches along the summit of the mountain tops. When the light finally came, what Bob saw stunned him, and he had seen a lot of fighting in Korea. There were dead Chinese everywhere, thousands upon thousands of them. He never saw so many dead bodies at one time. When he looked at the other Marines around him, he could see that everyone was numbed by what they saw. There was a silence that was more deafening than the sounds of battle. It was the silent sound of horror.

Bob got out of the foxhole and walked out onto the carnage amidst the frozen blood and guts and brains and body parts that were strewn all over. Because of the subzero weather and the drifting snow there was no smell to the carnage, and everything was turning white. The frozen corpses and body parts were like statues. This is what an artist should sculpt in white marble for some art museum, Bob thought. This is the art of war.

Bob heard some Chinese soldier below his feet moaning in pain. Bob took out his 45 and shot him in the head. He then emptied his 45 on anything that moved around him. He looked at faces upon faces grotesquely distorted in frozen agony, and he felt no remorse or fear. He only felt an absolute sense of victory as he stood on a pile of dead bodies and shouted, "You mother-fuckin cocksuckers, we are the Roman of the World, and we're going to kick your ass too!"

Behind him from the American lines, the snow monster roared.

Bob returned to his foxhole. His platoon had been hit hard. Bob Slattery, who he knew well, had been caught, like a lot of guys, with his shoes off. His feet were frostbitten. It looked bad. He could lose his feet. Hal Joyner was walking around with his eyeball dangling down his face. Two of the guys grabbed hold of him and led him down to the hospital tent. Human heads, body parts and shreds of clothing and human flesh were hanging from some the pine trees like Christmas ornaments. As far as Bob could figure, there were twenty-two casualties in the company and ten dead.

Jeff grabbed him and said, "Come on, it's our turn to go to the warming tents." Jeff's hands were shaking.

They walked down to the tents through the moans and screams and tears of the wounded and dying. There were a lot of guys hanging around a large bonfire that they had built outside one of the warming tents. Bob and Jeff decided to join the guys and listen to the scuttlebutt.

"Does anyone know what's going on?" Bob asked.

John Hanley who was a radio operator in the command post said, "The Chinese are pouring over the border. The Army on the other side of the reservoir was torn to shit. The guess is that they have lost over a thousand men. Charlie/7 is mouse trapped on Turkey Hill and Fox Company is pinned down at Toktong Pass. The road from here to Hagaru-ni is cut off. We're fuckin' sur-rounded by what they estimate to be two Chinese Divisions, maybe more. That's about two hundred thousand men."

"What do we got?" Bob heard someone ask.

Another guy who worked in the command post whose name Bob couldn't remember said, "We have two Marine regiments and three artillery battalions, and we're low on ammunition, food, and medical supplies."

Jeff laughed and turned to Bob and said, "We're in luck, Bob. Nobody's gonna be pissing in anybody's river for a while."

They had survived the first night at Yudam-ni and the massive attack by the Chinese that left the battlefield looking like a slaughterhouse. The next day, the brass, accessed their position, and the battle plan was laid out and passed down the ranks. They were in the 3rd Battalion 7th, and their job was to lead the breakout from Yudam-ni and seize the commanding heights on both sides of the road between which the two regiments would pass with all their equipment and the wounded. The battalion's first assignment was to seize Turkey Hill; and then as a separate fighting unit, their job was to break away from the main body and head over no-man's land to relieve Bill Barber's Fox/7 and secure Toktong Pass. They were supposed to do this all in twenty below zero weather.

Bob felt dishonored. They were retreating. He knew that everyone in the two regiments felt the same way he did, but according to the scuttle butt, there was nothing else that they could do. The 8th Army to the west of them was in retreat; the 7th Army on the east side of the Chosen Reservoir had been butchered; and Hagaru-ni, where they were headed, was surrounded and cut off from Koto-ri. They would have to fight their way back to the sea, which was one hundred fifty miles away; and there were two hundred and fifty thousand Chinese soldiers up in the hills and mountains around the Chosen Reservoir and only a couple of thousand Marines in Yudam-ni. All together there were only about twenty-five thousand Marine and Army troops in Yudam-ni, Hagaru-ni, and Koto-ri, and only half that number were combat troops. It was going to be a long walk home.

Bob's battalion moved out at sunset, and about one mile down the road, machine gun fire and mortar shells began to rain down from the hills. The battalion formed an attack line. Bob's company was on the left flank. On the road, Tapplett's battalion was forming a defensive position at the base of the hill. Bob's battalion was given the order to ascend the hill, and as they advanced, the Chinese intensified the machine gun fire and dropped more mortar shells down on the Marines. From the rear, a Marine artillery unit was firing on the Chinese position. Bob couldn't see much. Whenever a shell exploded or a flare was set off, he got a glimpse of the battlefield in the jagged light. Most of the forest had been lumbered out, but there were patches of trees and a strip of forest along the summit. The ridge above them was strewn with large boulders that looked like broken teeth, and as he and Jeff struggled through the knee-deep snow, Bob could hear the screams and moans of the dying and wounded, and he saw several bodies fly in the air in a flash

164

of red. Halfway up the hill they got pinned down, and they were ordered to take up defensive positions. Bob and Jeff dug in for the night.

In the morning, the Marine Corsairs came in and torched the Chinese position on the hills above with napalm. When the Chinese tried to reinforce their positions, the Corsairs fired rockets and then dropped napalm on the Chinese reinforcements causing them to withdraw. Bob's company tried to advance, but they were being held down in their position by machine gun fire.

Sergeant Mann stood up to lead the charge. "Let's go, Marines!" he shouted.

Bob, who was crouched next to the sergeant, saw the back of the sergeant's head fly off. Sergeant Mann fell back spread eagle into the foxhole with a bullet between his eyes. The death of their sergeant shocked the Marines. They froze in their holes.

Bob stood up and shouted, "You heard the man! Let's go!"

To his surprise the Marines followed him. Bob threw a grenade that was right on target and the machine gun ceased firing. Bob shot a Chinese soldier who came charging out of his foxhole. The Chinese were all around them. Bob looked for Jeff, and he saw him on the ground wrestling with a Chinese soldier. Bob hit the Chinese soldier with the butt of his rifle, knocking him off Jeff, and then he shot him dead. Over to his right he saw Ivan the Terrible, a huge black Marine, wielding an ax that he carried with him. He nearly split one Chinese soldier in half, the blood spurting out everywhere. The trees around them were on fire giving everything a blood red hue.

Able/7 came up from behind the Chinese, and the Chinese resistance began to break up. Bob shot one Chinese soldier as he tried to get away. The shot spun the Chinese soldier around and flung him to the ground, his right shoulder torn off. Bob put another bullet in his chest. The soldier's legs flipped up in the air and then he was dead. Bob watched Jeff, who was a great shot, take down a Chinese solder that was about one hundred yards away and running.

"Hell of a shot, Jeff," Bob said.

There was a lull in the fighting. Bob, who was standing next to a burning tree, looked all around him. There were burnt and charred bodies of Chinese soldiers who had been torched by the napalm. It was almost warm. Bob turned to Jeff and said. "This must be what hell is like on a good day."

Jeff nodded and said, "It's one hell of a cookout, Bob."

Down below, Bob saw Tapplett's battalion leading several thousand Marines and hundreds of military vehicles of various sizes and types out of Yudam-ni. The column looked like a giant bio-mechanical monster snaking its way down the road with thousands of heads and legs and wheels. In the hills on the other side of the road, Bob saw Marines walking the ridge line on other side of the heights. They had succeeded in their initial mission to establish a line screening the road from direct assault.

The 1st Battalion/7th next mission was to rescue Captain Bill Barber's Fox/7, a company that was surrounded by the Chinese at Toktong Pass. Once they rescued Fox/7, their job was to secure that potential bottleneck at the pass until Tapplett arrived with the column. In order to accomplish the mission, they would have to work their way across a no-man's land of frozen wilderness undetected and then fight their way through the Chinese lines to the surrounded Marines of Fox/7.

For the remainder of the day, they prepared themselves to be a strike force totally reliant on itself. They eliminated all their heavy gear except for two 81 mm mortars and six .30 caliber heavy water-cooled machine guns. All the men were given a double issue of ammunition, and every man had to carry one 81 mm mortar round in his sleeping bag. All personal gear was left behind, but Bob took some canned peaches for energy and then taped down everything that could rattle. He was ready to go.

When night came, they quietly stepped out. The moon appeared and disappeared into the clouds. The whole landscape had the ghostly feeling of another world. Icicles hung down from the trees like jagged fangs, and dark shadows played in the moonlight, death dancing with the snow. In some places, the snow was so deep, it was like wading through a swamp. At one point, where the snow was chest high, Bob had to pull himself from tree to tree to get through the snow. At another point, he had to climb a steep hill that was so trodden down by the troops who climbed the hill before him that it was slick as ice. Bob had to crawl up the hill on his hands and knees. The real enemy, however, was the bitter cold, but there was no turning back now, so Bob plowed on. Finally, Ray Davis, their commander, called a halt to their advance, and Bob fell right where he stood.

A few moments later, he felt a kick in the ass, and he heard Lieutenant Green say, "Come on, your assholes. I want a perimeter here, and start digging some cover for yourselves, or you're going to freeze to fuckin' death tonight."

He kicked another Marine who had also collapsed in exhaustion. "I said get the fuck up!"

The Marines responded. They established their perimeter and dug a deep hole to protect themselves from the icy wind and the thirty below zero weather. When Bob and Jeff finished, they crawled into their sleeping bags and huddled up next to one another like lovers for body heat.

Bob woke up at sunrise, and he was buried in the silent killer, snow. It came quietly at night while he was sleeping. He looked around. All the Marines appeared to be ghosts emerging from the underworld. Shaking himself off, Bob grabbed his rifle and joined the battalion as it stepped out on the last leg of the mission. The word was passed down through the ranks that they were only about five miles from Toktong Pass, so they moved forward quietly. All communications were done by hand signals or in low whispers. Half an hour later, they spotted the Chinese position. They were dug in around the trapped Marines, and it looked like most of the Chinese troops were still in their bunkers and foxholes asleep.

The two 81mm mortars were set up on the reverse side of the hill overlooking the Chinese position, and as the men in the battalion, one by one, passed the mortar position, they turned over to the mortar crew the mortar shell that they had been carrying in their backpack. The Marines then positioned themselves on the top of the hill, and when the 81's and the 30mm machine guns began to fire, the order was given to charge the enemy.

The Marines ran down the slope firing on the run. To Bob's surprise, there was no resistance. As he was running, Bob dropped a hand grenade into a foxhole, and Jeff shot the two Chinese soldiers who came out of another foxhole. When Bob dropped a hand grenade into the next foxhole, he saw that the Chinese soldiers who were lying down in the hole were still asleep. In front of him, he saw another Chinese soldier come out of a foxhole rubbing his eyes. He got cut to pieces by the machine gun fire.

Bob kept running and dropping hand grenades, one after another into the foxholes. There were explosions all around him, the shrapnel in the air whizzing by him. The objective was to cut a corridor through the Chinese lines into the Fox/7 perimeter. Once they reinforced Fox/7, they would wait for Tapplett's battalion and the troops on the west side of the road to show up, and then they would attack the Chinese in mass.

The resistance intensified when the Chinese realized what was happening. Bob was nearing another foxhole, and he was about to lobe a hand grenade into that foxhole when a Chinese soldier jumped out of the foxhole and aimed his submachine gun at Bob. The Chinese soldier was only about fifteen feet away when Bob, without thinking, lobed the grenade at the soldier, a gesture that probably sealed Bob's fate because if the machine gun didn't get him the exploding grenade would. Bob felt someone grab him by his backpack and fling him into a nearby foxhole as the grenade exploded and a moment later the Chinese soldier's dismembered leg fell on Bob's face. Half in shock, Bob threw the leg away and then turned to see who had grabbed him, who had saved his life. It was Jeff. Jeff smiled at him but said nothing, and Bob know that now they were bonded forever. This was man love, a love that you could only experience on a battlefield.

They looked over the edge of the foxhole to get their bearings and see where they were in their assault on the Chinese position and their attempt to link up with Fox/7. The enemy fire was furious, and it looked like their attack was stalled but then the Marines of Fox/7 attacked from their side of the perimeter opening the path to their lines. Bob and Jeff's company covered the flank and defended the door that they had opened until the rest of the column poured through. Moments later, they were inside Fox/7s position and safe for a while.

Amidst cheers and a lot of people slapping him on the back and shaking his hand, Bob looked back at a blood red path in the snow, and he guessed that they must have lost at least ten to fifteen men in the charge. He wondered if it had been worth it when one Marine hugged him and said, "God, it's so good to see you. Thank you. Thank you. I've never been so proud to be a Marine in all my life. You guys saved our lives. The Chinese were just about ready to finish us off."

Bob looked into the man's eyes. He was crying, and it was so cold that the tears were freezing to his cheeks.

A half hour later, Tapplett's and Harris's battalions showed up and encircled the Chinese. They had them sandwiched in. The

Chinese tried to surrender in droves, but the Marines had listened to stories through the grapevine about how the Chinese massacred the 7th Army on the east side of the reservoir. They heard that the Chinese had poured gasoline over trucks loaded with wounded and set the trucks on fire. The Marines were out for revenge. There would be no prisoners. They shot them all, every one of them even the one's freezing to death in their foxholes unable to move except to plea for mercy.

Bob had read somewhere that it got so hot in hell that, at its deepest depths, the fires of hell turn into ice. If that was so, then Bob was there. He was where the Devil lives, and he didn't feel anything but cold as he pulled the trigger again and again. Bob remembered his high school English teacher trying to explain to him what a paradox was. Somehow Bob felt like this was it. He was in the middle of a paradox, and the Devil was smiling. Bob pulled the trigger again. Killing was easy when you lost your soul in the cold, and you couldn't feel anything, but he also felt that this is what it means to be a man as he pulled the trigger again.

That night the two battalions positioned themselves on both sides of the road and waited for the column to arrive. The moon was nearly full, and from their position up in the hills, they could see the road very well. Bob heard someone singing. It was coming from the road. The singing grew louder, and then a Chinese soldier appeared from around the bend in the road. He was dead drunk, and he could barely stand. Bob and Jeff watched him stumbling along with a bottle in his hand, singing away, and totally unaware that there were over a thousand guns pointed at him.

Bob started to laugh and that got everyone else around him laughing. Soon everyone on both sides of the road was laughing. The Chinese soldier must have thought that it was the gods who were laughing at him, because he shook his fist at the sky, which made the Marines laugh more. The night air was full of laughter.

Nobody fired a shot.

They just let the Chinese soldier stumble on. When he was gone, it was quiet again, dead quiet, and at daylight the column arrived, and they moved on.

From Toktong Pass, it was all downhill to Hagaru-ni. About a mile outside the town, the battalion dressed ranks, and they marched into the base at Hagaru-ni as if they were on review. Bob smiled when the Marines at the base converged on him and the rest of the battalion. Marine after Marine slapped him on the back and shook his hand. Dave Tanner, a guy who he knew from boot camp, gave him a big bear hug, and now it was Bob's turn to cry.

Hagaru-ni was the main command post and supply depot for the X Corp, so it was well supplied. Hot food, a change of clothing, and new gear was waiting for them when they arrived. Hagaru-ni also had an airstrip to fly the wounded out. Bob gobbled down the steaming hot beef stew, corn biscuits, and coffee. He knew that this was a meal that he would never forget. After Bob and Jeff ate, they were led to a tent filled with cots, and in the relative warmth of the tent, Bob laid down and woke up ten hours later.

Haguru-ni was bustling with activity. The X Corp was preparing to bust out. Supplies and some reinforcements were being flown in, and the wounded were being flown out. The post was well for-tified. Earlier on, it had been under heavy siege, but they had fought off the attackers. Now the Chinese surrounding the base seemed willing to merely harass the X Corp with sniper fire and commando raids while they waited for the Americans to make their move. The word was that they were moving out soon. The next stage of their withdrawal was to battle their way to Koto-ri. Once they relieved Koto-ri, they would have to fight their way to Chinhung-ni where a fresh Marine Division was waiting to close the door on the Chinese. From Chinhung-ni, it was a truck ride to the seaport of Hungnam, and offshore, at Hungnam, the 7th Fleet was anchored ready to evacuate the troops to safety.

Several days after they arrived in Hagaru-ni, Bob, Jeff, and an Army infantryman named Eric Bossey were warming themselves at a fire burning in an empty oil drum. Bossey had been on the east shore of the Chosen Reservoir with the 7th Army when they were attacked and butchered by the Chinese.

"So, what happened to you guys, Eric?" Jeff asked. "How come you got beat the way you did?"

Eric was warming his hands on the fire, and at the same time he was balancing himself on two crutches and one leg. He had lost the other leg, and he was waiting to be flown out.

"We were all stretched out along the road when the Chinese hit us. There was no one in command. They just poured over our position and overwhelmed us with numbers."

Eric pointed to where he once had a leg and said, "I was one of the lucky ones."

"When the hell are they going to get you out of here?" Bob asked.

Eric pointed to the Dakota transport plane parked at the end of the runway waiting to takeoff. "They told me to be ready to board the plane in about half an hour. Shit, I should go over there now. Don't want to miss my ride home." Eric reached down to get his gear and duffel bag.

Bob grabbed Eric's duffel bag and handed his gear to Jeff. "How the hell are you going to carry this? Come on, we'll give you a hand."

Bob and Jeff headed for the airstrip with Eric hobbling along beside them. As they passed the command post, Major Richardson, an officer in the 7th Regiment who was standing in front of the command tent, called to Bob.

When Bob, Jeff, and Eric walked over to where the major was standing, the major said, "This is your lucky day, Sumner. You've hit the jackpot. The General is looking for heroes today. Come inside. You two can wait out here for him if you want to. This is going to be fast. The General's in a hurry."

When Bob went into the tent, he saw a bunch of soldiers lined up at attention. Standing in front of the soldiers was General Smith and General Almond, the Commander of X Corp. Almond was the Big Cheese, and Bob had seen him come in today in a helicopter. Also standing around inside the tent were some Marine and Army officers that Bob did not recognize. Behind General Almond were two Army photographers.

Major Richardson said to Bob, "Get in line, son."

Bob joined the line of soldiers and snapped to attention. The soldiers in line were from many different ranks. It took Bob a moment to realize that General Almond was giving out military medals and ribbons. The general had a pocket full of decorations and awards all shapes and sizes, and he didn't seem to care who got what. He didn't even look at the awards or decorations when he pulled them out of his pocket.

When the general came to Bob, Major Richardson said, "General,

Private Robert Sumner led a charge up Turkey Hill after his sergeant was killed, and his bravery was instrumental in securing the heights above Yudam-ni."

The general paused then reached into another pocket, pulled out a medal and ribbon, and pinned the award on Bob's parka as the cameras started flashing. General Almond saluted Bob, and Bob smartly saluted the general back. The General then addressed all the award winners, "Congratulations, gentlemen. You're a credit to the service, and we are all in your debt. Be proud. You have all served your country well." The general laughed and then said, "I don't know if you know this, but you've managed to advance in reverse. Why? Because on your way home in retreat you've managed kill over one hundred thousand Chinese soldiers and broken the back of their advance. This may go down as one of the greatest retreats in military history."

He then turned to General Smith and said, "I have to get back to Tokyo and report to the Boss. Good luck, Gentlemen. Keep up the good work."

Almond left the tent with the photographers and his staff. A moment later General Smith dismissed the men, and as Bob was walking out of the tent, he noticed one of the high -ranking officers take the medal he was awarded off his chest and throw it to the ground.

Outside the tent, Jeff was there to meet Bob, "Are you in trouble?" Jeff asked.

"No, I got a medal." Bob pointed to it. "I don't even know what kind it is."

Jeff grabbed hold of the medal to see what it was and said, "Jesus, Bob, you just won the Silver Star."

"What?"

Bob quickly took the award medal off to see it for himself. It was a silver star that hung from a red, white, and blue ribbon shaped like a shield. "Holy shit," he said.

Bob looked around for the crippled soldier, "Where did the Army guy go?"

"He got someone else to help him carry his shit to the plane. Look what he gave me." Jeff unbuttoned his parka and handed Bob a quart bottle of VO whisky.

"Damn, Jeff, we hit the jackpot today. We should go thank that guy."

"It's too late. That's his plane taking off now."

Bob and Jeff watched the Dakota transport plane taxi up the runway. Just about the time it was airborne it got hit by machine gun fire from the hills. The engine burst into flames, and the plane nosedived into the ground, and a few minutes later they heard an explosion.

"Jesus Christ," Jeff said, "the poor bastard, there's no way he survived that."

Bob put his medal in his shirt pocket and buttoned the pocket so that he wouldn't lose it and said. "Let's go get some chow, and then we'll find some place to drink this booze. It looks like we're going to a wake tonight." Bob laughed, "That soldier boy sure knew how to plan ahead."

They went to the food tent and picked up some food, and then they went to the warming tents to eat. Half an hour later, they came out of the tent and Jeff said, "I'll be damned. Do you see what I see?"

Bob looked to where Jeff was pointing and saw a guy being carried on a stretcher to a plane that was ready to take off. He was in a body cast, and his arm was in a sling. He had only one leg. Bob walked up to the stretcher to get a better look. "Damn," he said, "Is that you, Eric?"

Eric smiled. "I'm alive. Would you believe it? I only have three broken ribs and a broken arm."

Bob laughed, "Eric, you are the luckiest, unlucky son-of-a-bitch that I've ever met."

One of the orderlies said, "Hey, you guys, we have to get this man on that plane."

Bob and Jeff stepped aside, and they watched Eric being carried aboard the transport plane. A few moments later the plane took off without incident, and it disappeared into the horizon.

Jeff turned to Bob and said, "Things are really fucked up when a guy has three broken ribs, a broken arm, and no leg, and you envy him."

Bob laughed and said, "Come on, Jeff, let's go find someplace to drink this booze. We'll have a drink on the only Army guy I ever liked."

Bob and Jeff walked through what remained of the village of Hagaru-ni. Many of the buildings had been torn down for firewood or burned down in one of the many battles fought there. Bob noticed that there was smoke coming out of one of a wooden-shacks, and when he looked inside, he saw two Marines warming themselves at a small fire they had started on the dirt floor.

"Mind if we join you?" Bob asked.

One of the Marines motioned for them to come in, and the other Marine made room for them at the fire. They shook hands and introduced themselves. Rocco Pirro was from Sacramento, California, and Dave Sharp was from Buffalo, New York. They were both from the 1st Battalion, 11th Marines, one of the artillery battalions that fought their way back with Bob and Jeff and the rest of the Marines from Yudam-ni.

Bob pulled the quart bottle of VO whiskey out of his parka and

180

said, "You think you guys might want some of this?"

Rocco Piro's eyes widened, and he said, "Holy Mother of God, is that what I think it is?"

"Yep," Jeff took a swig and handed the bottle to Rocco, who took a swig and passed it on to Dave Sharp. They all savored the warmth of pure whiskey, and they began to talk. The artillery men complained about the weather and how the cold froze up the propellant in the shells and screwed up the accuracy of their guns. Bob and Jeff told them about Turkey Hill and how they relieved Bill Barber's Fox/7 at Toktong Pass.

Dave Sharp took a swig of the whiskey and said, "Listen to this. I saw these two things happen, all on the same day. I saw a Marine find a toddler nearly frozen to death and abandoned on the side of the road. I saw that Marine put the baby inside his parka and carry him as far as he could and then give him to the next Marine who did the same. They passed that baby from man to man and saved its life. On the same day, I saw a boy standing on the side of the road nearly naked. He was crying. He couldn't have been more than twelve years old, and he was freezing to death. I saw a Marine go up to him and put a bullet in his head and walk off as if nothing happened. What do you make of that?"

Jeff took the bottle and said, "War brings out the best and worst in people."

Dave nodded his head in agreement.

Two Marines poked their heads into the hut, and when they saw what everyone was drinking, they joined the party. Soon the hut was full of Marines.

A Marine named Patty said, "We're running out of wood."

"No, we're not," Bob said. He got up, grabbed one of the burning pieces of wood, and set fire to one of the walls.

"Hey, what the hell are you doing?" Patty shouted. "You're going to burn the damn building down around us."

Bob grabbed the bottle and took a big swig. "I don't give a shit. I just want to know what it feels like to be hot again. I want to sweat like I'm in fuckin' Florida."

The Marines laughed and passed the bottle as they watched the building begin to burn down around them. Bob could see the reflection of the flames in the whiskey bottle as they began to sing Marine fighting songs. They sang and drank until the smoke drove everyone out except for Bob and Jeff. Jeff wouldn't leave until the bottle was empty.

"Bob," he said, "are you still going to be a cop when you get out? Is that what you're gonna do?"

"I think so."

The roof caught fire. There was one swig left. Bob gave the bottle to Jeff. "Drink up, buddy. It's time to go."

Jeff, who was very drunk, took the bottle and said, "Bob, you don't really have any home to go to when you get out, do you?"

"Nope."

"Why don't you come home with me? My family would love you, and you can stay with us until you get settled. Our farm is in Spencer, but my brother is an auto mechanic in Ithaca. Ithaca is a good-sized city, and I bet you could get a job there. You got a Silver Star. I got to believe that any police force would love to have you. And there's the Sheriff's Office and the State Police. What do you think?"

Bob in his heart was very happy that he had a friend who loved him, and he had someplace to go, but he merely said, "Maybe. We'll see. Now come on. This place is burning down."

Jeff grabbed him. "No, not until you promise me."

Bob laughed at the same time he was coughing from the smoke inhalation, "All right, I promise, now let's get the fuck out of here." A piece of the roof fell in, and they rushed out of the hut laughing with the house collapsing behind them.

As soon as Bob heard the shot, he knew what it was.

It was a sniper. Jeff spun around. He had a look of wonderment on his face before he pitched forward. Bob caught him, and he saw the bullet hole in Jeff's forehead, and he knew that Jeff was dead.

Bob held Jeff in his arms and screamed. He screamed again and again. All the pain and sorrow and disappointment and anger and grief that he had been repressing all his life screamed out of him. He had lost his best friend, his only friend, the only person he loved. Bob cried and rocked Jeff in his arms like he was his baby. The Marines around Bob tried to comfort him. They all knew what it was like to lose a friend in battle. Finally, they managed to get Bob back up on his feet, and they led him to one of the tents and a cot. Bob cried himself to sleep, and the Marines around him listened and shared his sorrow in silence, listening to one man crying spoke for all of them. They all had enough. They all wanted to go home. A man can only take so much.

Bob heard his name called, and he snapped out of his recollections of Korea. It was the coroner, "The parents were shot three times, the boy twice and the girl once. Yes, she was raped. Then he pissed on her. The fire was started after they died, much later."

"God damn it. I knew it." Bob was mad as hell, and he felt warm again, the rage was the flame that held off the cold, the cold that had never left him. What did the Reverend call it? Oh, yes, a metaphor. Korea was just a metaphor for America. He never left the slaughterhouse; the slaughterhouse is here, a monster tail trailing along the snow into the bleak frozen wasteland that we are condemned to endure for eternity. Hell is our sun.

Bob stood up, got into his car, and made a call to the dispatcher.

184

He told the dispatcher to notify all ATM servers and local banks and credit card companies to be on the alert for any charges to the accounts of Keith and Elizabeth Van Gorder.

Bob saw a car pull into the driveway. It was the Police Chief, John Wright; his aide, Detective Tom Pickney; and the District Attorney, Ken Brown. The Chief was a large, over-weight African American who had a round face and cautious but probing eyes and a quick smile for people he liked. He didn't like Bob, and Bob didn't like him. When Bob saw the Chief, all he saw was black and the man who took a job that should have been his.

The Chief came up to Bob, "What do we have?"

Bob told him, and the Police Chief said, "Good, we'll take over here. What I want you to do is go around and see what you can find out from the neighbors. When you're done, call me, tell me what you have, then go to the station and fill out a detailed report. I'll see you in my office tomorrow morning at eight, and we'll all go over what we have then."

"Yes sir." Bob could barely get the words out of his mouth, but he had to swallow his pride because no matter what he thought of the Chief, no matter how much he felt that he did not deserve the job, and he wasn't qualified, Bob had to respect his authority. It was the chain of command, and it couldn't be broken.

Bob got in his car and headed down the road. He wasn't hot

anymore, but he knew one thing - he was going to get the son-of-a-bitch who had pissed on the American Dream.

Bob went from house to house interviewing the neighbors. They all knew the Van Gorder family. Phil Codington coached Pee Wee Hockey with Keith. Their sons were on the same team, and Phil and Keith Van Gorder took them to all the Cornell Hockey team home games. They were both members of the Chamber of Commerce. Ruth Codington worked with Liz at the book sale to raise funds for the Tompkins County Library.

Jay and Barbara Parks, who lived a quarter of the mile down the road, went to many a barbecue in the Van Gorder's backyard, and Barbara and Liz attended the Monday Tea and Cookie Exchange that Liz organized to get all the women together. Liz and Barbara were also active supporters of the City Dance Troupe.

Barbara Parks told Bob that Keith had worked in New York City for years. The Van Gorders had lived in Long Island somewhere. Huntington, she thought. They were delighted when Keith was given a promotion, and he was transferred to Ithaca, New York. Elizabeth put all her energy into their home. She chose the site, worked with the architect on the design and floor plans, and spent months traveling all over the northeast looking for the right antiques. She wasn't happy until everything was just right.

From Will Kelly and his wife Joan, Bob learned that Elizabeth was originally from Hersey, Pennsylvania. Keith was from Albany. They met in college, maybe Penn State, Will wasn't sure. He interviewed a few more neighbors, and it was the same story. The Van Gorders were wonderful people. Their neighbors were saddened and shocked by the tragedy. No, more than that, they were terrified. They had spent all their lives working to find the perfect place for their family where they could be happy and secure, and now this murder in their own backyard cast a dark shadow over their lives. Paradise had been invaded.

Bob put his notepad away. Except for some background in-formation and a list of people who may have worked for the Van Gorder's on and around their home, he didn't have much. Nobody had seen or heard anything out of the ordinary. One thing puzzled him though. Despite all their claims of intimacy and familiarity, none of the Van Gorder's neighbors left their house to see what the problem was at the Van Gorder home. They must have seen smoke. They must have seen and heard the fire trucks. Bob realized that he would never understand people like this, these academics and upper middle-class professionals, the so-called intellectual elite. They see themselves as morally superior to the vast majority of the American people, their hearts bleed for people thousands of miles away, and yet they wouldn't leave their houses to help a neighbor that could possibly be in danger. Bob didn't know one person at the

VFW who wouldn't come to the aid of a neighbor who they thought was in distress. Cold. They are all cozy killers at heart who don't want to see the blood that keeps them warm.

Bob looked back on the perfect pastoral scene and said to himself, "What fuckin' hypocrites." He then got in his car and called one of his informants. He told her to meet him at the inlet in half an hour.

A half an hour later, Bob pulled into a dirt parking space near the inlet. It was a quiet spot near the golf course, the city park, and the inlet to Cayuga Lake where people in the summer went fishing for trout, but it was late in the season. There was no one there today. Bob sat back and lit a cigarette. Soon a black 1987 Camaro pulled up beside him and Monique Wilson got out of the car. Monique was a prostitute who he protected in exchange for information when she had it, and often she did. Ithaca was a small town, especially the black community.

Monique was wearing jeans, sneakers, and a pull-over light blue wool sweater. She opened the door to Bob's car and sat down in the front seat and said, "Why the hell are you taking me away from my kids? You know this is not a good time of day to call me. I had to call my mother to come over and watch my babies. Jesus, Bob, I'm a mother you know. Have some consideration."

Bob smiled, "This is important."

Monique lit a cigarette. Her hands were shaking. She inhaled, blew the smoke out in a huff, and said, "What do you want?"

"I need information. A family's been murdered."

"Where?"

"Turkey Hill Road. A boy twelve years old, a girl sixteen years old, raped and murdered, the whole family, dead."

Monique put her hand to her mouth, "Oh, my God."

"I want you to ask around, keep your ears open for anything that sounds wrong. See if anyone has been trying to sell credit cards, stolen merchandise, or has come into some newfound cash, anything."

"Sure."

"Don't give me, 'sure.' I'm serious about this Monique. This one is very important to me. If I don't feel like you're putting out for me, our deal is off."

"All right, I get the message."

She was about to leave when Bob said, "Isn't this pay day?"

Monique sighed and reached down and began to stroke and message his penis as she went into the adoring whore routine that Bob liked so much. Bob once said that believing a whore was like believing in God. They were both a necessary illusion. A leap of faith.

Monique smiled wickedly and said, "Do I get to taste the power,

189

Bobby? Do I get to feel the force inside of me?"

She unzipped his fly and took his cock out. "You're the Man, Bobby. You're the Boss. Tell me what you want me to do. I'll do anything for you, Baby."

Bob didn't say anything. He just grabbed her by her hair and pulled her down until she took him in her mouth. Bob liked to look down at Monique sucking his dick. He loved her subservience to his power. She knew that, and she hated him for it, but she let him come in her mouth, and that turned him on more. He knew that she hated it.

Monique zipped up his pants for him and got out of the car. She stopped for a moment and said, "Why do you think the dude who murdered those people might be black?"

Bob smiled, "Because when I close my eyes, that's what I see."

Monique shook her head in disgust and said, "You know why I like to suck your cock, Bob?"

"Sure, because it's the biggest white cock in town."

"No, Sugar, it's because every time I eat all those red neck honky babies of yours, I figure I'm saving the world." Monique laughed and then walked away.

As she walked away Bob said, "Who got your boy off on a DWI? Do you know how much a lawyer would have cost you? You know the shit he would have gone through? And who got you out a jail for not paying your traffic tickets and driving without a license?"

When Monique got to her car she turned and said, "OK, you're not as big a racist prick as you make yourself out to be."

Monique got into her car and drove off, and Bob was smiling when he started his car. Bob liked Monique. He liked people who were fatally flawed and depended on him. Their common language of good-humored cynicism was as close to affection that Bob got before he withdrew back into his foxhole of a soul.

Bob drove to the station, and when he got to his desk, he called the Chief of Police and told him what he discovered from the neighbors. He then spent two hours filling out reports. Finally, he called it quits for the day and drove to the VFW.

When he entered the post, he saw that Charlie was still working on the floor. Brad Ferrell was behind the bar. The Reverend was talking to Dan and Melinda Wilson. Bob Ellis was sitting alone. Hank Wright and Chuck Babcock were playing shuffleboard, and John Masso and Bud Smith were watching the news on TV. The first thing Bob did was order a double shot of Jameson's with a beer back. As he looked about the room, he realized that just about everyone at the bar had a police scanner and listened to police dispatches. If he stayed at the bar he was going to be barraged with questions.

Bob looked over at the Reverend and said, "Come on, Reverend, let's play some pool. I've got some business to talk over with you."

The Reverend nodded his head in agreement then said, "This being a business meeting, can I assume that the next drink is on the house?"

Bob laughed and then motioned for Brad to get the Reverend another drink. He ordered another for himself, and when Brad served him, he walked over to the pool table and began to rack the balls.

The Reverend picked out a cue stick and said, "Sounds like a bad one out on Turkey Hill Road, Bob."

"Yeah, a whole family," Bob said as he smashed the rack sending the balls flying all around the table with the two-ball going in the corner pocket.

"Got any clues?"

"Some."

"Got any idea who did it?"

"My guess is that it is a black on white crime."

"How do you know that?"

Bob put the six-ball in the side pocket, "Because it was mean, hateful, and stupid."

"You're mean and hateful. Does that mean you did it?"

"No, but I ain't stupid."

"No, you're not stupid, but you are a bigot, and you tend to see everything in black and white. I pray every night that the love of Jesus will enter your heart, and you will realize that we are all God's children, black and white alike."

"If I'm right, tell that to the Gordons."

"But Jesus says -"

"Fuck Jesus. Jesus is a woman's version of a man, and you sound like a castrated monk."

"Bob, your problem is that you see everything that is humane, sensitive, empathetic, and caring as weak, and therefore feminine. Haven't you ever loved anyone?"

Bob ignored the Reverend and put the three-ball in the side pocket.

"Do you even love yourself?" the Reverend asked.

Bob was lining up the eight-ball for the corner pocket. He paused and said, "You know what I love Reverend. I love..." How did you say it? Oh, yes. I love fucking everything that's sensitive and caring. I love to fuck everything that is good. I love fucking love. I love to hear women scream and moan as I fuck them and embrace the pleasure of pain and self-sacrifice. I love to send them to Heaven and Hell at the same time in a human crucifixion. And I get off on the fact that it's not me on the cross. That's what turns me on."

"My God, Bob, what the hell happened to you over there?"

Bob slammed the eight-ball into the corner pocket to win the game then threw the pool cue down on the table and said, "And what the hell happened to you? How many times are you going to paint the bathroom white? If you put another coat of white paint on the walls, the walls are going to fall down. What the hell are you doing in there?"

"I'm writing my story."

"Then why are you painting over it every night?"

"To wash away my sins, all that is left in the end, is the word of God."

"In the shithouse?"

"Where else, everyone has to go there."

Bob could not stop laughing for a long time, but then he finally said, "You have to stop. People are complaining."

"I can't."

Bob smiled as he racked the balls again. "I'll tell you what I'll do. I'll cover for you if you go and see the Commandant of the Vietnam Veterans Association?"

The Reverend broke the rack, and the balls scattered in every direction. "No."

"You have to do it, Reverend. If we don't get the Vietnam Veterans to join, the post is going to die. All the World War II veterans are dropping like flies. We had six of them die this year. We need

194

new blood."

"What about the Gulf War vets?"

Bob shrugged, "I don't know. We got Jeff Sweet, Josh Norlander, and Leah, but that's it. They don't seem to be interested, and they're forming their own organizations. They're different."

"We're the last of the citizen soldiers, Bob. They don't trust us anymore."

Bob sank the seven-ball in the corner pocket. "Maybe for good reason. Maybe that's why they want to take our guns away from us. But damned, if we didn't have the social members, we'd really be sunk, and all they want is a cheap drink. You have to go talk to... What's his name?"

"Jack Pendelton."

"Right, go talk to him and tell him about the opportunities that they're missing." Bob missed the five-ball in the corner, just by a hair. "Tell him that we have a million-dollar property here. Tell him that we have two hundred and fifty thousand dollars in the bank, and we're tax free. Christ, in time, this is going to be all theirs."

"Cheap drinks and all?"

Bob laughed, "Cheap drinks and all the potato chips they can eat and throw in the hot dogs if you have to."

The Reverend sank the ten-ball in the side pocket. "He's going to tell me the same thing he told me last time. He's going to say that when they came home from Nam, we didn't support them."

"That's because they were losers." Bob stopped himself. "No, I don't mean that. They didn't lose that war. The politicians lost that war. We were wrong. We should have supported our brothers, but that's ancient history. They still can't be holding a grudge over that."

"Yes, they can, but I think it's something more than that. The leadership, especially Jack, doesn't want to give up their command." The Reverend sank the fifteen-ball.

"I want you to try." Bob thought for a moment, "Tell Jack that if they merge with us, each year we will set aside a third of the membership fees specifically for Vietnam War Veteran's Affairs. We will set up a board of directors to supervise the fund, and they will have to be Vietnam veterans to qualify for a position on that board, and only Vietnam veterans can vote for the board members. The first year will be a trial period, they can pull out after one year if they don't like it, and after five years all special considerations, like the Board of Directors for Vietnam Affairs will be dissolved, and we will all become one brotherhood again like we should be."

"Very neat, Bob. You're quite the politician when you want to be."

Bob smiled and ran three-balls and then missed the four-ball.

"Are you going to do it?"

"I'll try."

"You better do it, or I'll take your white paint away from you, and you'll die in mortal sin."

The Reverend's eyebrow rose, "You wouldn't."

"Yes, I would."

"I'll do it, tomorrow."

"There's one other thing I want you to do for me. Put a notice on the board for volunteers to go the Veteran's Hospital in Syracuse to visit the patients there. We should do that soon. It's been nearly three months."

"OK." The Reverend ran three balls.

Bob looked over to where Charlie was working on the floor. "How's he doing?"

The Reverend put another ball in the side pocket. "He's doing fine. He's a little slow, but he's doing a good job."

"Good, he can use the money."

The Reverend sank the eight-ball, and smiled, "We're even. Rack sucker."

Bud Gilbert and John Bergman wandered over, and they teamed up as partners. Bob continued to play for an hour or two and drank enough to relax and forget about the murders.

The Reverend left the game and saw one of his favorite people sitting at the bar. Leah Watkins was an African American Marine veteran of the First Gulf War who drove one of the tanker trucks that fueled the M-1 tanks on the frontlines. With each tanker truck carrying approximately 11,000 gallons of fuel, the tanker trucks were essentially bombs-on-wheels, and with very little protection, very little armor, these bombs-on-wheels traveled along open roads exposed to random fire, mines, and ambushes anywhere and everywhere at any time along the road.

Leah lost her leg when her convoy was attacked close to the frontlines from both the front and the rear of the convoy. The trucks that had been hit in the initial attack blocked the way. They were sitting ducks until the Black Hawk attack helicopters arrived, but it was too late for Leah. A missile from a hand-held rocket launcher ripped through the cabin of the truck, and a piece of shrapnel damaged her leg so severely that it had to be amputated. Her best friend and co-driver who ran shotgun with her was killed in that attack, and she watched her bleed to death unable to move and come to her rescue.

When Leah came back home, she went back to what she had been trained to do before she enlisted in the Marines. She became an elementary school teacher who taught 3rd grade at the South Hill Elementary School. The VFW was Leah's hideaway from the prying eyes of parents and the children that she has taught. Leah came to the post to drink and drown out the haunting memories of the war and the handicaps that she lived with day to day.

The Reverend saw that Leah was in a dark mood tonight and knowing what was dear to her heart, sat down next to her and said, "How are the little ones?"

Leah hugged him warmly, "They're wonderful, Reverend."

"You're fortunate, Leah, to be amongst the blessed, and they are fortunate to have you as their shepherd."

Leah laughed, "I do my best. They are all my children - black, white, pink, and brown. I embrace them all, and as far as I'm concerned, we'll never be a country at peace with itself until we recognize the simple fact that they are all our children."

Leah paused for a moment and her mood darkened when she said, "Will we ever be free of the nightmare, Reverend? How are we going to protect the children from what we saw?

"Leah, I only know one thing, that with every act of good and every act of love, Jesus is reborn, and though I despair..." The Reverend smiled and said, "I see you, and I believe again."

Leah smiled and to the Reverend she looked like an angel, but then she laughed and hugged the Reverend warmly and said, "You're such a sweetheart." She waved at the bartender, "Bobby, give the Reverend here a drink on me. He just saved another sinner from despair. And while you're at it, pour me another."

Bobby came over with the drinks and the Reverend raised his glass for a toast, and said, "The sun also rises."

Leah thought for a moment, "Hemingway, yes, I agree." Leah raised her glass to, "the sun also rises."

They toasted, and then the Reverend said. "There is something that I always wanted to ask you. I never understood why you joined the Corp. You were trained and educated to be a teacher. You love to teach. Why sign up to go to Hell?"

"Reverend, I believe, and I still believe that if we, as women, are not willing to sacrifice our lives for our country and die for what we believe in, we will never be free and equal to men, and asshole, like Bob, will always have the edge. I heard that son-of-a-bitch over there calling Jesus Christ a woman. That fool confuses manhood with sadism, and he deserves to go to Hell, but you, Reverend, why are you here? You need to get out of this hell hole. You've spent too much time here among the ghosts of past wars, the dead and the dying. You need to be born again in the light of the children. Come to one of my classes. You can teach them about language. Yes, that's it, tomorrow. I'll pick you up in the morning before I go to class. I'll drive right up to the door. You're safe with me." She laughed and said, "You can go to sleep in my foxhole."

The Reverend thought about it, and then said, "I need to go to the Vietnam veteran's headquarters tomorrow and talk to their leadership there. I promised Bob that I'd try to convince them to join us. If I go to school with you, will you go with me to see the vets, and then drive me back here?"

"It's a deal."

Leah finished her drink, left the VFW, and walked home to her apartment on State Street. When she got home, she finished up the next day lesson plans, had one last drink, and then went to bed and stared out into the darkness, alone with her memories.

It was night, but it wasn't night. Saddam Hussein had set fire to all the oil wells. The desert was blood red from the fire pouring out of the underworld, and the sky was a blaze with spirits, the black smoke from the inferno turned into swirling snakes with dragon wings and diamond stars for scales.

It was then that they came upon the Highway of Death to Bagdad. It was littered with thousands of horribly burned bodies and the mangled remains of the Iraqis tanks, trucks, and the civilian vehicles that had tried to escape the carnage. Rachael was bleeding oil. It was gushing out of her. She was drowning in black gold, the bitter-sweet fruit of abundance and sorrow in the Garden of Edan.

Leah screamed, "Stop! And she woke up and cried, "I want to be happy too," Over and over again she said it to herself until she cried herself to sleep, and the night took pity on her, and she dreamed no more.

Chapter Five

The next day, the Reverend woke up and cleaned up. He wore his best khaki pants, an ironed white dress shirt, and polished penny loafers. He even trimmed his beard to give it that Van Gogh look that Leah liked. He downed two cups of coffee, and he was eating a sugar doughnut for energy when Leah blew her car horn to let him know that she was there. This was it. He screwed up his courage and opened the exit door from the VFW. As Leah promised, she'd driven right up to the door, and she had even opened the passenger door to her car to make it easy for him. It was only a few feet away, but it felt like a chasm between him and the car. The Reverend reached out his hand and pressed it against the brick wall to steady himself and keep his balance, but the wall was no comfort. It had a pulse.

Leah leaned over to the passenger side so that he could see her. She smiled and said, "Come on, Reverend, you can do it."

He did. He was in the car. Leah was laughing at him, so in self-defense he said, "You may not know it, but the earth is revolving at 1000 miles per hour, and it is revolving around the sun at 67,000 miles an hour, and me, you, the earth, the sun and our whole galaxy is revolving around something out there at 144,000 miles an hour."

Still laughing, Leah started the car, put it in gear, and said, "It makes your head spin, doesn't it?"

"Exactly my point."

As Leah drove him to the South Hill Elementary School, the Reverend sat back so that he could see as little as possible. When they got to the school it was chaos, but it was not bad chaos like the chaos that was pulling the country apart. It was good chaos, the kind of chaos that was coming together, pouring out of the buses, laughing, shouting, giggling, and chirping like a massive flock of birds being herded into the school. Little feet and heads and backpacks swept him along through the halls to Leah's classroom.

Once they were in her classroom, they were like quantum photons hovering around Leah, their desks, the cloak room, and their backpacks. Leah rang an old-fashioned teacher's school bell, the kind with a handle, and she led her little flock to the friendship circle where they could share with the class their experiences. There were sixteen little packets of energy that sat like little Buddhas, or squatted, or laid about the rug in a semi-circle around Leah and the Reverend.

Leah had the Reverend introduce himself to the children, and he said, "My name is Mister Papa Bear, and this is my first day in class, and I'm afraid."

The children all laughed, but then one little boy named Jessie said, "That's not your real name. What's your real name?"

"Well, people have called me The Reverend, Doc, Sergeant Major, the Snow Ghost, James, J.B., and Mr. Brown. Around the world I'm known as…" The Reverend recited the same names in seven languages, then he said, "But I'm going to tell you a secret that I've never told anyone else before. Hiding inside of me is a little eight-year-old boy named Jimmy, and he created all these characters to protect himself from the meanies. You know who the meanies are, don't you?"

Many of the children nodded their heads in agreement. They knew, grownups.

"So, Jimmy has created Mr. Papa Bear so that he can play with you."

One little boy whispered to the little girl next to him, "He's crazy."

The little girl shook her head in disagreement, "No, he's a little boy."

"Very well, class." Leah said smiling, "Now that we know who Mr. Papa Bear is, who would like to share?"

A little boy named Omar raised his hand and said, "This weekend me and my family went to the Four Flags Amusement Part, and

I went on this ride they called, The Whip, and I went way up high and went faster and faster and it started to spin and whip around." Omar waved his arms around frantically then stopped.

"I threw up, and it smelled like a Chile dog, but then when I got off the ride, I had some cotton candy, and I felt better."

All the children nodded at the wisdom of the cure, and the Reverend raised his hand and said, "And if you put the cotton candy in your hair, you never have to comb your hair again."

All the children laughed, and another little boy told the class that his father owned an automobile dealership, and he had a new car every year. He passed around a picture of his father sitting in the driver's seat of a brand-new red Dodge Viper.

"Every year?" one little wide-eyed little boy asked.

"Every year."

"Wow."

Most of the little boys were really impressed. A brand-new car every year, that was close to what heaven meant to them.

A little girl named Leslie raised her hand and said, "See my new sneakers?" She raised her feet in the air to show the class, "And, look," she said as she flipped a switch on each sneaker and stood up, "When I walk around..." Her sneakers lit up like a cross between a blinking Christmas tree and a disco dancing floor.

"That's really neat," the Reverend said. "I want a pair of those."

He really meant it.

One of the children laughed and said, "You can't get those. Your feet are too big."

Another child disagreed, "You can find anything on the Internet."

Leah rang her school bell and said, "OK, class, it is time for our math segment. I want you at your desks. I want your worksheets out and want you ready to work. You have one minute. Go."

The Reverend was impressed with how organized the lesson plans were. The little ones were engaged in 15-minute segments with no loose time, but that didn't stop them from asking him for help. It was Mr. Papa Bear this and Mr. Papa Bear that, and Mr. Papa Bear everywhere. They tugged on his sleeve, on his pant leg. One little girl made him sit down next to her so that he would give her his undivided attention.

A little girl named Naomi tugged on his sleeve and whispered, "I have to go pee, Mr. Papa Bear."

The Reverend was confused, and Naomi kept looking up at him in expectation.

Leah came up to them and said, "That's OK, Mr. Papa Bear, I will take her." Leah rang her school bell and announced, "It's free time. Red Team is on the computers. Blue Team can play with building blocks, and the Green Team is at the Art Table."

Then she and Naomi disappeared.

In seconds the classroom turned into chaos, the little packets of energy containing the power of the sun were let free. One of the children ran out of the room and came back pushing a cart with computers for the Red Team, and there were fights over who was getting what computer. A tug of war started between two of the little ones. The Blue Team in the building blocks section were throwing building blocks at each other, and the Green Team had strewn crayons, color pencils, drawing paper, and coloring books all over the worktable and on the floor.

The Reverend tried to get their attention, but he was drowned out by the bedlam, and he didn't want to shout.

Someone tapped him on the back, and when the Reverend turned around, he saw that it was Jessie looking up at him. Jessie pointed to the light switch and said, "Flick it a couple of times, then turn the lights off."

The Reverend did as he was instructed, and the room turned immediately quiet. All the children returned to their desks and sat silently staring at him. You could hear a pin drop.

Leah returned to the classroom with Naomi, appraised the situation and said, "I see you found the panic button."

"That's amazing," the Reverend said.

"Us witches do have our tricks, Reverend." Leah rang her school bell again and said, "OK, children, we have a special treat today. Mr. Papa Bear is a writer and an expert linguist, and he is going to tell us what it is like to be a creative writer and artist."

The Reverend was at a loss as to what to say and how to say it. He believed that when an artist is writing creatively, the artist is not writing fiction. He is entering the quantum world where everything is possible, where you can travel back in time and forward into the future faster than the speed of light simply with the changing of tenses. It is a world where you can be everyone, everything, and everywhere. It is a world where you are at the core of the universe where infinite creativity dwells, and it is alive, and it is in all of us. How is he going to explain this to the children, he wondered, but then he looked at them staring at him like little Buddhas, and he realized that he didn't have to. They are closer to that world than we are, the so-called grownups. That is where they came from.

"I'm not a writer," the Reverend said. "I'm a sorcerer who casts spell, and with the proper spell I can be anyone, anything, anywhere at any time. I can conjure up with a simple spell, with my magic wand…" The reverend held up a piece of chalk in his hand, and with a flourish wrote on the board – "a cat."

"But this can't be just any old cat that I conjure up," he said. "Let's make it…" The Reverend with a flourish began to write again. "A purple cat with a…" He stopped and asked the class,

"What color is its tail?"

They got it. Shirley raised her hand, "A pink tail."

The Reverend wrote down "a purple cat with a pink tail named…"

He stopped and looked at the class and Timmy shouted, "Felix."

Mary said, "With yellow whiskers and green eyes."

They were getting excited; the little photons were moving about in anticipation of being free.

"Yes," the Reverend said, "Now watch this. I'm going to show you real magic," and the Reverend wrote, "Felix the purple cat with a pink tail, yellow whiskers, and green eyes, jumped out of a cloud of chalk into the lap of…" He smacked the board with the erase to create a cloud of dust and looked down at the little ones waiting in expectation. "Jessie!" he shouted.

Jessie caught Felix, petted him then passed it on to Tisha who let Felix lick her face. As they passed Felix from child to child Felix became more real. Shirley ran over to her lunch box and got a carton of milk, filled a bowl with the milk from the carton and put it next to the door. All the children watched Felix lap up the milk. They were doing it. They were, in an act of faith, leaping across the abyss of classic physics into the quantum world where it all began.

The bell rang for lunch and recess, and the children immediately forgot about Felix and got in line to be herded to the lunchroom and then to the playground for recess. After lunch, the Reverend watched them from Leah's classroom window return to the chaos from which they came. He watched them run madly around, climbing, falling, throwing balls, kicking balls, yet no one really ran into anyone else, no one hit anyone or got hurt. It was as if they had an internal radar or sonar system like some birds and animals and dolphins are said to have. When they finally came back to the classroom for rest time, the little photons were blinking out.

One of the little boys wanted to show him a picture book about the planets, so he laid down next to the little boy so that he could see the pictures. He was so tired. He was looking at a picture of our galaxy when he closed his eyes and dreamt that he was at the Palace of Versailles looking up at the mural of Venus, the muses, the cherubs hovering around Venus draping her with garlands of roses.

When he woke up, the children were hovering all around him, looking down at him like the cherubs in the mural, smiling, concerned, and wondering. One of them said, "It's time to go home, Papa Bear."

The Reverend had slept through the rest of the classes. He couldn't remember when he had slept so deeply, so peacefully. He was embarrassed, but once the children knew that he was awake, they just went about their business of getting their stuff together to go home. As they left, Jessie looked back and said, "Bye Jimmy."

After school Leah drove him to the headquarters of the veterans of the Vietnam War, and with Leah's help, Lou Penelton, their commandant of the post, agreed to meet with Bob. She then drove him to the VFW, right to the door. When he was getting out, she said to him, "Reverend, you were wonderful with the children today. They loved you." She then leaned over and kissed him on the lips, and the kiss lingered even when she drove away, and he was alone in the VFW. Something had changed. He was happy for the first time in a long time, and he didn't need a drink. The kiss lingered.

Chapter Six

W hen the sun splashed across the flowers woven into the handmade quilt bedspread, Charlie woke up and got out of bed. His work clothes were all washed and neatly folded on the dresser. Charlie showered, dressed, and then went downstairs to the kitchen where Daisy was making his breakfast.

He kissed Daisy on the cheek, "Good morning, Honey."

"Good morning, dear." Daisy slipped the spatula underneath one of the eggs. The yolk quivered but didn't break. Charlie loved his eggs light over easy like only Daisy could make them.

Charlie sat down at the breakfast table, and Daisy poured him a cup of coffee. He added cream and sugar and then reached for the *National Inquirer*, his favorite newspaper. The headline read,

Cops Offer Deal.

Mom Finally Cracks.

Her Confession Could Send Dad to Death Row.

Charlie looked at the picture of a twelve-year-old girl who was dressed up to look like a glamorous woman with makeup and lipstick and a full-grown woman's hairdo. He shook his head in disapproval and opened the paper to the article and began to read. "It looks like the father did it, and the wife was covering up for him."

Daisy placed a dish of bacon and eggs in front of Charlie and said, "Isn't it awful? Those people have everything. How could they do such a thing?"

"He's rich. I bet he gets away with it, just like OJ."

"Oh, I hope not."

Charlie pointed his finger at the picture on the front page of the twelve-year-old girl who was sexually molested and murdered in the basement of her parent's home. "I knew something was wrong when I saw what they did to that little girl, dressing her up to look like a sex pot and entering her in all those beauty contests. It's disgraceful. You knew something was wrong with those people from the start."

Daisy poured more coffee, and Charlie turned the page and read on. He read about how one star had cancer, and another was an addict. He read about one divorce after another and looked at the sad faces of the rich and famous and it made him feel better to know that even the rich and famous suffered. It made him feel that his life wasn't so bad after all, and maybe there was such a thing as divine justice. It would seem that even though these people may be above the law, they weren't above the law of God.

"Did you read about that poor little boy in Detroit," Daisy asked as she sat down at the table.

"What little boy?"

"The story is on page six."

Charlie turned to page six and read about a boy who was mentally retarded, visually impaired, and suffered from cerebral palsy. The father was unemployed, and the family couldn't pay for the child's therapy. There was a picture of the little boy smiling. There was so much hope in his eyes. Charlie's heart went out to him. The caption at the end of the story asked the family of *National Inquirer* readers to help.

Charlie looked up from the paper, "We should send some money, Daisy."

"I think so too, dear. Do you think that twenty dollars is enough?"

"Sure, there are a lot of good people out there who will help. We may not be rich, but together we can make a difference. For example, look at this."

He pointed to another article in the *Inquirer*, "A fifty-year-old crane operator and his wife found twelve thousand dollars on the road, and they gave it back to the man who lost it. The man's wife says here, 'We're regular folks. We don't have much. But that money belonged to someone else.'"

"See what I mean?" Charlie said.

Charlie looked across the table at Daisy, and she smiled at him much like she smiled at him when they first met, and she stole his heart. She wasn't the beautiful young girl he first fell in love with, but she was still beautiful to him. She had a beauty that radiated from within, and all her features expressed a generosity of spirit.

Daisy cleared the table and began to wash the dishes. As Charlie watched her, she seemed to be smiling to herself like she was somewhere else while she was there. "What are you thinking about, Honey?"

"Oh, I was just thinking about when we went to Coney Island, and I wanted to go on the parachute ride, and you were so frightened. You were like a little boy, and here you were a war hero and all of that. I thought it was so funny."

"It brought back bad memories, Daisy."

"I know, dear, but weren't those Nathan hot dogs good? We don't have anything like that here."

"They were delicious. I never had steamed hot dogs with sauerkraut and mustard before. I really liked that."

Daisy smiled, "And I also remembered when we first bought this house. I remember you saying to me, 'I finally got a home, Daisy.' It was so sweet, and I wanted so much for you to be happy,

215

Charlie."

She paused for a moment and then said, "We've done all right, don't you think, Charlie?"

"More than all right, Daisy."

Daisy smiled then dried her hands, poured herself another cup of coffee, and sat down at the kitchen table to read the Ithaca Journal.

Daisy caused Charlie to think about the home they made. Both he and Daisy loved the TV sitcom, *The Ozzie and Harriet Show*. The Nelsons were a real family. Ozzie was the dad. Harriet was the mother, and they had two boys David and Ricky. For the Nelson family everyday situations became a comic moment. They laughed at their everyday foibles and problems, and because they loved one another and had a sense of humor, their everyday problems never seemed to overwhelm them. There were some real-life lessons to be learned from Ozzie and Harriet and their children that Charlie and Daisy took to heart. Charlie wanted to be like Ozzie. He even had a wing back upholstered lounge chair in the living room like Ozzie's that everyone knew was Dad's chair, and though he couldn't wear a suit and tie like Ozzie did every day, Charlie always cleaned up thoroughly scrubbing every bit of the dirt off of himself before he changed into clean clothes. When they went out, he wore a white shirt and tie, well pressed pants, and a cardigan

216

wool sweater or a suit and tie like Ozzie, even when he went to the VFW. Daisy kept their house spotless because she knew Charlie liked it that way, and she always wore a dress around the house and an apron in the kitchen, just like Harriet. Charlie always loved to mess up Daisy's hair when they made love. It really turned him on because otherwise her hair never seemed to be out of place.

"Daisy," Charlie said. "I love you."

Daisy smiled, and she reached across the table to hold Charlie's hand. "I love you too, dear."

For a moment they just held hands, and Charlie was satisfied. After all these years and despite some hard times they were still best friends, and they still loved each other and that to Charlie made it all worthwhile. Charlie wanted to stay home with Daisy today, but then he looked at the kitchen clock and said, "Damn, it's eight thirty. I better go. If I get there too late, I'll never hear the end of it from the Reverend."

"Does he ever leave the post, Charlie?"

"Very seldom, and it is usually because Bob sends him on errands. 'Missions,' he calls them."

"That poor man, he's so bright and so good. I'm sure that the good Lord has forgiven him a thousand times over for what he did in the war, but he can't forgive himself. Men at war, it's a horrible thing."

217

"I know, Daisy. I feel sorry for him too, but he can sure be a pain in the ass. If I get there too late, he gets pissed off, but I can't get there too early either because, if I get there while he's painting the bathroom for the thousandth time, he gets furious."

"He's painting the bathroom?"

"Oh, Homey, you don't want to know. It'll just make you sad." Charlie had to be careful about what he told Daisy. Her heart wasn't as strong as it once was. She had a heart condition, and he didn't want to lose her. Charlie looked at the clock again, "I've got to go." He kissed Daisy on the cheek, grabbed the lunch that she had prepared for him and left the house.

Charlie drove his pickup truck to the VFW parking lot, grabbed his tools, and entered the post. As usual, all the TVs were on, and they were all on different channels. The Reverend was sitting at the bar drinking a Budweiser beer watching all the channels and listening to Jimmy Buffett on the juke box singing, *God Don't Own a Car.* Everything was spotless, and Charlie could smell the paint.

Charlie took a pair of earplugs out of his shirt pocket to block out the chaos, and as he was preparing his workspace, he found himself looking back on his life. The Reverend was right, it has been one hell of a roller coaster ride, he thought to himself. He has gone from being a happy child on Buffalo Street, as near to Paradise that he has ever been, to becoming homeless person and a hobo and

218

then experiencing the horrors of the Second World War. After the war, everything changed, and he experienced love, Daisy. He had a home, a family, everything he dreamed of when he was a hobo and when he was in the war. Now, he wondered if his life had meaning anymore. It seemed, today, no one cared about people like him and the values he believed in and fought for.

The Reverend may be right. There is an evil that has been set free here. He feels it too. He feels it lurking below the surface, in the darkness that laughs at the shallowness of his happiness and threatens to swallow up all that he loves and what little meaning that he possesses. What he feared most, however, is that the evil he feels is a part of him because, if he is being honest with himself, a part of him misses the war. Maybe it is because for guys like him, working class guys, the only time that we really feel that they are an important part of America and share in its power is when America is at war. For him, he knew that it was true. Despite the horror and the terror, or maybe because of the horror and the terror, he has never been nor ever will be again as high and powerful as he was there, and he loved it. This is what he shares with Bob, this is what haunts the Reverend, and this is what makes him feel guilty. It is a truth that has never been resolved, and even now, as he tears up the floor, he can hear the roar of the "Cyclone" engines that powered the Flying Fortress.

The Big Ass Bird was in a long line of bombers running up their engines ready to take off, and when Lady Luck rolled up the runway, the Cap pulled The Big Ass Bird into position behind her. As soon as Lady Luck was in the air, the Cap walked The Big Ass Bird down the runway alternating throttles until all the engines were in sync. Weighing fifty thousand pounds, the bomber strained against the laws of gravity. Slowly she picked up speed and faster and faster she went until she reached one hundred and fifteen miles an hour. Then, in a magical moment, she was airborne, lighter than air, a graceful giant that soared into the stratosphere. At nine thousand feet, the 100th was joined by the 390th and the 95th Bombardment Group, and they took up a position behind the Third Combat Wing. They were on their way to Bremen, Germany.

"Hey Guys." It was Bagel Man. "Why don't witches wear underpants when flying on their broomsticks?"

Rock Head took the bait, "I don't know, Bagel Man. Why?"

"For a better grip."

Charlie burst out laughing with the rest of the boys, but he felt a bit uneasy because he didn't feel you should be disrespectful of women.

"This guy goes into this bar," Bagel Man said, "and he hears a piano playing, but there's no one at the piano playing it. So, he goes over to the piano to take a look, and when he gets closer, he sees a twelve-inch man standing on the piano bench playing the piano. "He goes back to the bar and says to the bartender, 'Hey, there's a twelve-inch man over there playing the piano.'

'Here,' says the bartender handing the man an old oil lamp. 'Rub this.'

"So, the man rubs the lamp and out comes a genie.

'What is your wish, Master?' the genie says.

'A million bucks,' the man says without hesitation.

'Granted,' says the genie, and he claps his hands and disappears.

"The man checks his wallet and finds the same five-dollar bill he came into the bar with, but a moment later a million ducks came flying into the bar from the streets. Flabbergasted, the man says, 'Hey, I didn't ask for a million ducks!'

'Do you think I asked for a twelve-inch pianist?' the bartender asked."

A lot of the guys laughed, but Charlie didn't get it.

"OK, you assholes," Billy Boy said over the intercom. "No more jokes. This is kiss and tell time. I'm talking to you, Pops."

"Yeah Billy."

"You're an old guy. You've been laid a lot, right?"

Pops laughed, "I guess I've had my share, Billy."

"Tell me, Pops, who was your best piece of ass and why?"

Pops was quiet for a moment then said, "That's easy. When I

221

was eighteen years old a couple of my friends and I went to a Lake George in Upstate New York to party on the 4th of July. We got real drunk going from bar to bar looking for girls. I spotted this one girl wearing a tee shirt and jeans. She was the kind of girl I really liked, thin with big tits, great body but not too pretty, so I thought I might have a chance.

"I asked her to dance. She was drunk too, so it was lust at first sight for both of us, and in no time, we had our tongues in each other's mouths. My buddies were making it with her girlfriends, so we all decided to go over to the motel that the girls were staying at. On the way over, we made out. We were both so hot to fuck that when we got to the motel room, she took me directly to the bedroom, closed the door, and took off her tee shirt. She had the most beautiful tits I'd ever seen in my life, but just as I unbuckled the belt on my pants, the state troopers broke in. The guy who owned the motel called them, the old prick.

"I jumped out of the window and hid in the woods. A half hour later when I thought the coast was clear, I went back to her cabin and tapped on the window. There she was again. She opened the window, and I began to climb in. Her arms were open to receive me. Oh, my God, those tits, they were so beautiful. It was all I saw, and I wanted to put my mouth on those babies so bad I was salivating, but right then when I was nearly in, I heard the owner of the motel shout, 'I knew you would come back, you little bastard.'"

"I was off and running and I never saw that girl again."

"Hey, but Pops," Number One said, "This is about the best piece of ass you ever had. You never got that chick."

"Pee Pee, when you get to my age, you'll realize that the best piece of ass you ever had was the one that got away. You'll be masturbating over her for the rest of your life."

"What about you, Meatball?" Hayseed asked.

"For me, first is always best. When I was seventeen, I had this girl friend, Carmella Morelli. She was an angel. In fact, she was so religious she saw the statue of the Blessed Virgin Mary at Saint Mary's Church come alive. She saw the Madonna open her arms. No shit. Italian Catholics believe virgins are pure and can see things like that."

"Like the Vestal Virgins," Cap said.

"The Vestal what," Meatball asked.

"Never mind, Meatball," Billy Boy said, "the Cap is showing off his education. Tell the story."

"Anyway, Carmie was my girlfriend, and I was always trying to get in her pants. When we went to the movies we sat in the balcony, way in the back where it was dark and neck, but every time I tried to get my hand up her dress, she'd stop me. But one time, we went to a movie that she liked for a change. It was really corny and romantic. There was no shooting in it or anything, and I was really bored, but right in the middle of one of the love scenes, I put my hand up her dress, and she let me do it. She opened her legs, and I touched her panties and felt how wet she was, and I came right there. It was the first time I ever touched a girl there, and it was the best."

"I don't know about this first is always best stuff," Bagel Man said. "My first piece of ass was so fat she needed a building permit to put on her girdle."

The guys moaned.

"I'm not kidding. She measured 36-24-36 and the other arm was just as big. God, she was so fat-"

"OK, that's enough, Bagel Man," Pops said. "Let's hear from Charlie. Are you still there, Charlie, or did you bail out?"

"I'm here."

"So?"

Charlie never had sex with a woman, but he didn't want to admit to that, so while the other guys were telling their stories Charlie was trying to make up a story of his own. "I was on the bum," he said, "going from house to house asking for food. At this one house, in this real nice neighborhood, this girl comes to the door."

Charlie looked up at the picture of Betty Grable that he had hanging up on the side wall of the fuselage. Betty Grable was his

Madonna; the girl he dreamed about. She was the girl he wanted to see spread her arms for him.

He began to describe her. "She had beautiful blonde hair, blue eyes, and she was wearing a tight cashmere sweater, and she had beautiful boobs, not too big, not too small. And her legs, I'm not saying that she was flashy because she wasn't. She was just right, not too much, not too little. Anyhow, she was kind and nice, and she felt sorry for me, so she asked me in. She said that she needed some work done in the house."

Charlie couldn't go on. He just couldn't turn Betty Grable into a slut.

"Well, what happened Charlie," Pops finally asked.

"Nothing."

All the guys laughed.

"We got to get Charlie laid guys,' Billy Boy said. "That is a number one priority when we get back."

"All right, men," the Cap said, "let's get serious. It's show time."

Things quieted down, and everyone was scanning the sky looking for German fighter planes. Charlie was beginning to believe that they had lucked out today, but as they neared the target, Charlie heard Bagel Man shout, "Holy shit."

Charlie tried to see out the window, but he was at the tail end of the bomber, and he couldn't see anything ahead. "What's going on?" he asked.

"There's so much antiaircraft fire over Berman, Charlie, it looks like a black cloud covering the whole fuckin city." Hayseed said.

Oh shit, Charlie hated this, mainly because he couldn't see what was coming, and even if he could, they couldn't do anything about it except stay in-formation, dump their load, and get the hell out there.

He saw the flak now. It was exploding all around them, and there was so much smoke he couldn't even see the fortress that was flying beside them in the formation until it exploded into flames. Another explosion jarred the Big Ass Bird, and the plane seemed like it was shaking in fear as the Cap tried to keep her under control amidst the multiple concussive explosions around them. Charlie kept telling himself what they kept telling him at the briefings to relieve his fear. On the average, it takes 3000 shells from an 88 to take down one bomber. That made him feel better until he felt a jolt that thrust the Big Ass Bird upwards, and he heard Billy Boy shout, "We've been hit. Bagel Man, are you all right?"

The next jolt threw Charlie against the Plexiglas window, and they began to dive.

"Oh, Jesus, this is it," he heard Hayseed cry out.

Billy Boy shouted at the Cap to pull her up. They were diving faster and faster, and the Big Ass Bird was screaming like a banshee. The G-force of the airplane pinned Charlie against the rear of the plane, and he was beginning to panic. He couldn't even reach his parachute; and to make things worse, he could hear the bombs rattling around in the bomb bay.

Over the intercom, he heard Meatball praying to Mary Mother of God. Rock Head was crying. Hayseed was singing the gospel song, *Amazing Grace*, and Pops was telling everyone to keep cool. He told them that The Bird was built to take more G-force than this, and he was right. Charlie could feel the Big Ass Bird pulling out of the dive. They weren't going to crash. As they pulled up, he could see the rooftops of Bremen, and as they gained altitude and leveled off, he heard Cap shout to Bagel Man to unload the bombs.

Bagel Man shouted, "Where?"

"Any fuckin' place, we need to get light fast. Just push the fuckin' button. I don't care where."

Charlie felt the bombs unloading and then the concussions from the explosions. Bombs were exploding all around them. Flying this low they were part of the target zone. They were the target. Cap banked the Bird out and away from Bremen flying higher and higher, the Big Ass Bird straining until Charlie swore he could hear rivets popping. The plane was being torn apart, but they finally leveled off at 30,000 feet and everything calmed down. They were out of the range of the anti-aircraft guns.

227

"Father Bob," Meatball said, "you did it."

"All right," Cap said, "I need a damage report, and everyone needs to check in. Pops help me out here please. Check everything."

"Will do Cap, but how are things up there?"

"Billy and I are banged up a bit, but we're OK. Bagel Man is hurt bad. His arm looks mangled. Rock Head has shot him up with morphine and stopped the bleeding. He looks stable. The front canopy is shattered so it's a bit windy up here, and the best news for last. Engine three is gone."

"OK," Pops said, "Here's the news so far from here. Overall, the Big Bird has a lot of holes in her, but it doesn't seem fatal. The right elevator is ripped up badly, and you better check all your controls, Cap. There are a lot of loose wires back here. I'll try to trace them."

Cap went through the roll call. Bagel Man was hurt bad. The rest of the crew was banged up too, but nobody was seriously hurt. The big problem was that they had to get home now on their own with one engine out. Cap was making for the clouds when Charlie heard Cap shout, "Here they come!"

They came out of the clouds, and they were upon them before Charlie could reload his 50s. He frantically jammed a new belt of ammunition in when he heard Number Two shouting, "Charlie, ten o'clock."

Charlie looked up, and a Messerschmitt was overhead, but he could only get a few quick bursts off before it turned away to circle back for another pass. Another fighter came in from nowhere, and a burst of canon fire shot off a piece of the Big Ass Bird's dorsal fin. It looked like a shark had bitten off a chuck of meat.

Number One shouted, "My brother is hit! Jesus Christ, Harry. Oh shit! Harry is all bloody. Oh Jesus, I need help!"

"Man your gun, Fred," Cap said. "I'll get someone back there to help you. Don't leave your gun. You know the rules. Rock Head get back there!"

"I'm on my way."

"Watch out, Charlie!" Hayseed shouted, and Charlie spotted a Messerschmitt come up from under the tail wing, and this time he was prepared. Charlie fired into the fuselage, and the Messerschmitt burst into flames, and he watched the plane come apart, piece by piece. A moment later clouds began to envelop The Big Ass Bird within a cloak of invisibility, and for a moment, they were safe.

The Cap ordered everyone to report in. Number One had taken a piece of shrapnel in the leg. Bagel Man was hurt, and Meatball had a big gash on his head that he got when part of the nose canopy was shattered by enemy fire. The number three engine was still out, and Pops thought that one of the hydraulic fluid lines to the brakes had ruptured.

"All right," the Cap said. "This is the story. The Bird is hurt, but she's still in one piece. We have one engine out. I can't get her to go over one hundred and fifty miles an hour, and she doesn't want to climb much either. Fortunately, guys, it's a shitty day all around, and we have a lot of clouds up here, so we're going to be playing hide-and-go-seek with these fuckin' Krauts. And when we run out of clouds, well... Those sons-of-a-bitches are going to be in real trouble."

Rock Head laughed and then said, "You got it, Cap. Those Krauts don't know who they're fucking with today."

To confuse the German pilots, Cap changed his course while they were still in the clouds. However, when they cleared the clouds, it was only a few minutes before Pops shouted. "Here they come again!"

They were coming at them from all angles. One Messerschmitt dove down from above and exploded to the starboard side. Pops shouted, "I got him," but the Kraut and his plane nearly got them as the wing from the Messerschmitt flew right past Charlie almost hitting The Big Ass Bird.

Then Charlie heard some bullets piercing the fuselage behind him, and he heard Rock Head shout, "We have a fire back here. I need some help."

"I'm coming," Billy Boy shouted.

Charlie panicked. A fire was one of the worse things that could happen on board a bomber. The Big Ass Bird was loaded with ammunition and gasoline, and all sorts of inflammable stuff. One spark in the wrong place could set her off like a bomb. Charlie grabbed his fire extinguisher and made his way to where there were flames. The rear end of the fuselage was full of smoke. Through the smoke, Charlie saw Rock Head spraying the flames with foam from a fire extinguisher, and Billy Boy was pissing on it.

Billy Boy smiled at Charlie and said, "We have it under control, Charlie." Charlie laughed then threw Billy Boy the fire extinguisher and went back to his post.

Repeatedly the German fighters attacked The Big Ass Bird as she flew from one cloud bank to another for cover, zig zagging as best the Big Ass Bird could to confuse the German pilots. At one point, one German fighter got so frustrated that he dove into the clouds after them. When Charlie saw him, it was as if the clouds had become a monstrous ghost, a machine nightmare. "Holy Shit," Charlie shouted as they nearly collided.

At any moment Charlie expected to see another fighter appear, but the cloud cover stayed with them. Nobody said anything. It was as if they believed that if they said something, the Krauts would hear them like in a submarine. Thirty minutes later, when they came out of the clouds again, the German fighters were gone. They must have been running low on fuel.

Charlie let out a sigh of relief just when The Big Ass Bird was rocked like it had been kicked by a mule. Charlie looked down, and he saw flak mushrooming up around them. "Jesus Christ," he said. "We're over a city."

"Hey, guys," the Cap said. "I want some altitude here. Throw out everything we don't need and that includes flak pads and armor. We have to get above this crap."

A few minutes later Pops appeared, "You have anything to throw away, Charlie?"

The only thing that Charlie had was the armored plate that he was sitting on. "Just this Pops," He pointed to the plate.

"Give it to me."

"Pops, I don't want to loss 'em before I use 'em!"

Pops laughed, "That's the funniest thing you ever said, Charlie, but if we don't get some altitude, we're going to get our asses blown out of the sky anyway."

Charlie handed the armored plate to Pops. Pops pointed at the twin fifties. "If you run out of ammunition, disassemble your guns and throw them overboard too."

Pops left, and a few minutes later, The Big Ass Bird began to climb. They were climbing out of the range of what seemed to be midrange anti-aircraft guns. Over the intercom, Charlie could hear Rock Head say that the last hit had torn off one of the bomb bay doors, but otherwise they were fine.

An hour later, they made the coast. Below them they spotted Lady Luck piloted by Captain Dave Wittlin.

"Hey, Dave," Cap said into the radio. "Are you all right?"

"I think so, Bob. We're shot up pretty bad, and we're flying on two engines, but I think we're going to make it."

They flew for a while with Lady Luck below them to provide her with some protection, but Lady Luck was flying low above the water, and Cap needed speed and altitude if he was going to save his crew.

Charlie was wondering what the Cap would decide when he saw them first. "We got company," he shouted. The decision was made for them.

"How many, Charlie?" the Cap asked.

"I see four."

They were Focke-Wulfe 190 fighters. Charlie thought it was a better fighter than the Messerschmitt, not as much armor but a hell of a lot more maneuverable and difficult to hit. They went after Lady Luck first, and the crew of the Big Ass Bird tried to give her some cover fire, but it was hopeless. After the first pass, Lady Luck lost another engine, and she was smoking badly. Charlie saw a parachute but one of the fighters swooped down under Lucky Lady and hit the parachutist with cannon fire and tore off his lower body. It was a hell of a shot, and it was true what everyone was saying. The Germans were after the Bloody 100. They were showing no mercy.

Two more parachutes appeared, but Lady Luck had lost so much altitude that the two parachutes barely opened before he two airmen plunged into the icy ocean. They were goners. Dave Whitlin sat Lady Luck down on the water as if he had landed it on solid ground. It was a beautiful landing, and the guys on board might have survived if the Germans let them be, but they came in to finish them off, riddling Lady Luck with bullets. The water around the bomber was turned into a boiling cauldron of machine gun fire, but some glorious bastard in the top gun turret of Lady Luck kept firing as the bomber sunk into the water and dis-appeared.

"You sons-of-a-bitches, you no good bastards," Charlie shouted.

Charlie had never felt the kind of rage that he felt at that moment. He wanted the Germans to attack him, and when he realized that they were going to attack from the rear, he was happy. "Come on, you bastards. Come on. Here I am. You want the Bloody 100th. You got it."

Charlie started firing when the fighters were about three hundred yards away. He blew the propeller off one of the fighters, and he kept on firing at it until it disintegrated. Bullets were tearing through the Plexiglas window and the fuselage, but he didn't notice it. He turned his guns on another fighter and got it as it was side slipping to the right. It went into a spinning dive and plunged into the water below.

"Pops is hit," Number Two shouted.

Another fighter exploded, and then Charlie heard the Cap shout, "The last one is going to try and take us head on."

That was one of the weakest spots of the Flying Fortress. The F model had no front gun turret. If the German came in straight on the nose there wasn't a gun on The Big Ass that could hit him.

"All right, Hayseed, this Kraut is yours."

Charlie felt the plane bank. The Cap was giving Hayseed a shot at the Messerschmitt from the belly turret, but at the same time, he was exposing the bottom of the ship. It was one gun against one airplane. No one else would be able to get off a shot, and if Hayseed missed the shot, the fighter would gut the Big Ass Bird.

Charlie couldn't see anything, and all he could do was listen to the gunfire from both planes, and then Charlie saw the Messerschmitt come flaming by. Hayseed had done it! The pilot bailed out, but he didn't have a chance. Everyone fired at him. He was dead when he hit the water. They had won!

Everyone was cheering, but then they heard the Cap say, "We've lost another engine, boys, and we're losing altitude fast. Every-thing has got to go, guns, ammo, everything."

Charlie dismantled his guns and threw the guns and the ammo out of the plane. He then made his way to the mid-section of the bomber, and what he saw horrified him. The Big Ass Bird was rid-dled with bullet holes. There was blood all over, and Pops was sitting down holding his guts in with his hands as Rock Head tried to tape him back together with gauze and surgical tape. Rock Head was bleeding also, and he was so nervous and frightened that he was shaking like a leaf. Number One had a huge gash in his leg, but he was helping Number Two throw out the guns and ammo and anything else that wasn't bolted down. Charlie went forward to help up front.

It was just as bad up front. The nose canopy had been shot away, and Meatball's bandaged head was soaked with blood. Bagel Man was out on morphine, and his arm looked terrible. Charlie could see a bone sticking through the skin like a broken chicken wing.

Billy Boy grabbed hold of Charlie. He had a first aid kit in his hand. "I'll fix you up, Charlie. Let me help you take off your jacket."

Charlie didn't know what Billy Boy was talking about, but then he saw the blood. He'd been shot in the arm. He almost fainted right there.

Billy took off his jacket for him, and Charlie asked, "Is it bad?"

"I don't think so, Charlie. I think it went straight through without rupturing any artery or hitting a bone. You're not bleeding that bad."

"Jesus, Billy, I don't want to lose my arm."

"It's not that bad, Charlie. Don't worry."

Billy wrapped Charlie's arm and sat him down against one of the bulkheads in the radio compartment. Everyone was coming forward to where the bulkheads were for some protection against a crash landing. Number Two and Rock Head carried Pops into the radio compartment. They were a bloody mess. Pops was unconscious. Charlie started to cry. He couldn't take it anymore. He wasn't crying because he was probably going to die. He was crying because it was all too terrible.

"We're going to make it, guys," Billy Boy said, "But we don't have enough gas to make it to our own home base, and the radio is out, so we're going to land wherever we can."

Billy went back up front to help the Cap. Fifteen minutes later they were flying over England. Charlie wanted to see what was going on, so he went up front to look. The gas gauge looked like it was on zero.

"I know there's an English air base around here somewhere," Cap said.

Billy Boy pointed, "Over there."

"Right," Cap smiled. "I got it, Billy. Fire a flare to let them know that we're hurt and coming in."

The Cap turned to Charlie and said, "You better get back there, Charlie. This may be rough."

Charlie didn't move. He was tired of being in the ass end, not knowing what was going on until the plane had landed. He wanted to see this.

"OK, Billy, keep an eye out for traffic," Cap said. "I'm going in. Put the turbo on and drop the wheels."

"Got it."

"Make sure the intercoolers are off."

"Check."

They began the turn into the descent. Billy Boy fired another flare. Charlie estimated that they were about two miles away

"Lower the flaps one quarter and reduce speed," Cap said.

"Check."

"What's our speed?"

"One-twenty, Cap."

Charlie watched the runway get closer and closer, and for the first time he finally felt what it was like to be in control, to be a part of the Big Bird's massive wings, the pull of the propellers, the pounding of her heart beat, cylinders firing. He was flying! He wanted to be the pilot. He wanted to fly this plane and land her in the face of death. Somehow, he knew that this was as high and as low as he was ever going to get in his life.

"Full flaps, shut down the throttle," Cap said. "Come on Big Bird, just this one last time."

The ground came at them so fast Charlie thought they were about to crash, but their fall turned into a thump and then a bumpy slide, the wheels skidding like a car on ice. The Big Ass Bird bounced twice as if she was trying to take flight again, but then she was on the ground speeding down the runway. Even Charlie knew they were going too fast.

"I got no brakes!" Cap shouted.

The Big Ass Bird raced down the runway going seventy-five miles an hour with no way to stop. Charlie should have found a safe spot, but he couldn't move. He was fascinated by the immensity of the moment. He felt he was still a part of the Big Ass Bird when the wheels collapsed, and they were now skidding down the runway. Sparks were flying all around them. Charlie could feel pieced of The Big Ass Bird being torn apart. It felt like pieces of him were being torn away. They skidded off the runway into a muddy field, and they were still going fifty miles an hour when the right wing hit a tree. The tree sheared off the wing and spun the Big Ass Bird around. She skidded and spun for another fifty yards.

Charlie's head was spinning too. He felt like the Big Bird was dancing on the brink of oblivion before she came to a stop.

It was so quiet that Charlie could hear birds chirping like nothing just happened. "We made it!" Charlie shouted. "Holy shit, we
made it."

The Cap and Billy Boy smiled at one another and shook hands.

Charlie rushed back to the radio room to see if the boys were
OK. He opened the door, and shouted, "We made it! You should
have seen it. It was..."

Charlie stopped in mid-sentence. Pops was dead.

The fire engines and the ambulances arrived, and the crew was
helped out of the plane. They had landed at a British air base. The
English crews gathered around the wreck, and they were amazed
that The Big Ass Bird had made it. One British airman said that he
counted over a thousand bullet holes in The Big Ass Bird and then
gave up counting. Another British airman patted Charlie on the
shoulder and said, "I'll tell you one thing, Yank, I'm never going to
make fun of a Flying Fortress again."

Charlie, who was being helped into an ambulance, looked back
at The Big Ass Bird. One wing was torn off. She was riddled with
bullets. There was a big bite out of her nose and tail. She was done
for. Charlie felt like he had lost an old friend. Then he remembered
something. He turned to the guy who was helping him into the

ambulance and said, "I'll be right back."

Charlie ran to The Big Ass Bird and crawled into the plane. He went back to his tail gunner's position. He was looking for Betty Grable. She had been torn apart, but Charlie gathered up her remains, her face, her breast, a piece of her leg, her ass, and some other indiscernible shreds that were like the sacred bones of a dead saint to Charlie.

They took Charlie to the hospital. He had lost a lot of blood, tore a tendon in his arm, and his shoulder bone had been chipped by a bullet fragment. When Charlie felt well enough to get up and walk about, he went looking for the other members of the crew that were in the hospital. Number Two, Meatball, and Rock Head were going to be okay. They were scheduled to be discharged from the hospital about the same time that Charlie was.

Bagel Man was more difficult to find. He was in another part of the hospital, but Charlie finally found him. When Charlie walked into Bagel Man's room, Charlie had a big smile on his face, but then the joy of seeing his friend alive turned to shock. Pete Lowe had lost his arm.

Charlie didn't know what to say. He sat next to Pete, and without thinking he reached out for the hand that wasn't there, "Gee, Pete, I'm so sorry."

Bagel Man laughed, "What do you have to be sorry for Charlie?

241

I'm the one who lost the arm. Hey, Charlie, I got a joke for you. Why did the moron jump off the Empire State Building?"

Charlie tried to look cheerful, "Why Bagel Man?"

"Because he wanted to make a big hit on Broadway."

They both laughed, but Pete's laughter turned into tears when he said, "I don't care what anyone says, Charlie, when I get home, I'm going to marry the farmer's daughter, and I don't care how many traveling salesmen she fucked."

Charlie was crying too. He was crying for Pete and Pops and for himself, for the boy in him that died with The Big Ass Bird and Betty Grable. There was no more adventure left in him. He wanted this war to be over. He wanted to go home.

When Charlie got out of the hospital, he went straight to the barracks to look for the boys, and they weren't there. They had gone to London, so he caught a train to London and went to The Stars and Stripes Pub where he hoped to find them. When he walked in the front door of the Stars and Stripes, he heard his name called. It was Billy Boy.

They were all there, The Cap, Hayseed, Number One, and Number Two. Even Meatball and Rock Head were there. Billy introduced Charlie to the two new guys that were going to replace Pops and Bagel Man. Their names were Sam Ericson and Jack Woods. No one knew them well enough to give them nicknames, but they seemed to be okay guys to Charlie.

It was good to be back with the boys, but it wasn't quite the same. Everyone was trying to be cheerful and devil-may-care, but it wasn't working. Finally, Billy Boy, who was drunk, said what was on all their minds. "I'm going to miss Pops and Bagel Man. They were the best."

Cap ordered shots of whiskey for everyone, and when they came, he raised his glass, "To Steven Gilbert and Peter Lowe, the best of the best. And may Pops rest in peace."

The boys clinked glassed, downed the whiskey in one gulp and ordered another round of whiskey and more pitchers of beer. This was the first time that they were all back together again, and the new plane was due to arrive in a few more days. There was going to be a lot of drinking tonight.

"Remember the big fuck up?" Rock Head said. He turned to Jack and Sam, the new guys, and said, "We weren't always the best god damned bomber crew in the United States Air Force. Get this. We were supposed to fly a simulated bombing run from Hamilton Field in California, to Kearney Air Base in Nebraska, and we got lost."

Hayseed laughed and said, "Boy, were you a fucked-up navigator back then, Meatball."

"What do you mean? They gave me the wrong co-ordinates."

"Wrong coordinates my ass," Billy Boy said. "You couldn't read coordinates then."

"He still can't read coordinates," Cap said. "The only reason we get where we're going is that he follows the other planes."

"Fuck you guys. They gave us the wrong coordinates."

"Anyway," Rock Head said. "We're lost, and by the time we figure out where we are, we're flying over Texas! We don't know what to do. Then Pops comes up with this idea. We have to land, so why not land near this town in Texas where he knows this girl who's got the hots for him. A minute later, over the intercom, I hear the Cap say, 'Why not?' Half an hour later, we land at the Huntsville airport. Remember that, Cap?"

"Sure do." Cap smiled, "I was thinking then, what the hell. We had to land somewhere. Pops was right. Someone might as well get laid, and who knows, she might have friends."

"See, that's why the Cap is our leader," Rock Head said. "He's got reason. So anyway, we land at this airport. God, you should have seen the looks on those people's faces when they came out to look at The Big Ass Bird. None of them had ever seen a Flying Fortress for real before. It was like we were celebrities from outer space.

"So, there we are, and Pops calls this girl, and she still has the hots for him. She has some friends too, so we all go out and have a great time. Pops, he's all over this girl. She's a good looker too. The only problem is that she lives with her mother.

"So, Bagel Man says to Pops, 'Why don't you take her back to the bomber, Pops. I'll go back there before you do and put a mattress in the bomb bay for you.'

'You'd do that for me, Bagel Man?' Pops says.

'Sure, Pops. We're buddies.'

Pops is really drunk now, and he slaps Bagel Man on the back and says, 'I'm never going to forget this, Bagel Man.'

"So, Bagel Man does like he said he was going to do, and he goes back to the airport, finds a mattress, and puts it in the bomb bay for Pops. Pops and the girl go back to the airport. We all go back to the airport except Number One and Billy who scored with the girl friends.

"Pops takes the girl out to the bomber, and they climb in. Bagel Man tells us to take some of the mattresses that the people at the airport have given us to sleep on and follow him out to the bomber. Quietly we put the mattresses under the bomb bay doors, and Bagel Man sneaks into The Big Ass Bird. Pops and the girl are too drunk and too busy fucking to hear him, and, man, were they fucking away. Pop was banging her so hard that The Big Ass Bird was bouncing up and down. The girl was really into it too. She was moaning and screaming and pumping away. They were really

245

building up to a crescendo. Like this was going to be a big ex-plo-sion. And just as they came, Bagel Man opens the bomb bay doors."

Rock Head laughed as did everyone else. "It was bombs away! Boy was Pops mad. Stark naked Pops chased Bagel Man all over the airstrip, but then he just started laughing. The girl was a good sport too. She just told us to fuck off and went home, but not before giving Pops one last big kiss, just like in the movies."

There was a pause in the laughter, and everyone grew silent again until the Cap raised his glass and said, "Here's to The Big Ass Bird. She held together until she brought us home."

They all raised their glasses and drank to The Big Ass Bird.

"Are we going to name the new plane, The Big Ass Bird," Number Two asked.

"Nah," Cap said, "that would be disrespectful."

"Anybody got any ideas?" Billy Boy asked.

"How about Betty," Charlie said.

"Shit, Charlie," Meatball said. "There are too many bombers named Betty already - Gorgeous Betty, Betty My Love, My Girl Betty. What's that other one, Bill Blade's plane?"

"Betty Boobs," Number Two said.

"Yeah, see. We need something more original."

"How about, She's My Momma," Hayseed said.

Cap nodded his head in approval, "Not bad."

246

"How about the Bearded Lady," Number One said. "The new chin turret on the G model makes it look like it's got a beard."

"We're getting the new G model?" Charlie asked.

"Yah, Charlie, and the big change is that it has a chin turret. No more weak spot in the nose."

"All right, so the Bearded Lady is in the running along with She's My Momma," Cap said. "Any other suggestions?"

"I got an idea," Meatball said. "What was the name of the girl who Pops banged in the plane?"

"Yeah," Number Two said. "That's it."

"So, what was her name?" Cap asked.

"Janice," Hayseed said.

"No, that wasn't it," Number One said. "It was Sandra or something like that."

"No... No, it was Mary," Rock Head said. "It was Mary or maybe Mary Ann. Oh shit, I don't know, but I know it wasn't Sandra. My sister's name is Sandra, and I would have remembered."

Charlie knew her name. He would never forget. She was the first girl that Charlie had ever heard fuck or seen naked. "Her name was Sally," Charlie said.

"That's right," Cap said. "I remember now. It was Sally."

"Yep," Rock Head said. "It was Sally. Charlie is right."

"So, we'll call her Bomb Bay Sally," Billy Boy said. "How does

247

that sound?"

Everyone was happy with the name.

The Cap raised his glass. "So be it. Here's to Bomb Bay Sally our new girl."

They all lifted their glasses to toast, "Bomb Bay Sally."

Charlie heard someone in the bar shout, "Hey, there's Ass End Charlie."

Charlie heard his name and looked up and saw William Stewart, the Brit who befriended him the night that they had a big fight in the bar. It looked like the whole crew was with him. Charlie wondered if they were going to have another fight.

William extended his hand, "Good to see you in one-piece, old boy. It was our airfield where you landed that wounded bird of yours. We saw it all. Bloody good show."

"Who's the pilot here?" another English airman said. "That was some good flying there, I'll say."

Cap introduced himself and introduced the rest of the crew. Everyone shook hands.

An English gunner named Bret Harrison shook Charlie's hand and said, "I hear you blokes took on the whole German Air Force."

Rock Head who was sitting next to Charlie said, "Charlie shot down four German planes on his own, no lie."

Charlie was embarrassed, "We were just fighting our way

248

home."

"Why don't you guys join us," Cap said. "Have a drink on us. Have two. We're celebrating the christening of a new ship and mourning a dead friend."

"I have a better idea," the English pilot said. "Let's mourn the whole damn war."

"That's a great idea," Billy said and ordered more rounds of whiskey for everyone, and when they all raised their glasses, Billy raised his glass and toasted, "Fuck war."

The next day, Charlie woke up in the barracks with the worse hangover of his life. To make things worse he discovered that they were back on the line, and they were going out on the next mission, and that mission was the Big B, Berlin. Charlie didn't want to go. Why couldn't their last four missions be milk runs? Why Berlin now? The Germans would throw everything they had at them. Charlie wasn't the only one on the crew who felt that way. Billy Boy was drinking heavy. On some of the practice flights he was shaky. Even Cap seemed quiet and withdrawn, and when Cap told them that the target would be Berlin, Charlie could see that the Cap was not happy. He was burnt out too. The whole Bloody 100th or what was left of them seemed burned out.

When Charlie was in the hospital, thirteen planes from the 100th went on the mission to Munster, and only one came back, Rosie's

Riveters. There were so many new guys and new planes in the 100th that Charlie could hardly recognize anyone. Most the guys that Charlie knew were either dead or prisoners of war. However, The Memphis Belle had completed its tour of duty. Maybe Bomb Bay Sally could do it too. Charlie remembered the day the Memphis Belle came home on its last mission with flares flying and everyone on the ground cheering. They had made it. They had beaten Death.

On the morning of the Berlin raid, waiting to take off, Charlie listened to the Cap going through the preflight check list. The Cap kept checking and rechecking everything. Charlie knew he was looking for something, anything that would justify his order to pull Bomb Bay Sally off the line. Charlie knew that everyone was praying that he would find something, but he didn't find anything. On the intercom, Charlie heard the Cap get the go ahead to taxi onto the runway. A few minutes later, they were up in the air again and heading for Berlin and a party with the Devil.

There were five hundred Flying Fortresses and three hundred and fifty Mustang fighters as escort on this mission. Everywhere Charlie looked he saw bombers and fighters. The bombers, Charlie figured, covered five square miles of air space, and there had to be at least three million pounds of bombs on the way to Berlin. The Mustangs were welcome companions. Finally, after all this time, they had escort fighters that could go the distance.

The magnitude of this mission seemed to have quieted everyone down. There was no longer the usual chatter and humor, just the deafening roar of the engines and Cap periodically warning everyone to stay alert. Charlie missed Bagel Man and his humor, and Pops was always a steadying influence. When morale was down, like it was now, Pops would step in and cheer everyone up. He would convince them that everything was going to be all right, there was an adult present. When Charlie went into the midsection of the plane to check the ammunition feed lines, he saw Billy Boy with his head stuck out the side gun portal throwing up his breakfast.

Charlie thought about Betty, and he wished he was in her arms surrounded by her warmth and softness, but up here he had to watch out because the enemy was out there, and they were looking for anything soft to penetrate and rip apart. It was strange, he thought, how different men and women were. Women gave birth to life, and here we were in a bomber pregnant with bombs about to give birth to death. Charlie wished he was an educated man because it all was so confusing to him. He didn't even know what madness was except that he thought that this must be it.

"Here they come," Cap shouted.

"Where," Charlie asked.

"Everywhere," Cap said.

"Jesus Christ. Holy Mother of God," Meatball shouted.

Charlie saw them now. There had to be hundreds of German fighters in the air, and they were probably only the first wave. In minutes, all hell broke loose. The fighters were attacking from every direction and angle. Some were maneuvering about a thousand yards outside of the formations and firing cannon shells and rockets into the formations. Other German fighters were diving into the middle of the formations, and right behind them flew the Mustangs giving chase. There were so many targets that nobody on the crew was talking to anyone else. Everyone was just firing at anything that moved. It was like a Fourth of July fireworks display of bullets and tracers, cannon and rocket fire, exploding planes and flaming parachutes, shredded flesh like confetti celebrating the death of life. A man's severed head hit the side of the window with a thud and bounced off like a basketball. Charlie barely noticed.

One part of him was a cold mechanical part of a killing machine, and the other part of him was horrified and frightened and firing at the whole god damned war. He was praying to God to save him when the plane was hit so hard that it threw Charlie backwards, and he was slammed against the fuselage. He heard metal tearing apart and then an explosion inside Bomb Bay Sally's mid-section. Charlie knew immediately that they were going down. He grabbed his parachute and struggled to strap himself in, and when he exited

252

the rear end of the fortress to enter the med-section of the airplane where he could bail out… he froze on the edge of an abyss.

The tail section of the plane had been completely severed from the rest of the plane. In the distance, he could see the midsection of the bomber, for a moment, suspended in space without her tail. Number One was in the midsection, standing on the edge of nothing, still holding on to his gun and looking at Charlie in absolute terror.

Charlie rushed forward and dove out of what remained of the tail end of Bomb Bay Sally, and all that he could think of was Bagel Man's joke about the moron who jumped off the Empire State Building. The chute opened, but his relief was short lived when he realized that the sky was raining blood and bullets, body parts and planes. A flying fortress in flames passed right over his head, and he saw a propeller that was whirling through the air sever a parachuting airman in half. He was terrified that something or someone would hit him or his parachute, and he would become part of the rain of death.

When Charlie hit the ground, he rolled just like he had been taught. He quickly took off his parachute and looked around. It was bedlam. There were parachutes everywhere on the ground and airmen running in every direction, and they were being chased by German civilians. He was about to surrender, but then he saw an airman hit the ground, and when he raised his hands to surrender, the German civilians attacked him. He watched one German jam a pitchfork into the airman's belly and another man club him in the head. Charlie ran for the woods nearby, and when he entered the woods, he stopped dead.

"Oh, my God."

Above him was a dead airman who had been hanged by the Germans from the limb of a tree with the cord from his own parachute. It was Billy Boy.

Charlie heard shouts, and he took off again running blindly through the woods until he was so exhausted that he had to stop to catch his breath. Think, Charlie, think. If you keep running like this, you're going to get caught. You don't know where you're going. Charlie took out Dick Farris's compass and got his bearings. He had to be ten to fifteen miles outside of Berlin. Where the hell was he going to go?

Trains.

There had to be trains coming in and out of Berlin from all directions, and if there was one thing that Charlie knew about, it was trains. During the depression he hopped hundreds of trains. For three years, they were his only home. All he had to do now was find a train heading east, and he was on his way. Charlie figured that if he walked north or south, he had to run into tracks heading east or west. Cautiously he moved on, and when he came to the edge of the forest, he saw that he was in a semi-rural area, and a couple of miles down the road he saw a village. Farmhouses dotted the countryside, and it would have been quite beautiful if it were not for the fact that he was running for his life. In the distance he saw what he was looking for, tracks running east and west. Charlie moved along the edge of the forest and followed the tracks to a point where a road crossed the railway. The train would slow down at the crossing.

Charlie looked for the best place to wait for the train. He couldn't stay in the forest. It was too far from the tracks. He'd never make it when the train came. He had to get closer, and the only place he could see that would provide him with any cover was a shed and a feed trough close to the intersection. The shed and feed trough were on what seemed to be a dairy farm fenced in by barbed wire.

Charlie started running. With his flight suit and boots on it was slow going, but he made it to the shed without anyone seeing him. He had to hide somewhere until the train came, but where? The shed was not a good idea. That would be the first place they'd look. The feed trough was a better idea, he thought, it was full of feed grain and if there were dogs, it would hide his scent. Charlie slid into the trough and buried himself in the feed. He cautioned himself that he had to stay alert, but he was so tired that he couldn't keep his eyes open and soon he was asleep dreaming of Betty again. She was licking his face when he was awakened by the sharp piercing sound of a train whistle.

It was dark, and he was staring into the huge black eyes of a monster. Charlie cried out, but then he realized that it was a cow. Charlie laughed, but then he heard the train whistle again. Oh, my God, he was going to miss it!

Charlie bolted out of trough and ducked under the barbed wire and ran along the tracks parallel to the train. Luckily, it was a freight train, and it was heading east. He looked for a box car with an open door, but he couldn't see one. He was losing ground and running out of time. When a flatbed appeared, he grabbed for the side rail and swung himself up onto the wood platform. Beau Blue hadn't lost his touch. He was on the train, and he quickly looked around for a guard, but he didn't see anyone. There were probably guards on the train, but he bet that they were nothing like Blackjack Fenner, the cinder-bull who nearly killed him.

Charlie cautiously worked his way along the flatbed, climbed up onto the top of a box car and cat walked his way to the middle of the train. He climbed down from one of the flatbed cars and using the coupling between the cars as a precarious support, he lowered himself carefully onto the support braces between the wheels of the car. He was under the train only inches from the gravel bed and death, but he felt safe. Nobody would look for him here.

Charlie relaxed. The train was like an old friend. It reminded him of the Old Uncle Remus story that he saw in a cartoon movie where Brer Rabbit got caught by his arch foe, Brer Bear, and he convinces Brer Bear that the worst thing that he could do to him was throw him in the briar patch.

"Oh, Brer Bear, please, please, don't throw me in that there briar patch."

Brer Bear just smiled and looked at the sharp knife-like thorns that would pierce Brer Rabbit's body, and he threw him as far and as high as he could into the briar patch.

Brer Rabbit landed, but he didn't scream in horror and pain. He just laughed and said, "Oh Brer Bear, what a big fool you are. I was born and bred in this here briar patch."

Charlie took his belt off and strapped himself to a support beam so that he wouldn't fall off his perch if he fell asleep. As he worked, he sang one of the songs from the movie, "Zip pity do da, zip pity day, my oh my what a wonderful day. Plenty of sunshine, plenty of rain, zip pity do da, zip pity day. It's the truth. It's actual. Everything is satisfactual."

After hours and hours of sitting in one position strapped to the wheel supports, Charlie was stiff and aching all over. He was cold, but this was nothing new to a tail gunner in a Flying Fortress. He was always cramped and cold. It was a way of life for Charlie. Hours later, the train entered a large city.

When the train stopped there was a lot of movement around him and voices. It sounded like a whole army out there. He couldn't figure out what was going on until he felt the jolt of his car being uncoupled. His box car with a lot of other cars was being dis-connected from the train. He didn't dare move. He had no idea where they were taking the cars, until another jolt told him that he was being hook up to another train.

A half an hour later, the train pulled out of the train station, and he had no idea what direction the train was going. Christ, he could be going in the wrong direction. He could be going deeper into Germany. Then what would he do?

When the train went over a viaduct, he had his first clear look at the city he was passing through. It was completely bombed out. The city was reduced to mounds of stones and skeletal homes. Heat from the incendiary bombs had melted the cobble stone streets. A ruined cathedral looked like a melted ice cream cake with a bent cross sticking out of the topping. All the signs indicated that there had been a fire storm and the consequences were monstrous. There was no escaping it. The families who hid in their cellars thinking that they would be save from the blast and the falling debris, probably suffocated to death. A firestorm of this magnitude would have literally pulled the air out of their lungs. This was the first time that Charlie had ever seen up close the damage that a bombing raid could do, and he felt ashamed. All these people couldn't be Nazis. God, he didn't even know what a Republican or a Democrat was.

Several hours later they slowed down again. It was light now, and he had to get a better look at where he was and where he was going. With much effort he climbed back up onto the flatbed, and he saw that they were coming into a rural town, and judging by the signs, he was in France. Thank God, at least he won't be hanged or clubbed or pitch forked to death by angry Germans. That was the good news. The bad news was that they were coming into what looked like a farm depot. They would be stopping there. He had to do what he did as a hobo. Get off the train before it stopped and pick it up again on the other side of town.

Charlie waited for the train to slow down sufficiently and then he jumped. When his feet hit the ground, he rolled down the embankment and then scrambled into some bushes by the side of the tracks to hide. He couldn't stay here.

Charlie made his way to a nearby wheat field where the wheat was high enough to provide good cover. He waded through the wheat to an old stone farmhouse where he spotted some clothes on a clothesline. Sneaking up to the house, he grabbed a pair of pants and a shirt off the line and a pair of muddy work boots from the porch, and using the wheat field as cover again, he changed his clothes and buried his uniform. He then worked his way to the edge of the field so that he could get a good look at the landscape and see what he was dealing with. Once Charlie got his bearings, he realized the scope of his problem. He was in open farm country. Farmers didn't like trespasser even in good times. The only way to the other side of town was right down the farm road ahead, and he had to hope that he could pass through a small town where everyone knew each other without being noticed and jump another train on the other side of town. He was in civilian clothes. That was good, but if the Germans caught him in civilian clothes, they probably would shoot him right on the spot, no prisoner of war for him. That was bad. The way he saw it, he had no other choices, not if he wanted to remain a free man. Charlie shrugged and stepped out onto the road and started to walk.

Walking along the road, he felt good. He was almost resigned to being captured or shot, so he enjoyed the view, his last moments of freedom. Everything felt so alive that he felt the trees around him breathing in the air. The colors of the flowers and the vegetation were vivid, and the farmhouses looked tranquil. The wind was murmuring through the leaves of the trees, and the birds were chirping away in the bright sunlight. The whole setting seemed to be saying, this is peace and quiet and the rest doesn't matter. See what a fool you are?

Charlie was so absorbed in the countryside, that he didn't even hear the German jeep coming down the road. By the time that he knew they were there, they had pulled up alongside of him.

There were two of them and judging from how they were dressed they were officers. They were talking to Charlie in German, or at least it sounded like German. Charlie was frightened to death. He didn't know what to do, but he decided to play the French farmer who didn't understand German.

Every time they spoke to him, Charlie just shrugged.

They tried again and again. Charlie thought he could hear some French words mixed in with the German. He grimaced, the expression on his face seemed to say, 'My God, that's not French. I can't understand a single word you are saying." One of the officers was getting angry, and the other one was pointing down the road.

Then Charlie got it! They were asking for directions. Charlie pointed down the road and said, "We."

The two German's smiled and said what sounded like, "Thank you," and then they drove in the direction that Charlie had sent them.

When they were gone, Charlie should have run and hid

somewhere, but he didn't. He didn't care. He continued to walk down the road. He passed several farmhouses. As he passed one farmhouse, he noticed a chalk mark on the edge of the sidewalk leading to the house. He walked about fifty yards more down the road then he stopped dead.

The chalk mark was the same mark that hoboes used back in the Depression to tell other hoboes that this was a good house to go to and beg for food and money and shelter. For a hobo, this was the jackpot. Could it be that a downed airman, who had been a hobo during the Depression, stopped at that farmhouse and asked for help? Could he have left that sign for other airmen who had been hoboes? Only a hobo would know what that sign meant. Could it be possible? Did he dare go to that house and knock on the door and ask for help?

Charlie heard the train whistle. A train was coming. He had to decide. He heard the train whistle again, and then he saw the train. He saw a clump of trees where he could hide before he jumped onto the train. If he was going to hop that train, he had to run, now.

Damn. That sign on the side of the house was telling him in hobo language that it was a five-star restaurant, and he was starving. He watched the train come closer and closer, and he watched the train pass. He watched the train disappear down the tracks, and he wondered if he was watching all his hopes of escaping disappearing down the tracks with the train.

Warily, Charlie walked up to the farmhouse. He knocked on the door, and when a man opened the door Charlie simply said, "Hello, sir, my name is Charlie Tremaine, and I'm an American airman. I wonder-"

The man grabbed Charlie and pulled him into the house. Five days later Charlie was back in London.

Charlie was awarded the Congressional Medal of Honor. He finished his tour of duty, and he was sent back to the states as a gunnery sergeant to train new tail gunners. Six months later the war was over, and he was out of the service and back home. He decided to go back to Ithaca. It would be the first time that Charlie had been in Ithaca since the day he hopped a train to go west and make his fortune. He was sixteen years old then. Now he was twenty-one years old. His mother was dead. She had died while he was in the service. His grandfather and grandmother were dead, and he wasn't quite sure why he wanted to go back to Ithaca except that it was the only home that he had ever known.

He took a room in the house that he was born in. It was a rooming house now. The room he was living in had been the cook's room. The flowered wallpaper was stained, and the walls were cracked. The room looked out at what once had been the garden, but it was overgrown now, and the fountain was broken. The cherub had lost its head, but Charlie could still take walks back into the forest behind the house and look out over the gorge and down into Cascadilla Falls. The falls were beautiful and the gentle flow of water over rock was soothing to him. Charlie was a member of the 52-20 Club. As a veteran he got twenty dollars a week of un-employment for fifty-two weeks, gratis of Uncle Sam. It gave him time to think.

Charlie didn't know what to do with his life, and at first, when he got out of the service, he liked doing nothing. He liked taking long walks through the gorges, swimming at the falls, and fishing in the inlet, but it depressed him to live in the ruins of his parent's home. Why did he rent a room there? He wasn't sure except that it was his only tangible tie to Ithaca, his parents, and his past.

Charlie needed to change his life, so he reached out to God. Maybe his dad was right. Maybe they had sinned. Maybe he had sinned by abandoning his mother. He wondered if God would ever forgive him for killing all the men he killed. He wondered if he even believed in God anymore. He had seen so much suffering. Despite his doubts, he went to mass every Sunday at Saint John's Episcopal Church, his parent's church. He liked being around nice people, and he liked the feeling of something being sacred. He finally got to wear a suit and tie for the first time in his life, and it made him feel like a respected member of the church and the community.

One Sunday during the mass, he saw Daisy for the first time. He saw her in profile looking down at her song book and singing along with the choir. She was wearing a pretty yellow dress with blue flowers, nylons, and white high heel shoes. In that setting, with the light from the stained-glass window shining down on her long blond hair, she looked like an angel crowned with a golden halo. For some reason, she must have sensed that he was looking at her because she turned towards him, and when their eyes met, he knew that he was in love and that Daisy was his salvation.

After the mass they had a Sunday brunch in the church basement. There was coffee and fresh orange juice, and all kinds of pastries that the women brought to share. Charlie saw Daisy across the room. She was talking to Father Baker, and when she saw Charlie, she whispered something into Father Baker's ear and then laughed at what looked like the confession of an innocent sin.

Father Baker motioned for Charlie to come over.

Oh, my God, Charlie thought, what do I do now?

He walked over to where Father Baker and the girl were standing. Father Baker put his arm around Charlie's shoulders and said, "Daisy, I would like you to meet, Charlie Tremaine, a real live hero. Charlie, this is Daisy Miller."

Daisy extended her hand. It was soft and gentle, almost weight-

265

less except for the touch of her bare skin. He looked into the most beautiful blue eyes that he ever saw. They were the kind of eyes that poets wrote beautiful words about, like in Hallmark cards. Charlie wanted to say something witty and charming but all he could do was smile and say, "It's really nice to meet you, Daisy."

Father Baker patted him on the back and asked, "What's it like to be a hero, Charlie?"

"Embarrassing."

Father Baker laughed and said, "Modesty magnifies the deed tenfold." Then he waved to someone in the crowd and said, "I see Carol Jones over there. I must talk to her about some parish business. Please excuse me." He touched them both affectionately and said, "You two should get to know one another."

Father Baker left, and Daisy smiled and said, "Would you like some coffee, Charlie?"

"Yes."

Daisy poured him a cup of coffee, asked him if he wanted cream or sugar, and then she served him. Every movement she made expressed the simple beauties of life and the cream seemed creamer than cream. After that ritual was completed, they just stood there and stared at each other. It was as if her spirit was passing into his spirit, and his into hers. For Charlie, it was like a holy communion. He had to ask her out, but he couldn't find the courage. He had won the Congressional Medal of Honor, yet this slight almost ethereal girl terrorized his soul.

Finally, he blurted out, "Would you like to go to the movies with me?"

"Yes, I'd love to."

On their first date they went to see the movie, *A Place in the Sun* starring Montgomery Cliff, Shelly Winters, and Elizabeth Taylor. They held hands throughout the movie about a boy from nowhere like Charlie who tried to reach too far for too much and did not appreciate what he had all along, and the movie ended in tragedy. It was a sad story, and Daisy put her head on his shoulder and cried. He put his arm around her, and he knew then that he had finally come home from the war. He was going to marry Daisy and put all the love he was feeling into her and his family. They would be everything to him, and he and Daisy and their children would be secure, safe, and happy.

After that they went to the movies every Saturday. On Sunday they went to church together, and then they would go to the ice cream parlor or take a walk in the gorge. Sometimes they would go on a picnic. It was obvious to Charlie right from the beginning that kissing Daisy and holding hands and dancing very close was as far as he was going to get with Daisy, and he loved and respected her for it.

One particularly hot summer night, he took Daisy to an open-air concert at Stewart Park. They sat under a weeping willow and looked out at the lake that was like a quivering mirror of light and darkness dancing together. In the park, they heard children laughing, and they saw the children's shadowy figures as they raced about chasing after fireflies. The band was playing *Moonlight Serenade* when Charlie proposed to Daisy. Daisy accepted, and they were married a month later by Father Baker, the matchmaker.

Charlie had a whole new future to plan now. He had to do something with his life. Though Uncle Sam would pay for it, he gave up the idea of going to college. For what, Charlie didn't have any idea what he would go to college for, so he decided to take advantage of the loan program for veterans going into business. He borrowed two thousand dollars and bought a truck and the tools and the equipment that he would need to lay down floors. Because of the GI Bill, millions of veterans were taking advantage of the government's home loan guarantee for veterans, and the building and construction business was booming. Charlie had all the work he wanted. He even had someone working for him. In one year, Charlie was able to buy a house and a car. Everything was new in their lives. Daisy got a job working as a secretary at Cornell University, and at the same time, she raised two children and built a home around Charlie full of toys for everyone to play with. It was happy days for him and most of America.

Charlie remembered when they bought their first TV set. He even remembered the first show that they watched. He brought home ice cream for the occasion, and they watched The Milton Berle Show. He even remembered Uncle Miltie dressing up as Carmen Miranda and clowning around on the stage. It was totally silly, but Charlie loved it. His daughter, who was two years old then, spilled her ice cream on the floor, and she began to cry. She was heartbroken. When Charlie tried to soothe her, he remembered the sounds of dying men, and he began to cry too, but they were tears of joy. He was so happy to be where he was surrounded by his family with his child in his arms crying over spilt ice cream.

Charlie set the last tile for the day on the floor at the VFW. The floor was three quarters done, and he felt good. He felt strong. This job had done wonders for him. He cleaned up his workspace, put away his tools and supplies, and went to the bathroom to wash up. He looked into the mirror and thought he looked younger.

When he came out, he went to the bar and sat next to Bob Sumner. "How's the murder case going Bob?"

"We know what the killer looks like. The dumb son-of-a-bitch takes the credit cards he stole from the Van Gorders and goes on a shopping spree. We have pictures of him and an older woman from an ATM money machine. We also have several salesclerks

269

who sold merchandise to them at a department store in Syracuse who can identify them. They used the cards again. How fuckin dumb can you get?"

Bob shouted at the Reverend who was sitting on the other side of the bar talking to Pete Jeff. "I told you that it was a black on white crime."

"How come you only remember when you're right, Bob?" the Reverend asked.

"Are you sure?" Charlie asked.

Bob nodded, "Almost sure."

"Couldn't they have sold the credit cards?"

"Maybe, but the pictures taken at the ATM money machine were taken on the same day as the murders. I think it's them."

"What next?"

"We'll look through mug shots, show the pictures around, and see if anyone recognizes them."

"Have you had any luck yet?"

Bob shook his head and said, "No." There was a pained look on his face.

Charlie saw Daisy come in, and he waved to her. She walked over to where Bob and Charlie were sitting, and she gently ran her hand through Charlie's hair. He had forgotten to comb it when he cleaned up.

"Would you like a drink, Honey?" Charlie asked.

"No, Charlie, my stomach is bothering me. I've had heartburn all day. If you don't mind, dear, I would just as soon go home."

"I don't mind. You don't even have to cook tonight if you don't want to. I'll pick up a six pack and a sub at the Seven Eleven."

Charlie dug into his wallet and pulled out some money and left it on the bar for his drink. He looked at the clock. It was 7:00 PM. He slapped Bob on the back and said, "I hope you catch the bastard, Bob."

"I will."

As Charlie and Daisy were walking to the door, the Reverend shouted, "When are you going to finish the floor, Michelangelo?"

"Tomorrow."

The Reverend looked at the floor and said, "No way."

"I'll bet you a beer."

"You're on."

Charlie and Daisy waved goodnight to everyone and left.

When they got home, Charlie and Daisy went out onto the patio. Charlie ate his meatball sub and drank some beer, Daisy wasn't hungry, and she didn't want anything to drink. She seemed content to look out at the night, the stars, and the fireflies flying all about just like the night he proposed to her. The crickets next to him in the flower bed were making a racket.

Charlie reached out and grabbed Daisy's hand and said, "You're the best thing that ever happened to me, Daisy."

Daisy squeezed Charlie's hand and said. "I love you, Charlie."

"I love you too."

Daisy got up from her chair and kissed him on the forehead. "I'm going to go to bed early tonight, Charlie. Goodnight dear."

"I hope you feel better tomorrow, Sweetheart."

"I'm sure I will."

Daisy entered the house, and Charlie opened another beer. He felt tired. He had worked ten hours today. When he finished the beer, he went into the house and watched television for a while, and then he went to bed.

The next morning, he woke up, turned over and touched his wife's shoulder. She felt cold. Charlie sat up and stared at his wife. Daisy was staring at the ceiling.

"Is there something wrong, Daisy?"

Charlie touched her, and she didn't move. Charlie shook her, and she didn't move.

Daisy was dead.

Charlie just sat there and stared at his wife staring at the ceiling. He sat there for an hour or two, and then he got up. He had to go to work. He had to finish the floor.

Chapter Seven

Bob Summer woke up the next morning on the couch with a terrible hangover. He was still wearing his clothes from the night before, and he had a terrible hangover. One beer and one shower later he felt a little better. He put on his blue suit and tried to button the jacket, but he couldn't. He looked into the mirror. He had always been a good-looking man with blond hair, blue eyes, and even features. He was six feet tall, and in his prime he weighed a hundred ninety pounds. His girlfriends, over the years, often said that he looked like the hero sheriff in a cowboy movie, but now he was thirty pounds overweight, and he looked like shit. He was drinking himself into the toilet, and he didn't care.

Bob heard a vehicle on the gravel road approaching his home, and he looked out the window and saw Doug Fairbanks in his new Ram pickup truck pull into his driveway. Bob opened the door before Doug could ring the doorbell. "You should have called and got clearance before you came. You've broken protocol."

"I did. I called you several times, left messages, but you didn't call me back. We need the rifles and the ammunition for our new members. We've been training them with paint and air guns, but we need to get them on the rifle range with the real thing."

"I hope you are being careful when you recruit these guys."

"Of course, Bob, most of them the members have known for years, and those that we don't know very well, we have passed on to you and Steve, and you guys have been a great help running them through law enforcement data banks. Their all good men, Bob, eager to join The New Minute Men and do their duty.

Bob was the commander for this sector, and he wanted to sound enthusiastic and encouraging, but he was still hungover, so he only managed to say, "Do you have the money?"

Doug handed him a bag from MacDonald's filled with money that could have as easily been filled with Big Macs. Bob didn't bother to count it or even look at it to see if it was there. He just tossed it on the couch. They were brothers in arms.

Bob went to a false wall panel in the living-room. When he re-moved the baseboard, the false panel turned into a sliding door that revealed what once had been a small bedroom but was now filled with military arms, munitions, combat equipment, and supplies. Doug helped Bob carry a crate of M16 rifles and a crate of ammunition to Doug's pickup truck, and when they finished loading them, Doug pounded his chest with a closed fist in an ancient Roman salute and said, "Call to duty."

Bob went back into the house, grabbed his gun and badge off the kitchen table, and picked up the papers from the Van Gorder murder file. They were strewn all over the floor. On the way to the VFW, he reviewed the case. The perpetrators who had murdered the Van Gorder family took their access cards to an ATM and used the cards to draw out six hundred dollars. The camera at the ATM got a shot of a black male accessing Keith VanGorder's bank account. The man was wearing a hooded athletic warm-up jacket and a knit cap pulled down low over his head. His features were blurred, black on black, but judging from the angle of the shot he was probably five feet ten inches tall with a slim build. Bob estimated that he probably weighed around one hundred and fifty to one hundred and sixty pounds.

A few moments later a black woman, who was wearing glasses with thick tinted lenses that veiled her eyes, used Elizabeth Van Gorder's access card and withdrew another three hundred dollars. Again, the picture was not a good one, but she looked much older than the man. She was wearing a quilted winter jacket with a hood, so it was difficult to determine her weight, but her facial features indicated that she was probably thin, maybe one hundred pounds, maybe less, about five feet tall.

The next day, the two suspects did something even more foolish. They drove to the Syracuse Mall and purchased a Panasonic VCR,

275

a Sony 27-inch television, a man's black medium wool sweater, a dress, size small, and two women's sweaters, one medium, one large. They also purchased three pairs of Nike sneakers, the most expensive kind. Bob hated the Nike ad that said, "Just Do It." The attitude was completely amoral. If you feel like mugging someone, just do it. If you feel like murdering a family and raping a fifteen-year-old girl and pissing on her body, just do it.

The salesclerks who waited on the two suspects described the male suspect as black and being somewhere in his twenties. The woman was believed to be in her late forties or early fifties. Their height and weight were approximately what Bob had estimated from the pictures taken at the ATM.

A police artist, working with the salesclerks who waited on the two suspects, drew up some sketches of the suspects. Bob couldn't recognize anyone he knew from the sketches. He flipped open the Van Gorder files. He quickly looked at the sketches again. Nobody had been able to recognize the two suspects from the sketches. The clerks who had waited on them looked through pictures of known offenders, but they could not make a positive ID, not even close. Bob didn't have much faith in composite sketches, but he noticed one thing that was quite curious to him. The man and woman looked alike. They both had high cheek bones, elongated features. They could be related. Could the woman be the killer's mother?

276

Jesus.

Bob pulled into the driveway at the VFW, parked his car, and entered the building. The Reverend was at the bar watching four different TV shows. On one of the channels, the newswoman was speaking Italian, and on another, it sounded like Chinese. Why the hell did he ever buy that satellite dish for him? Bob didn't know if it helped or made things worse for the Reverend, but he seemed to like it, and it calmed him down. However, it drove Bob crazy, and it drove some of the other members nuts too. Charlie was working on the floor.

The Reverend walked behind the bar. "What do you want, Bob?"

"What do I want? I've been drinking the same god damn drink for the last ten years. What the hell do you think I want?"

The Reverend poured Bob a double Jameson whiskey straight up, handed it to him, and said, "Some people change their minds, Bob."

"Yeah, right, and some people can't even make up their minds about what fuckin' TV channel they want to watch."

Bob's hand quivered as he raised the glass to his lips. He downed it in two gulps, and he felt much better. He lit a cigarette and looked over to where Charlie was working. Observing Charlie more closely, Bob realized that Charlie wasn't working. He was just kneeling on one knee staring at the floor. He had a tile in his hand. Bob watched Charlie for a few more moments. Charlie didn't move.

"What's wrong with him?" Bob asked.

"I don't know. He came in a while ago, didn't say hello or anything, started working, but then he just stopped. I thought he was thinking about something. Maybe he's sick."

The Reverend walked out from behind the bar and walked over to where Charlie was kneeling on one knee. He knelt next to Charlie. Bob couldn't hear what they were saying, but then he saw the Reverend put his arm around Charlie's shoulder, and for a moment they both stared down at the torn-up floor and seemed to be praying. The Reverend said a few more words to Charlie then got up and walked over to where Bob was sitting.

"What's wrong?" Bob asked.

"Daisy's dead."

"Oh, Damn, where is she?"

"She's home in bed. She died in her sleep. He's in shock. He thinks that if he finishes the floor everything will be all right."

"I'll call the coroner and get an ambulance over there to pick her up. I'll call Decker's Funeral Home. He's Charlie's cousin, right?"

"Right, I'll stay with him."

Bob made the appropriate calls, and when he got everything

arranged, he came back to the bar. The Reverend had managed to get Charlie to stop working. They were sitting at the bar, and the Reverend was talking to him.

"Charlie," the Reverend said, "Daisy was the last of her kind. Women like Daisy brought love and kindness into our lives. Everything we value in our lives we owe to women like Daisy."

Charlie took a swig of his beer and said, "I don't know if I can go on without her, Reverend. I don't know if I want to."

"Charlie, you have to go on. Your son and your daughter both need you."

"I don't know about that, Reverend. Timmy has Judy to take care of him, and my daughter never calls, and she never comes to see us. She doesn't even want to know me. I'm an embarrassment."

"She'll get over that when she has children of her own, and then she will appreciate how much you loved her and how much you sacrificed for her. And Timmy and Judy, they still need you. In fact, they could come to live with you. They would love that."

Bob whispered into the Reverend's ear, "I have to go to work. I've arranged everything. Can you handle this?"

The Reverend nodded and said, "I'll try to get ahold of his daughter. It's time for her to come home."

Bob left the VFW, got into his car, and drove away. Last night at home, when he was going over the Van Gorder file, he tried to picture the two suspects. He saw them as the kind of poor blacks who never went anywhere. If they lived in New York City, they never left Harlem. If they worked, they probably worked for shit wages and blamed white people for every problem that they ever had. Fuck white people. If you kill one or two or three, and their children too, so what, they got no soul, just do it.

If they moved here from out of town, he thought, they probably moved into the black neighborhood on the south side of the city and never left the block, yet, he was certain that they had been to the Van Gorder house before the crime. They knew the house. They knew the Van Gorders. This was not a random crime. They either worked for the Van Gorders in some capacity or worked for some-one else who worked for the Van Gorders. It would take weeks, but Bob was certain that when he went through the records of can-celed checks that were waiting for him in his office, he would eventually come up with something to tie the suspects to the Van Gorders. He also had another possible lead that he had to follow up on.

They had found the Van Gorder's van abandoned at the East Hill Plaza. Bob was almost certain that whoever did this crime was so dumb that they parked the van somewhere they had been before, somewhere that they were known. Maybe they went shopping at the supermarket after they parked the van, and then they took a bus home. There was a strong possibility that the suspect didn't have a car. There were no tire tracks at the crime scene except from the Van Gorder's cars. They did find some bicycle tracks. Was it possible that the son-of-a-bitch was so poor and hateful that he rode his bicycle out there to kill a whole family?

It was mind boggling to Bob how crazy people are in America today. It seems like some criminals want to get caught. All they want to do is get their names or pictures in the newspapers or see themselves on TV. Their lives are so pathetic that they'll do anything to get noticed, even commit the most horrible crimes.

Bob pulled into the East Hill Plaza parking lot. He went from store to store showing the clerks and managers the ATM bank pictures and composite sketches of the two suspects. An hour later, he still had nothing. He was disappointed, but he was not ready to give up. He had five more places to check out. One of them was Jason's Bowling Alley. He knew if he went to Jason's Bowling Alley that Jason, the owner, would slip a shot of whiskey into his coffee, so he decided to go there first.

Bob walked into the bowling alley. The place was empty except for a few early boozers at the bar. The bowling alley seemed eerie, almost haunted without the sound of squeaking bowling shoes and bowling balls rolling down the alleyway then smashing into bowling pins that went flying in every direction.

Bob entered the dining room. Jason was behind the bar, and his wife Molly was setting the dining room tables for lunch. Jason, who was counting money and putting it in the register, looked up and said, "Bob, how you doing?"

Bob sat down at the bar, "Fine, Jason, do you think I can get a cup a coffee?"

"No problem." He shouted across the room, "Molly, Bob needs a cup of coffee?"

Molly looked up from her work, smiled, waved, and then disappeared into the kitchen. A few moments later she reappeared and placed a cup of coffee in front of Bob. She kissed Bob on the cheek and said, "How are you doing, Sweetie?"

"Just fine, Molly."

Jason came over with a bottle of Jameson's whiskey and poured a shot into the cup of coffee. Bob pretended not to notice it.

"How's the Van Gorder murder case going, Bob," Jason asked.

"That's what I'm doing here, Jason. They parked the Van Gorder's van in the Plaza parking lot, so I thought maybe someone saw them. Maybe they went into a store to buy something. Maybe they've been here before."

Bob showed Jason and Molly the ATM photos and the composite sketches, "Have you ever seen these two or someone, anyone, who looks anything like them?"

282

Jason studied the pictures and the sketches, "No, can't say that I have, Bob."

Molly looked at the pictures and the sketches too, and she shook her head in the negative.

Tom, their son, who worked in the kitchen, put down a tray of glasses that he had just brought into the dining room for his mother. He looked over Bob's shoulder.

"You know," Tom said, "If he had a beard, he might look like Ron Foster."

Jason looked at the picture again, "Jesus, Tom, you might be right."

Bob's heart skipped a beat. "Who's Ron Foster?"

"He worked here a couple of years ago, cleaned up the place in the morning. Worked here for about a year, but he had a beard."

"Jason, give me a pencil," Bob said.

Jason handed Bob a pencil, and Bob handed it to Tom and said, "Give him a beard."

Tom took the pencil and sketched in a beard. Tom studied the picture for a moment then said, "He always wore a baseball cap. Never took it off."

"That's right," Jason said.

Bob took the sketch and the pencil from Tom and drew a baseball cap. He handed the sketch back to Tom.

"Could be," Tom said. "Can't say for sure, but it could be. What do you think, dad?"

Jason shrugged, "Maybe."

Molly nodded her head in agreement.

"So how tall was this guy?" Bob asked. "How much did he weight?"

"He wasn't very big," Tom said. "I'd say about one fifty, maybe one sixty and about five foot eight or nine, maybe five ten, but not much bigger than that."

"Can you tell me anything more about him?"

"He worked for us for about a year," Molly said. "He never said much to anyone. Did a good job, but then one day he quit. Told me he was going back to New York City for a while, said he was going back to school."

Bob put the pictures and the sketches back into the folder. "Do you know where he lived?"

Both Molly and Tom gestured negatively, and Jason said, "It's been a long time, Bob."

Bob got up, "Do you think you might have his address in your records?"

"Maybe," Jason said, "but it's going to take some time to find it."

"That's all right. I need to go down to the station and run this guy through. I'll call you later." Bob smiled broadly, "You three have been a great help."

He nearly ran out the bowling alley, he was so excited. When he arrived at the station, he put Ronald Foster's name into the computer.

Bingo! Ronald Foster had a record. He'd been arrested on one count of robbery, two counts of burglary, two counts of assault, and one count of drug possession. He did some time in a juvenile detention center for assault and robbery when he was fifteen; and a couple of years back, he did one year in Elmira for burglary. He even had a probation officer in town and a local address.

Bob hadn't felt this good in a long time. He'd show the Chief who the best cop was. That dumb bastard had this guy right under his nose, and all he was doing was sending crap to the FBI labs to show everyone what a smart black man he was. Bob would show him. Bob looked at the picture of Ron Foster that had just come off the printer. He was dying to go into John Wright's office and stick the picture of Ron Foster right up the Chief's nose, but Bob decided to wait. He was going to put it all together and then hand it to the Chief at the right time and the right place so that nobody would have any doubts about whose collar this was.

Bob made some phone calls to the stores at the Syracuse Mall where the suspects had charged merchandise. Three of the clerks who had waited on the suspects were on the job. He made arrangements to meet them, left the station, and drove to Syracuse. On the way to the mall he contacted another employee who agreed to meet him at the mall.

Three out of four of the clerks identified Ron Foster. He immediately drove back to Ithaca. On the way, he called Jack Wells, his ex-partner, the only guy in the department that he could trust. Jack had been busted back down to a beat cop by the Chief because he wouldn't kiss his black ass. He replaced Jack with Tom Pickney, alias the Pucker. This was going to be divine justice.

Jack answered his car phone.

"Jack, this is Bob Sumner. When do you get off duty?"

"In another hour, Bob."

"Great, here's what I want you to do. When you get done, pull the file on Ronald Foster off the computer." He gave Jack the file number, and then he gave him Ron Foster's address.

"I want you to stake out the place. Don't tell anybody what you're doing, nobody."

"What's going on Bob?"

"I have the guy who murdered the Van Gorders."

"No shit."

"I have three positive IDs. We're going to make the Chief and The Pucker look like assholes."

"I love it."

"Jack, I want to know if the son-of-a-bitch is home. If he's not home, you wait until he gets home, and then you call me. I want to make the bust today before the Chief can wiggle his fat ass around the case and make it look like he did it all."

"You got it."

Bob drove back to the station. When he got to his office, he uploaded the banking records of the Van Gorder family from his computer. A half an hour later, bingo, there they were, two checks written out to Ronald Foster, and three checks to Beverly Foster. He checked the probation files again. It's his fuckin' mother. He's got 'em.

Bob called Steve Bedosky, the State Police Commander for Tompkins County and told him that he wanted to see him immediately, that it was urgent. Bob drove over to the station and laid out the case to Steve. He knew that Steve would want to be in on what could be one of the biggest arrests of his career. Now Steve owed him, and the pay back was that Bob wanted to play a lead role in the arrest and make the Chief look like a fool. Bob didn't have to tell Steve what he wanted. Steve knew the story. Every cop, one time or another, had been down that road. It was called, fuck me, fuck you.

The phone rang, and Steve picked it up and handed it to Bob. It was Jack.

"Bob, Ron Foster just rode up to the house on a bicycle. I checked it out. The house is a duplex. The mother and grandmother live in the first-floor apartment, and the son lives in the second-floor apartment. They don't seem to have a car."

"He's home," Bob said to Steve. Steve nodded and got on another phone.

"What should I do, Bob?" Jack asked.

"Stay right where you are. If he goes out again don't follow him. Call me and then wait for him to come back. Steve and I are going to the station and lay this out for the Chief. We have a plan, so all we need to do is brief the Chief and get the warrant. We should be there, in force, in about an hour."

When Bob hung up the phone, Steve got up from his desk and said, "Let's go see your Chief." Then he smiled and said, "He's not going to like this, Bob."

"Steve, I went strictly by the book. We have a dangerous criminal located. You've been in on this case from the beginning, and we need the manpower and your special expertise. I was in pursuit, and we're still in pursuit. I didn't have time to go looking for the Chief."

"You didn't have any trouble finding me."

"You were where you belong, in your office working."

Steve laughed and then said, "Come on, Bob, let's get this show on the road."

They drove over to the station. The Chief was in his office, and The Pucker was with him. Bob enjoyed seeing the surprise in the Chief's eyes when he saw Bob walk in his office with Steve Bedosky.

Bob sat down like it was his office, and he was in charge, "I have the murderer in the Van Gorder case."

"What do you mean you have the murderer?" the Chief asked.

Bob opened his file and showed it to the Chief. He showed him Ron Foster's file, the positive identifications by the clerks, and the canceled checks.

The Chief looked up from the file, "Why wasn't I told about this earlier?"

Bob shrugged, "I was in pursuit, and I couldn't find you." Bob knew where the Chief had been all along. He had been at the Rotary Club giving a bullshit speech. The Chief was not about to admit that. Bob was in control. He was the boss now.

"Who is at the suspect's house?" the Chief asked.

"Jack Wells."

"Why the hell is Jack there?" Tom Pickney asked.

Bob smiled at the Pucker and said, "I had to get the man most qualified for the job."

Tom Pinkney's face was bright red. He was about to say something when Steve Bedosky said, "Shouldn't we be getting a warrant, John?"

The Chief reached for the phone, called the judge. When he hung up, he said, "Wallace is amenable, but he wants to see the evidence. This is a high-profile case, and he doesn't want any blowback. Pickney, take what Bob has and get that warrant, and get it fast. We need to act now and be in place."

"Steve, do you have a surveillance team in place?" the Chief asked.

"Yes, the house is on Etna Road across from the fair grounds. It's a rental property, a two-family house. The mother and grandmother live on the first floor, and the son lives on the second floor. One of my officers contacted the owner of the property, and we should be getting the layout of the house at any moment. We have eight men at the scene. Two of them are in a gas and electric utility truck near the front of the house, a couple of men are in the woods behind the house, and there are four men in two cars on standby."

"OK, I need to do the paperwork on this and organize the manpower, and I..." The Chief looked over at Pickney. "What the fuck are you still doing here. Go!" He turned to the rest of the group, "I'll see you all in the meeting room in fifteen minutes."

Fifteen minutes later, the Chief took charge of the meeting. He laid out the plan. It was Bob's plan. The Ithaca police would make the arrest. The State Police were to provide back up. When it looked like the Chief was going to cut Bob out, Steve Bedosky spoke up for Bob. In front of everyone, he gave Bob the credit for putting the case together, and he made it clear that he thought that Bob should be the arresting officer.

The Chief looked around the room. Bob could read his mind. The Chief knew that everyone in the room was aware of the animosity between him and Bob. If he didn't make Bob the arresting officer, his decision would be viewed as being personally motivated and vindictive. Bob watched the Chief eat crow, and he felt like a winner for the first time in long time. When the meeting broke up, Bob was leading the pack, giving orders. This was what I was born to do, he said to himself.

A half an hour later they were in front of the house on Etna Road. The house was a rundown graying old farmhouse with rotten wood siding, peeled paint, and a tar-paper roof. The one-family home had been cut up into two apartments. Ron Foster lived in the upstairs apartment, and his mother and grandmother lived on the ground floor. For Ron Foster, there was only one way in and one way out, the front door. There was no fire escape, and though there was a back door to the downstairs apartment, they had the place surrounded. The Fosters weren't going anywhere. They had them. Bob looked at his watch. Where the hell was the Pucker?

Waiting there, waiting for the action to start, caused Bob to think about Korea again, to the moment he became who he is today. It was two days after Jeff was shot dead that X Corp made its move to break out of Hagaru-ni. Marine, Navy, and Air Force aircraft plastered the Chinese positions. Bob hadn't seen so much air power since Inchon. They blasted the Chinese off the hilltops and back into the mountains, and then they burned down the forest around them. When Bob's battalion once again secured the hills on the east side of the road, there were so many charred and dismembered bodies of Chinese soldiers that one of the Marine's joked that it smelled like a Chinese restaurant gone bad.

In the background, Bob could hear explosions going off at Hagaru-ni. The Marine and Army engineers were blowing up the supplies and equipment that they were leaving behind at the depot. Bob saw Chinese soldiers running through the depot trying to salvage what they could, and they were being blown up too, but they didn't seem to care. Bob realized that, in some ways, the Chinese were probably worse off than the Marines. The Americans controlled the air. The Chinese had to resupply themselves by foot and mostly at night. They had no artillery except for mortar, and though their light quilted uniforms were surprisingly warm, they wore pathetically flimsy sneakers. Bob had found many of them with their feet frozen solid, but they still outnumbered the Americans, and at night or on cloudy days when the airplanes couldn't fly, they continued to attack the American defense lines in large numbers. They kept coming, and Bob kept firing, and it got colder and colder. The temperature was reaching record lows for the region, but Bob didn't care.

He didn't feel anything anymore. He wasn't afraid anymore. He didn't even feel the cold anymore. The cold was his friend, his lover, and the more he embraced it, the stronger he got.

Halfway to Koto-ri they came upon the remains of the Drysdale convoy. When the convoy had attempted to relieve Hagaru-ni, they were attacked and destroyed by the enemy. The road was strewn with twisted wreckage and frozen bodies. Some of the men were frozen in firing positions like statues of ice and snow. Some of the statues perpetuated for eternity the agony of the moment of death. In the abandoned Chinese foxholes up in the hills, they found bits and pieces of Christmas wrappings and discarded boxes that had contained Christmas presents for the troops of the X Corp, presents that had never been delivered. It was only seven days until Christmas.

The rest of the way to Koto-ri was quiet, and when they got to the base, the troops at Koto-ri greeted them with cheers. It was like a party, but Bob preferred to stay up in the hills, alone. Even when he was periodically relieved to go down to the base and get a hot meal and some rest, he didn't leave the hills. After a while, every-one left him alone in his grief. Nobody even seemed to give him orders anymore. He just did his duty day after day and stayed at his post. His job was to kill Chinese, and he was doing it efficiently. An officer who interrogated prisoners told Bob that one prisoner told him that Bob had become a legend to the Chinese. They be-lieved him to be a mogwai, an evil spirit who, if he consumed you, could chain you to the pain of eternal reincarnation.

From the hills, Bob watched army engineers build an airstrip and fly out the wounded. He watched a work crew unload truck after truck filled with the bodies of dead Americans. They were stacked one upon the other and then buried in a mass grave that was plowed over by a bulldozer. In his company, there were only twenty-five men left of the two hundred men that first marched up the Chosen Reservoir on their way to the Yalu River, but the long journey back was nearly at an end. Chinhung-ni was only about twelve miles away, and the Army's 3rd Infantry Division was wait-ing for them there. If they could make it to Chinhung-ni, they were safe and on their way back home to the sea, but the road to Chinhung-ni was steep and treacherous, and three miles outside of Koto-ri, they came to a place where a bridge spanned a two thou-sand feet deep chasm adjacent to the Changjin Power Plant. The bridge had been demolished.

Up in the hills they found hundreds of Chinese soldiers frozen to death in their foxholes. A Chinese soldier, who they captured and interrogated, told them that nearly a battalion of Chinese soldiers had been force-marched across the same wilderness that Bob's battalion had crossed to relieve Martin's Fox/7 at Toktong Pass. Their mission had been to blow up the bridge and intercept the Americans. The night that the Chinese arrived at Fuchilin Pass, the temperatures dropped again to record lows, and most of the Chinese soldiers froze to death in their own sweat. Some of the Chinese soldiers did survive, but barely. The Marines found them in foxholes and bunkers. When Bob came across these soldiers, he shot them without remorse.

Down below on the road, the Marines faced their final challenge. They had to replace the bridge across the thousand-foot drop into nothingness if the X Corp and its fifteen-hundred vehicles and trucks were going to reach Chinhung-ni as a fully equipped fighting force. Bob watched Air Force cargo planes parachute six bridge sections down to the X Corp. One was damaged and another was captured by the Chinese. The word that came up to him through the lines was that the bridge sections were too short, seven feet two inches too short. The gap across the chasm was twenty-nine feet, and the steel-tread-way-bridge was only twenty-two feet from end to end.

295

Bob got curious. He walked down to where they were assembling the bridge. The army engineers were bunched up near the edge of the gorge, and they were talking to a Marine general.

Bob watched the chief engineer point to the other side of the gorge and say, "That ledge over there is almost eight feet below the surface of the road and about ten feet wide. As you can see, General, we've taken hard wood timbers and built an open crib on that ledge all the way up to the level of the road. I think that will do it. If we fill the crib with earth to form a solid base; and we then place the steel-tread-ways on the crib, they will be long enough to cross the gorge and reach the solid roadway on the other side."

"Will it be stable?" the General asked.

"Yes sir, we can place a four-inch-thick plywood sheet between the steel beams. We're going to be fine, sir."

"However, General, we have one problem," another engineer said.

"What's that?" the General asked.

"The dirt to fill the crib, sir, the ground is frozen like a rock. We will have to blast the dirt free with explosives. It will take several days, and we could start a rockslide if we did it anywhere around here."

They all stood silent in the swirling snow and freezing cold groping for an answer. Nobody could come up with a solution, but it was obvious to Bob. There was a Chinese prisoner standing on the road nearby. Bob raised his rifle and fired, hitting the Chinese soldier right in the heart. The Chinese soldier fell back into a mound of snow.

Bob looked the General straight in the eye and said, "Dead weight. You have hundreds of them up in the hills frozen to death." Bob picked up the dead Chinese soldier and threw him in the crib.

"There's your fuckin fill."

Bob walked back up into the hills and came back again and again carrying the frozen bodies of the dead Chinese soldiers over his shoulders like sacks of dirt. He carried each of them to where the engineers had built the timber crib that would form the base and threw them over the edge of the precipice as landfill. With every dead body he threw over the precipice, it became clearer and clearer to him. Death rules here. We all consume each other, and death consumes us all. Our agony is its food, and our tears are its fountain of youth, its immortality. And love, he thought, as he threw another Chinese soldier over the edge into the precipice, love is a pathetic illusion to rationalize our submission to oppression and turn it into a virtue. We glorify self-sacrifice and embrace Death as our lover. Bob was liberated from all of this. He was the ice and the snow. He was the cold. He felt nothing. He was nothing. He was free.

The General watched Bob fascinated by what he was doing. There was a lesson here, and he wanted everyone to see it. Finally, the general said, "I like that soldier's style. Who the hell is that cold son-of-a-bitch?"

Bob heard someone say, "Bob Sumner, sir."

The General looked at one of the engineers and said, "Is that it? Will it work?"

The engineer walked to the precipice and looking over the edge to see what the results of Bob's efforts were, and he then turned to the general and nodded in the affirmative.

"Get to it," the General said, then walked away.

Squads of Marines went up into the hills to collect the dead Chinese soldiers as land fill. Bob watched the engineers span the gap in the road with the steel beams and then put the plywood down. Everything looked like it was going well until a bulldozer slipped off the beam, and its heavy earth pan smashed through the plywood. It looked hopeless. It looked like they never would get the bulldozer off the bridge without moving the steel beam and causing the bridge to tumble into the gorge, but then some Marine engineer climbed onto the bulldozer, and he managed, inch by inch, to get the bulldozer back on the beam and off the bridge without a disaster.

They took the plywood out of the bridge and narrowed the

width of the beams. Now there was no center board to support the smaller vehicles. Now the wide Pershing heavy tanks had only about two inches of surface on either side of the beams to ride on, and the jeeps had only a half inch of surface on the inner edge of the beams. It was going to be a real high wire act. Bob watched for hours as fifteen hundred vehicles inched their way across the chasm. As it got darker, it got more dangerous. The bridge was lit up like a circus tent, and in this bizarre eerie lighting, Bob watched the bio-mechanical monster that they called X Corp crawl to safety on its own steel entrails.

By daylight they were on the other side. The road was open. The rest of the way to Chinhung-ni was easy. When they got to Chinhung-ni, they were put onto trucks and rode the rest of the way to the twin cities of Hamhung and Hungnam where they were put aboard boats. From the boat, Bob could see the engineers blowing up the seaport. Explosions were going off everywhere as they destroyed the docks and everything of value to the enemy. It was Christmas day, and the Marines onboard the ship were singing Christmas carols to the King of Peace. Bob smiled, King of Peace, my ass.

Bob heard a tap on the window. It was Pickney waving the warrant at him. Bob got out of the car, and he moved quickly and decisively. He wasn't a plodder like the Chief. This he wanted everyone to see. All the officers took their positions as Bob, Tom Pickney, a state police detective named Bill Bradley, and a young trooper named Pete Jeff headed for the front door of the house. They were all wearing body armor. The Pucker and Bill were carrying shot guns. Bob had his old Colt revolver, and Pete Jeff was carrying an M-16.

Bob didn't hesitate. He climbed the steps to the porch, opened the entranceway door to a stairway that led to the second-floor apartment. He cautiously but quickly climbed the carpeted steps to the second-floor apartment. The carpet on the steps was old and worn but it muffled the sound of their footsteps. The door to the apartment was made of cheap plywood.

Bob looked back to see if everyone was ready, and then he reached for the doorknob and turned it slowly. The door was locked. Bob stepped back and gave the door a hard kick, and it flew open banging against the wall like a gun shot. He swung his gun to the right to where the living room was located. No one was there. He quickly swung his gun to where the bedroom was supposed to be. The door was open.

Bob had been pursuing a dark image from a bank surveillance camera, a composite sketch, and a police snapshot. The real Ron Foster was sitting on the bed. Next to the bed, propped against the wall, was a cut down twenty-two rifle with a pistol grip and a

300

silencer. Ron Foster was wearing a baseball cap, and he had a baseball glove in his hand. Bob recognized the baseball glove. It was a Rawlings, and it was brand new. It was the Gordon boy's baseball glove, the one his parents had given him for his birthday.

Ron Foster looked up. He smiled. It was a weird smile, Bob thought. It was as if Ron Foster believed that by having the dead boy's baseball glove, he possessed his spirit, and now he was twelve years old, and Bob was his dad. He smiled like he had been a bad boy, but he was so cute that daddy had to forgive him. Bob stared at the boy coldly, and the colder he got the further he went back in time to where it all began.

Bob pulled the trigger, and the back of Ron Foster's head splattered against the wall. The baseball glove flew in the air and landed on the floor. Ron Foster was sprawled out on the bed in a pool of blood. One foot jerked and then he was still.

Bob turned to the three men behind him and said, "He went for his gun."

The young trooper was white as a sheet, and Bill Bradley, the detective from the state trooper station, just shrugged his shoulders and said, "I couldn't see it from where I was."

Bob noticed a trace of a smile on Bill's face. He would support him.

"What the hell are you talking about?" Tom Pickney shouted.

"He never moved." The Pucker looked at the young trooper and said, "Isn't that right? You saw it."

The young trooper was throwing up.

The Pucker turned on Bob and said, "I knew someday you would fuck up big. All I had to do was wait."

Bob sniffed the air and then turned to the detective from the state trooper station and said, "Hey, Bill, I think someone shit their pants. Pucker, you got to tighten up, man. You're losing it."

"You're gone, asshole," The Pucker said, then pushed by Bob and stormed down the stairs.

Bob turned to Bill Bradley and said, "Come on, Bill, let's get this job done."

Bill nodded.

Bob put his hand on the shoulder of the young trooper who was still shaken up. "Come on, son. We'll show you what to do."

Bob and the two troopers went through the apartment. They found the new TV and the VCR that were purchased at the Syracuse mall. Ron was wearing new sneakers. Downstairs in the other apartment, they found the rest of the merchandise that was purchased with the Van Gorder's credit cards. The grandmother was wearing one of the sweaters, and when they tried to take it off her, she screamed that it was her birthday present. The mother was handcuffed and dragged away screaming. The grandmother cried

302

out repeatedly, "Who's going to take care of me?"

Bob went to his car, sat down in the driver's seat, and lit up a cigarette. He shot that kid in cold blood, and he didn't care. He had to do it; he was tired of retreating; he was tired of backing off. Somehow, he knew that it was the last shot he was ever going to get at the enemy, and he had to take it. Bob called the social services and told them that there was an old lady at the house who couldn't take care of herself. He asked them to send someone over to look after her.

Bill Bradley came over to the car and stuck his head in the car window and said, "Your buddy, Tom Pickney, is spilling his guts out to the Police Chief. I'll stick to my story, Bob, but I don't know about the new kid. He's pretty shaken up, and I don't know him well enough to talk to him."

"I understand, Bill. Thanks a lot."

Bill patted Bob on the arm, "That scum bag deserved it."

Bill left, and a few minutes later the Chief came over to the car and said, "I want you to go back to the station and fill out a full report, everything in detail, and I'll see you in my office in two hours."

Bob started the car and said, "Yah, sure, what are you going to do, give me a medal?"

Bob drove to the station, filled out his report, and waited for the

Police Chief.

When the Chief arrived, he called Bob into the office, read through the report, threw it on his desk and said, "This is bullshit, Bob. I have written statements by two officers on the scene saying that the boy did not make a move for his gun, and you shot him in cold blood."

"Whose statements do you have?"

"Tom Pinkney and Pete Jeff."

"They're wrong. The young trooper is inexperienced, and Tom was too busy shitting his pants to see anything."

"I don't think a board of review or a court of law will see it that way."

The Police Chief sat back in his chair and said, "Here are your choices, Bob. You can go into your office right now and fill out a request for early retirement, or I turn this report over to a board of review, and you'll go to trial and probably go to jail on a manslaughter charge."

"You been waiting for this for a long time, haven't you, John?" Bob said.

"No, that's not how this is going down, Bob. The way I see it, I'm giving you a break. I don't have to do this. I could fuck you good, but, despite all our differences, we're both cops here, and I know what it's like to be on the front line. I know what it's like to be that shield."

"Do you?"

"Bob, I know you think you're a better cop than me, and you think that you should have been appointed Police Chief, not me. But I wouldn't have done what you did. Even if the prick was a bigoted, red neck, prejudiced, son-of-a-bitch like you, I wouldn't have shot him in cold blood. I would have done my job."

Bob was pissed now. "You're god-damned right that I think you have my job. And you have the job because you're black. You didn't have the experience nor did you have the record, and you know that's god-damned true, but you took your shot, and I've died a little bit every day because you have the job that belongs to me."

Bob got up from the chair and walked to the door. "So, let me ask you something, Chief. You took your shot with affirmative action, and you killed a good cop. I took my shot and killed a scum bag. Who's the murderer around here, you or me?"

Chapter Eight

The Reverend woke up feeling like he had been hit on the head with a hammer. He stumbled off the couch and staggered into the bathroom. Once again, the bathroom had been painted over and was perfectly white except for a neatly scripted passage written on the wall above the urinals that said,

In Memory of Our Daisy

Daisy was a loving heart who brought life and love to all of us. Her hopes and dreams, her gift to us, is best expressed in her favorite prayer.

Lord, make me a channel of thy peace

That where there is hatred, I may bring peace

That where there is wrong, I may bring the spirit of forgiveness

That where there is discord, I may bring harmony

That where there is doubt, I may bring faith

That where there is despair, I may bring hope

That where there are shadows, I may bring light

That where there is sadness, I may bring joy

Lord grant that I may seek to comfort rather than be comforted

To understand rather than be understood

To love rather than be loved

For it is by self-forgetting that one finds

And it is by dying that one awakens to find Eternal Life

Amen

The Reverend washed, shaved, and changed his clothes. He then waited for Bob to take him to Daisy's memorial service, but Bob didn't show up. The Reverend called him repeatedly, but he didn't answer the phone. He called Leah but there was no answer, and there was no one at the VFW to drive him to the service. He finally realized that he would have to leave the bunker and go out on his own. No matter how much he was horrified by the prospect of going out in the world, he had to do it. He couldn't miss Daisy's funeral. Charlie would never forgive him.

The Reverend walked into the bar-room and turned on the four TVs, the radio, and the jukebox to prepare for the fragmented chaos that lurked outside the bunker; he drank several cups of coffee, downed a shot of whiskey, and ate one doughnut for nourishment. Then he faced the door. This was it. He decided not to take the keys to the VFW with him. Once the door closed behind him, he was locked out. There was no turning back.

The Reverent opened the steel door and stepped outside into the world and closed the door behind him. The lock snapped shut. Immediately he was flooded with stimuli. The world was spinning around him so fast that he was barely able to keep his balance. The air was vibrant with a collage of whirling colors, and his ears were assaulted by the constant growl of traffic. There was a stench in the air of anxiety and despair. He felt unhappiness clinging to him, afraid to be swept away and the chaos of emotions. The Reverend gathered his courage and walked forward, one step at a time, but by the time he reached the street, he was lost.

He had no idea where he was or which way he was going, but he had been in the land of nowhere before. He knew that the only thing to do was to go with the flow and read the signs, so when a sign said, stop, he stopped, and he went the opposite direction. At the next street corner, the light was green. He crossed the street and continued walking on the same path until he came to a red light, and he changed directions again, keeping to the green. He walked two more blocks and then followed the arrow on the one-way street. The people on the street looked like the living dead with their eyes turned inward to avoid what he could see, the world without repression. He wanted to run for shelter, but the buildings around him seemed to be bursting apart, and he felt nature below the concrete sidewalk licking away like a cat licking spilt milk. He heard birds chirping, and he saw jewels of light flashing through the branches of a tree, and he knew it was a sign from God. Follow the light.

He walked toward the light, toward the trees, and when he saw tombstones in the distance, he knew where he was, he was back to where the dead lived. He sat down on a bench next to one of the large tombstones, closed his eyes, and all the sounds and smells of the world around him were swept away by the sound of the whirling blades of a helicopter. He was back in Vietnam, and he was with Rocker.

Rocker was sitting next to him in the helicopter, and they were on their way to Saigon for five days of R&R. When Rocker and Doc landed at the airport outside of Saigon, they took a small blue and white Renault taxicab with a torn canvas top and ripped upholstery into the city. The taxi rattled so much that Doc was worried it wouldn't make it to Saigon. On the way, they passed a refugee camp that was built on top of an Army dump where the refugees had dug tunnels down into the dump as if it were a gold mine.

Soon the ring of shanty towns and shacks that laid siege to Saigon gave way to what was once French colonial Saigon with its tree lined boulevards, parks, and French colonial architecture and Romanesque public buildings built in the grand empire style of France's faded glory. The influence of the Americans' presence was beginning to be felt. The smell of French and Chinese cuisine, the sound of bicycles and birds, and the quiet elegance of French Saigon was giving way to cars, trucks, motor scooters, and gas fumes. Speed and more speed were the American way, and the pace of life was accelerating as more Americans arrived. The sound of rock and roll was drowning out the sound of violins and grand symphonies. The air was electric.

Doc and Rocker checked into the Hotel Majesty, a faded gem from the French colonial era with its ornate and swirling touches of rococo that merged with palm trees and jungle vegetation, marble floors, and peeled paint. Their room had sixteen-foot-high ceilings and French windows that opened out onto a balcony and the sound of the ever-increasing chaos.

Doc stepped out onto the balcony, and from there, he could see the river and Saigon Harbor. Over the rooftops he could even get a glimpse of the countryside and the jungles and the mountains beyond. Vietnam extended some twelve hundred miles from the south China border to the Gulf of Thailand, an area about the size of California. The country was shaped something like two rice baskets hanging on the ends of a bamboo pole, much like the burden the Vietnamese peasants carried on their shoulders day after day. Vietnam was a beautiful country of mountains and plains, deep valleys, lush green fields, and flat treeless grasslands. Almost half the country was jungle, and nearly four-fifths of the land was covered by trees and tropical vegetation. Climatically, it fell between Miami and Panama.

If Doc were a tourist, Vietnam would have been a beautiful and fascinating country to see, but he was a soldier fighting in a war, and Vietnam was a country that was ideal for guerrilla warfare. There were impenetrable forests and inaccessible mountains, a vast river delta of endless rice fields crisscrossed by canals and a spider web of footpaths with safe havens across the border in the jungles of Laos and Cambodia. During the summer monsoon season that lasted from June to December, it was hot as hell and humid, and sometimes it seemed as if it would never stop raining. It was a great place for the American war machine to get stuck in the mud.

Doc and Rocker took a shower and changed into their civilian clothes. Rocker wore a floral Hawaiian beach shirt that he bought in Florida and a pair of khaki pants and brown cordovan shoes. Doc wore a white short-sleeved dress shirt, khaki slacks, and a pair of brown penny loafers like the ones that he wore in high school. They left the hotel, and as they walked up Dong Hoi Street, they walked by department stores filled with American merchandise, massage parlors that were fronts for brothels, French cafes, and black market stands that sold cigarettes, liquor, and hard to find electronic goods. The street was jammed with bicycles, pedal-cabs, motor scooters, trucks, and cars. The blue gray smoke of cheap gas pervaded everything. Two homeless children were asleep next to a trash pile that they had laid claim to, and a woman was washing her clothes in the gutter.

Doc talked Rocker into stopping at an outdoor café where they sat down at a table near the street and ordered food and drink. Sitting back in his chair, relaxed, Doc took a swig of his beer, and listened. He liked to listen to the Vietnamese people talk. Generally, they talked about the same things that we all talk about. At the table to his right, the man and woman were complaining about rising prices. At the table to his left, a woman was complaining to her husband about her mother-in-law, and the toddler next to her was chewing on a paper napkin and throwing food on the floor. The mother said what every mother in the world says in that situation, "I can't take my eyes off of you for a minute."

As he listened to the conversations, Doc watched the young Vietnamese girls strolling down the boulevard. Most of the girls wore graceful, flowing, silk ao dais dresses. Doc thought that most Vietnamese women were quite pretty. They had very fine features and well-proportioned bodies, and they moved gracefully like cats.

Rocker, who was eating a pork and egg bun and drinking a beer, said, "What the hell do you want to sit here for, Doc?"

"We're in a foreign country, Rocker. Don't you want to sit back, relax, and get a feeling for where you're at?"

"I know where I'm at. I'm in a fuckin' country where you have beautiful women walking around with hand grenades stuffed up their cunts dying to sit on my lap."

Rocker stood up and put some money on the table, "Come on. Let's get out of here."

Doc shrugged and got up from the table. If he was going to do any touring of the city, he was going to be doing it alone. Rocker hated Vietnam, and for the most part, he didn't like the Vietnamese people. Rocker graduated from Ohio State with a civil engineering degree, and he probably came to Vietnam thinking that he could fix it.

They walked to *Uncle Sam's*, a bar that the Special Forces and Special Ops guys frequented in Cholon, the Chinatown of Saigon. There were two Nungs tribesmen at the door to provide security for the bar. The Nungs were a Chinese tribe that nobody liked, but they were loyal to their pay, and the Special Forces and Special Ops guys liked to use them as bodyguards. A month ago, a Viet Cong guerrilla had casually walked *by Uncle Sam's* and placed a bomb satchel under one of the tables. Fortunately, one of the Nung tribesmen spotted it. Now, the large open-air windows that looked out into the street were always shuttered, and even in daylight, the bar was dark and brooding with deep shadows and artificial lighting. As an added security precaution against acts of terror, no Vietnamese were allowed in the bar except for the owner, his staff, and the prostitutes and strippers who worked there. The CIA spooks screened the staff. The prostitutes and strippers worked for a high ranking general in the South Vietnamese Army, and the owner of the bar was a black marketer. Nothing was what it should be in *Uncle Sam's*. Even the booze was watered down.

When Doc walked in the door, he heard someone shout his name. It was Bob Sutherland, an old friend. Bob and Doc had come to Vietnam together, and they had both been assigned to a Special Forces unit responsible for setting up strategic hamlets around the Saigon area. Bob was sitting at a table in a corner of the bar with Fred Wyman and Chuck Strickland who were Navy Seals in a Special Ops 35 unit. Special Ops 35 was running missions into North Vietnam, and there were even rumors that they had gone into China.

On the wall, behind the table where Bob was sitting hung a large posture of John Wayne and another of Marilyn Monroe. John Wayne was dressed as a cowboy, and he had a smirk on his face, the one he got when he was about to give the bad guys a lesson in American frontier justice. The posture of Marilyn came from a movie where she played a demented babysitter with voluptuous lips. She was wearing a bathrobe, partially open, exposing her bountiful breasts and the slip underneath. She was Mother Nature in a cheap hotel, and you felt that all she needed was a good man and a child of her own and everything would be all right, but in your heart, you knew you were wrong. You could never satisfy her. Something was wrong. Something was missing, and until you found it, nothing would ever be right again. Both John Wayne and Marilyn Monroe were bathed in the purple, orange, and green light coming from the stage behind the bar where a stripper was dancing with a wooden dildo that was carved to look like a Vietnamese devil with a very big head. Rocker and Doc sat down and joined the three men at the table.

"How're things going on the trail?" Bob asked.

"Hot as hell," Rocker said. "Ever since LBJ started bombing North Vietnam, North Vietnamese Regulars have been pouring down the trail. Shit, it's not even a trail anymore. They're building a fuckin highway. Someday they'll be driving tanks down it."

Chuck Strickland, a big, burly, blond-haired Ivy Leaguer who played college football at Princeton University smiled and said in a low voice, "We had something to do with that."

Bob Sutherland laughed and said, "What did you do, Chuck? Tell LBJ to bomb the bastards? I didn't know you and LBJ were asshole buddies like that."

"I'm serious. We were running an operation in North Vietnam. Our target was a radar station on one of the offshore islands in Tonkin Bay. The operation went very smooth. We blow up the damn thing, but on our way out, who do we run into, the god damn Navy. They decided to run maneuvers in Tonkin Bay while we were running one of our operations. It was one big fuck-up. The North Vietnamese were mad as hell because we blew up one of their radar stations, and they thought that the Navy ships in Tonkin Bay were part of our operation, so they took a shot at the *Maddox*. LBJ gets pissed off and used the incident as an excuse to start bombing North Vietnam, and now we got a hot war with North Vietnam, and it is all because nobody knows what anybody else is doing." Chuck Strickland laughed, "I guess you could say that we just sort of bumped into this war. Sorry."

"How do you know it wasn't a set-up?" Bob asked. "All your operations have to be approved by the Secretary of Defense. The President had to know."

Chuck Strickland thought about it for a moment, "No, I don't think they're that smart. Like I said, maybe after the fact they used the situation as an excuse to do what they wanted to do all along, but they never planned it."

"I don't care who the hell started it or why," Rocker said, "but I got the solution. Bomb the shit out of them and turn this whole fuckin country into a parking lot."

Doc raised his glass, "Here's to good old American know-how."

Chuck Strickland filled everyone's glasses and said, "Forget about the VC and the NVA. Let's not forget the prime objective." Chuck raised his glass, "We're here to get laid."

Everyone raised their glass and drank, and Chuck got up, put some money in the jukebox, and five minutes later he came back to the table with the stripper who had been dancing with the devil dildo and four other prostitutes.

A prostitute named Spring Flower sat on Doc's lap. Spring Flower smelled like orchids, and she had big breasts, which was uncommon for Vietnamese women. She ran her fingers up and down the zipper to his pants and said that she liked him because he spoke such beautiful Vietnamese. Three full glasses of whiskey later he was staggering out the back door into a dark courtyard with Spring Flower. He nearly fell over a pile of garbage, and then he walked into some wet clothes hanging on a clothesline. Spring Flower helped him up a flight of stairs and then led him into a room that was dimly lit. He could hear a baby crying behind a pink screen that partitioned off the room, and he realized why Spring Flower had such big breasts, she was nursing a baby.

"Where are you from?" Doc asked.

"I'm from Ben Cat."

317

Doc knew the area. It was northwest of Saigon, and it had been one of the first areas that his Special Forces unit had tried to pacify. "Why did you leave?"

Little Flower helped Doc off with his pants and said, "My father was a village chief. When the VC came into our village, they accused my father of being a collaborator. They tied him to a pole in the center of the village, and then they gutted him while my mother and I watched them pull out his intestines. He was still alive when they chopped off his head, and then they shot my mother. When the South Vietnamese Army returned, they burned down our village because they said we were harboring the enemy."

Doc was about to ask her another question when she put his cock in her mouth and that ended all talk about the war and the horror that he paid her to forget about. It was back to business, and when she got him good and hard, she straddled him and gave him her breasts to feed on. He sucked on her breasts like a baby, and when he came, he had her milk on his mouth.

Doc fell back on the bed. He was very tired, and he was about to fall asleep when Spring Flower nudged him and gently informed him that if he paid her an additional twenty dollars he could stay for the night. Doc gave her the money and passed out.

When Doc woke up the next morning, Spring Flower was sitting at a table breast feeding her child. Through the window the

318

sunlight poured over her bare breasts. Framed, it was a beautiful portrait of mother and child. The reverend remembered the taste of her milk on his lips, and he felt like a thief.

Spring Flower smiled at him and asked him if he would like tea.

"Yes, thank you."

Doc got up and washed his face in a basin, and all and all he didn't feel that bad. He had some tea with Spring Flower, and when he got up from the table to leave, Spring Flower kissed him on the cheek and said, "You will come back."

"Yes."

"Promise."

Doc smiled, "I promise."

"And I'm your very special girl?"

"Yes, you're my very special girl."

Spring Flower kissed him on the lips. It was a kiss that a woman would give her husband when he went off to work.

Doc went down the stairs to the courtyard and entered *Uncle Sam's* through the back door. He found Rocker sitting at the bar drinking a cup of coffee. Doc slapped Rocker on the back and said, "You look like shit."

"I feel like it. Let's go back to the hotel. I need a bath."

They left *Uncle Sam's* and looked for a cab, but there were none in sight, so they walked in the direction of the hotel. It was early in the morning, and the streets were quiet and peaceful. As they passed a small park, a child's laughter filled the air. He was being chased across the grass by his mother. Doc smiled, but then he saw two Vietnamese teenagers riding a motor scooter, and as they approached, Rocker reached for a forty-five pistol that he had tucked in his waistband. Doc was unarmed. The scooter got closer and closer and then it passed by; the boys were totally unaware of the Americans. Rocker was probably right. You never really get to relax in Vietnam, not even in Saigon. That was the nature of terrorism and guerrilla warfare, that was the strategy, never let your enemy relax, always keep him on edge, wear him down, and then strike. When he turns to fight, run, leaving him only with his anger, his frustration, and his dead.

Doc spotted a blue and white cab, and he waved at the cab driver to stop. Fifteen minutes later Doc and Rocker entered the Majestic Hotel, and when they got to their room, Rocker immediately filled the old porcelain bathtub with water, undressed, and took a bath. When he was done, Doc filled the bathtub back up again and climbed in. He slipped down into the water and rested his head on the back edge of the tub. It felt great.

Doc heard Rocker say, "I've had it with this fuckin' war, Doc. When my DEROS comes up, I'm out of here."

Rocker was on his second tour of duty, and for a while, Doc

thought that Rocker might become a lifer. He was curious. "What are you going to do when you get back home?"

"Maybe I'll go to work with my father. Take over his construction company someday. What the hell, there's nothing wrong with building bridges, right?"

"Nothing wrong with bridges."

"What are you going to do?" Rocker asked.

Doc thought for a moment and said, "I don't know. Maybe I'll finish up at Cornell, go on to graduate school and specialize in linguistics and the philosophy of language. My parents will love that." Doc couldn't decide whether he was joking or not.

"You should do that, Doc. You're a really smart guy." There was a long pause, and then Rocker said, "Doc, have you ever been in love?"

Doc thought about it for a minute, "No, not really."

"I think I want to fall in love before I die. You know I use to make fun of my mom and dad because they were so boring. I think I want to be boring too. I've had enough excitement in my life. I want to be in love, and I want to be boring, and I want to build bridges. What do you think about that, Doc? Do you think a girl would go for a guy like me?"

"Hey Rocker, it's called stability, security, dependability. Girls love that. They go out with exciting guys like we go out with

321

whores, but in the end, they fall in love with stable guys like you, guys who build bridges, guys who want to fall in love and live happily ever after."

There was no response from Rocker. Doc got out of the tub, toweled himself off, brushed his teeth, and shaved. He went into the bedroom to change, and he saw that Rocker was asleep on the bed. Despite the risk of going out alone and wandering around Saigon, Doc decided to do some of the things he wanted to do and see some of the places he wanted to see. Doc looked at his image in the mirror, and he could not help but be frightened by how slight a figure he projected. He wasn't much over five foot ten inches, and he barely weighed in at one hundred and sixty pounds. In fact, with his well-trimmed van Gogh beard, his overgrown crew cut, his oversized head, and his fine English and Scottish features, he looked more like a college professor on safari than a member of a special forces kill team.

He pulled his shirt out and let it hang loose, and as he tucked his forty-five caliber service automatic into his waistband, he posed in front of the mirror like his father had posed for a picture on the jacket cover of one of his books entitled, *Man and Identity, the Sociology of Meaning.* He laughed at the absurdity of it all, and he left his room and the hotel.

Doc casually walked the streets of Saigon like a tourist. He stopped at a café for coffee, and then he bought a book of poetry written in Vietnamese at a bookstand. When he came to a Buddhist temple that interested him, he opened the gate and entered the temple garden. At the center of the garden was a large statue of a sitting Buddha surrounded by bursts of color and cultivated harmony. Doc sat at a stone bench and studied the statue. He wished he could possess the serenity of a Buddha amidst all the war and horror around him. The Buddha's got it right, the Reverend thought. Life's a mud puddle. Splash around in it, and it gets a little muddier. If everyone splashes around in it at the same time, it's a shit storm. Academics call it a historical era. The whole idea is not to move. In the stillness of the Heavenly waters everything is clear.

A Buddhist priest who Doc estimated to be in his seventies sat down next to Doc on the bench. They sat there quietly for a moment, then Doc said in Vietnamese, "It's so peaceful here, Venerable Father. I wish I could stay here forever."

"You can, my son, if you carry the garden with you."

"How do I do that?"

"You will learn."

Doc laughed, "I love your religion. It turns life into a lesson. If you get it, you go on. If you don't, you have to repeat the course."

The priest laughed and said, "What religion are you, son?"

"I'm a Christian of sorts."

323

"Christ achieved Nirvana and Buddha enlightenment, and he taught the way in the simplest of terms. Follow the way of a loving Jesus, and you will follow the way of Buddha."

"If that is so, Venerable Father, why do Buddhists and Catholics in this country hate each other?"

"History, my son, history, before the French came, Vietnam was a Buddhist country made up of common-lands and peasant farmers. When the French took over, they embraced the Catholic minority and made them a privileged class. If you were Vietnamese, you had to be Catholic if you wanted to go to the best schools or if you wanted a good job with the government. In return the Catholics were loyal to their masters. The French also took the land away from the peasants, and they created a landlord class. Now the Americans are here, and nothing has changed. The country is still run by a Catholic minority, a corrupt government, and a landlord class. Everything remains the same. What do you think the lesson is, my son?"

Doc thought for a moment and then said, "You think we're backing the wrong side?"

"I only voice my humble opinion, but I think that if everything remains the same, you will lose the war. Most Buddhists do not want to become Communists, but they do not want to be landless and poor either, nor do they want to be persecuted and discriminated against by the Catholic minority."

The priest stood up, bowed, and said, "I must go now and prepare myself. Tomorrow I graduate. I wish you well in your journey, and I hope you find peace in love."

Doc smiled and said, "Thank you."

He watched the old priest walk away and disappear into the temple. Doc left the garden and returned to the hotel. He woke Rocker up, and they took a cab to *Uncle Sam's* where they went through the same rituals that they had gone through the night before. They bullshitted with their buddies, told war stories, traded information, got drunk, picked up a prostitute, and got laid. Spring Flower made him promise once again that she would be his one and only whore. It was something like going steady.

The next day, Doc was ready to go through the same routine again. He left the hotel early in the morning, walked the streets for a while, and then he went to a museum and looked at Vietnamese art and pottery from different periods of Vietnamese history. Chinese influences were very apparent especially in the pottery. He then looked at a mural depicting the battles of Tran Hung Dao. Tran Hung Dao in the thirteenth century had defeated five hundred thousand Mongol invaders using the same military tactics that the guerrillas were using today.

Walking back to the hotel, Doc came to Le Van Duyet Street, and in the distance, he noticed a crowd of people marching down the street carrying banners. As they came closer, he could see that the procession was made up of hundreds of monks and nuns chanting supplications. A police car was clearing the street for the pro-cession, and at the front of the procession, a gray Citron led the way. The procession stopped, and the marchers formed a circle around the car. Doc watched a young monk get out of the car and place a small brown cushion on the pavement. What he saw next truly surprised Doc. The old Buddhist priest that Doc had talked to in the temple garden got out of the car and sat down on the cushion in a lotus position and began to pray. He was as serene and peaceful as he had been when Doc last saw him in the garden, and he radiated with holiness. Another priest opened the trunk of the car and took out three gasoline cans. The two monks carried the gasoline cans to the center of the circle, and they poured most of the contents over the priest's head and shoulders then stepped back and joined the others who began to chant the sacred words, "Nam mo amita Buddha. Nam mo Amita Buddha," that meant in English, "Return to the eternal Buddha."

Horrified, Doc watched the old priest strike a match and set himself on fire. As the flames engulfed the priest, many of the monks and nuns prostrated themselves before the burning sacrifice while others held back the white-clad police who had rushed to the scene and were trying to rescue the old monk. The flames seemed to roar forever as the old man sat there calmly, hands folded in his lap, without a cry of pain.

Over a loudspeaker Doc could hear a monk say repeatedly. "A Buddhist priest burns himself to death. A Buddhist priest becomes a martyr for you and me. A Buddhist priest sacrifices himself for peace." The sweet stench of human flesh filled the air, and finally the old man fell backward, his charred legs kicked out for several moments and then he was still, enlightenment. Now he knew what the monk meant when he said, "Tomorrow I graduate."

Doc walked the rest of the way back to the hotel in shock. He realized that the old man had told him what he was going to do, but he was too stupid to get the joke. When he got to his room, he found Rocker throwing clothes into his duffel bag. He was wearing his combat fatigues.

"Jesus, Rocker, you won't believe what I just saw. I saw a seventy-year-old Buddhist priest burn himself to death."

"You think that's bad," Rocker said. "I got a phone call when you were gone. They want us back to the base, immediately."

Doc and Rocker packed their gear, checked out, and took a cab to the airport where a helicopter was waiting for them. When they got back to the base, everything was in turmoil. Helicopters were flying in and out of the landing strip stirring up a whirlwind of dust and dirt. It looked like every team on the base was being mobilized.

"I don't like the looks of this, Doc," Rocker said.

"I'm hip."

They entered the command bunker to report for duty. Their commander, Major J. B. Lewis, was with the sector commander, Colonel James Farley. There was a third man with them, a civilian carrying a thirty-eight-caliber revolver in a shoulder holster who Doc knew to be a CIA spook. The three men were looking at a large map spread out on a table.

Major Lewis looked up from the map, saw Doc and Rocker, and said to his adjutant, "Tell Lieutenant Cowen that his unit can stand down. They're back."

"Come over here," he said to Doc and Rocker, and when Doc and Rocker approached the table, the Major pointed to a spot on the map, "Is this where you saw the trucks?"

Rocker studied the map for a moment. It was a map of Laos and the border areas between Laos and Vietnam. He looked more carefully at the spot that the Major was pointing to and said, "Yes sir."

The Major pointed to a spot much further north and said, Intelligence tells us that there's a large truck convoy up here heading south. We want you to go back to where you were two days ago. We believe that the convoy is heading there."

"Why?"

The CIA spook, whose hands were stained with nicotine, made a large circle around the area that Doc and Rocker had been in. "We think there's a large depot down there somewhere, and they're building up for something big. We figure they are going to launch from there."

Major Lewis pointed to the map again. "You've been there once before, so they'll be looking for you. But, if we insert you here," The major pointed to a spot about ten miles from the target zone, "you're far enough away from the road and so deep into Laos that we don't think they'll be looking for you there. It's a hump, but you should be able to penetrate their defenses and reach the target zone by 01200 hours tomorrow."

"When are we leaving?" Rocker asked.

"In one hour, son," Colonel Farley said.

He pointed to the map. "We have two hatchet teams landing here and here as decoys. They will work south, and away from the target. They should draw the NVA to them and clear the way for you. When you get to the target, you report in. If you spot the convoy, two other hatchet teams will be on standby. You will order the teams in, and you will then attack the convoy in coordination with the two hatchet teams. Your goal is to demobilize the convoy and withdraw when it gets dark because we're bringing Puff the Magic Dragon in for a night attack. When Puff is done with them, we're calling in a B-52 strike."

Colonel Farley took a drag off his cigar, stared at the map and said, "Charlie doesn't build a fuckin' highway down the Ho Chi Minh Trail. That's a fuckin' no-no."

The Colonel then smiled and said, "Get this right, and you two are on your way to Thailand and an extended leave."

"Yes sir," Rocker said.

Rocker and Doc were dismissed, and they left the command bunker and walked to where their unit was camped. Happy, Sleepy, and Sneezy and the new Grumpy were ready to go. Doc put on his gray fatigues, and he loaded his rucksack down with ammunition. He attached four ammunition pouches to his pistol belt, and he grabbed eight grenades and attached four to his sack and four to his Stabo harness. He then attached two canteens of water to his sack. Water and candy bars were all that he would bring with him to eat and drink. They weren't going to be dining out on this mission. This was an all-out assault, and they had to be ready for a sustained fire fight. Doc grabbed a LAW rocket launcher and attached that to his sack. The LAW was light and portable, and he could throw it away after he fired it.

Doc looked around. Everyone was loading up with fire power. They were throwing a whole SOG unit at the enemy today, and they were just the prelude. After them came Puff and the B-52s.

Uncle Sam wasn't fucking around.

Doc looked at the new Grumpy and laughed. Grumpy not only had his usual AK47, but he also had a LAW and a M76 grenade launcher attached to his pack. "Jesus, Grumpy," Doc said, "You can't carry all that."

Rocker stopped stuffing his pack, looked at Grumpy, and said, "Doc's right. You can't lug all that shit. You have so many grenades on, you look like a fuckin' Christmas tree. Get rid of some of those grenades and just carry the launcher, forget about the LAW. Give it to Doc. He can carry two, they're small."

Rocker Took the LAW from Grumpy and handed Doc the one-shoot, two-foot-long fiberglass bazookas that weighed only five pounds. It was one hell of a throw-away. Rocker then checked everyone's pack. Satisfied, he told the team to saddle up. The helicopters were waiting. A half hour later they were given the go signal, and they were airborne.

Happy shouted over the sound of the helicopter, "What's a B-52?"

"You've never seen one?" Doc said.

"No."

"They're the biggest, nastiest, killer birds in the sky. They fly way above the clouds up there, and they carry forty-eight thousand pounds of explosives each. They'll probably be traveling in threes,

331

and you won't see them coming until it's too late."

"Forty-eight thousand pounds of explosives, how much is that?" Happy asked.

"That's just about all the shit in the world. And we don't want to be anywhere around when those big birds take a dump."

A half hour later they reached the landing zone. The helicopter hovered over the landing site using the wash from the helicopter blades to separate the elephant grass. Doc and Rocker looked for any signs of danger. When they were reasonably certain that the ground was safe, they signaled the pilot to touch down, but even then, when they hit ground, they moved cautiously through the grass looking for mines, booby traps, and any signs of the enemy. At any moment they expected to be fired on from the jungle bordering the landing site. The helicopter gun ship that accompanied them hovered nearby to give them cover if they needed to withdraw.

When they reached the edge of the jungle, they waited and listened...nothing.

Rocker took the microphone for the Puck 25 radio that Happy was carrying, and he ordered the helicopters to leave. The team moved out slowly and cautiously, stopping every fifteen minutes to listen. They remained perfectly still for five minutes, then moved out again. On and on they went, starting and stopping, repeating

332

over and over again the cycle of movement and stillness. It was a painful pace. The jungle was like a furnace, but they kept on humping, scanning the jungle for anything out of the ordinary. It took most of the day, but they were nearing the target site.

Suddenly, Sneezy, who was walking point, froze in his tracks. Everyone ducked for cover. Sneezy didn't move. He just stood there. Doc, who was fifteen yards behind Sneezy, cautiously moved up to a position a couple of yards behind Sneezy. They were standing at the edge of a clearing in the jungle where the leaves and branches of the giant trees formed a vaulted ceiling. Bands of light crisscrossed the floor of the jungle like in a cathedral, and on the floor of the cathedral were the bones of what seemed to be prehistoric animals, huge fossils, maybe dinosaurs, but then Doc realized that it was an elephant graveyard.

Doc walked up to Sneezy who broke their code of silence and said, "This is bad luck."

Doc didn't say anything. He just stared. There had to be at least ten to fifteen skeletons huddled together in what seemed to Doc to be an almost human grief, a need even in death to be among your own, not alone.

The other Dwarfs had come up to look. They were frightened. Rocker motioned for them to go forward and spread out.

They all refused to move.

In sign language Doc said, "Let's get out of here, Sneezy. We're exposing ourselves."

"Not through there," he said.

"OK, not through there. We'll go around, but let's go. This place gives me the creeps too."

Sneezy nodded, and he led them around the graveyard. A half an hour later they found a foot bridge built six inches under the water line of a large stream, and further on they found some steps built into the rocks along the edge of a ravine. They had found a branch of the trail, but they were still quite a distance from the road, and it was getting dark, so they began to look for a campsite for the night. They would complete the trip in the morning when they were rested.

They found a good camp site on a rise near the trail. It was protected by some boulders and had good cover, but they followed their usual routine, and they didn't stop there. They continued on to another site, set up camp, and then when it got dark, they quietly moved back to the spot near the trail. Doc was so exhausted that he immediately went to sleep.

Doc woke up when he felt a hand over his mouth.

It was Happy. He could see him in the vague light of a waning moon that barely seeped through the jungle ceiling. Happy put his fingers in front of Doc's face, and in sign language, he told him that they had company. Doc quietly followed Happy to the clump of boulders at the edge of their camp site overlooking the trail. The Dwarfs and Rocker were there. Doc looked down onto the trail, and at first, he couldn't see anything. However, when his eyes got used to the dark, he saw what looked like fireflies dancing through the jungle. It took him a moment to realize that he was looking at a procession of VC or NVA soldiers walking down the trail. The light came from little lanterns that they were carrying in the palms of their hands. The lanterns were little glass containers filled with gasoline that had a spring feed wick. The enemy used the leaf from a plant to protect their hands; and, at the same time, it acted as a shield to direct the light. Doc could make out silhouettes of men. He could even see flashes of their faces as they marched silently by, barely making a sound. They were about thirty to forty yards away. Normally, they would follow them, and in the morning call in the hatchet teams or an air attack, but not tonight. They had their mission.

When the last man passed, Doc asked, "How many?"

"It looks like a company, maybe two hundred," Rocker said. "They're heading south."

"Or they're after the decoy teams, and they could be coming back," Doc said.

"Maybe."

Nobody got any sleep for the rest of the night, and when morning came, they moved out even more cautiously than they had previously. They were nearing the target, and for every five minutes that they were on the move they stopped for five minutes and listened. Doc smiled to himself. The Buddha is right. If you stay sill long enough and listen, even an insect has footsteps.

It was a snail's pace, but they finally reached their target, and they were on time. Doc could see and hear the trucks now, and as they moved along the road, he counted at least twenty to thirty trucks down there. Doc watched them drive to the end of the road, unload their cargo, and then turn around and head back north. The CIA intelligence was right, for once. Rocker got on the Puck 25 radio and called in the hatchet teams. They would attack the convoy from both ends, and Doc's team would attack the middle. The idea was to jam up the convoy and make them sitting ducks for Puff the Magic Dragon and the B-52s.

Doc's team situated themselves at a point above the road where they could get a clean shot at the convoy.

They waited.

Forty-five minutes later the hatchet teams Cobra and Cougar made contact. They were in position at both ends of the convoy. Cobra was to the north, and the Cougar team was to the south. The primary responsibility of the Cougar team was to keep the main body of the NVA pinned down at the end of the road where they were all busy unloading the trucks. They would commence their attack when they heard Rocker fire.

Rocker pointed to two trucks idling side by side, one facing north and the other facing south. He whispered to Doc, "I'll get the one on the far side. You get the one on the near side."

Rocker motioned for the Dwarfs to spread out. Grumpy and Sneezy, who also had grenade launchers, would team up with Rocker to form what was essentially an artillery unit. Doc, once he fired the two LAWs he was carrying, would coordinate the teams and join with Happy and Sleepy to provide infantry fire support.

Rocker loaded his M76 grenade launcher. Watching Rocker fire a M76 grenade launcher was like watching a pro quarterback throw a touchdown pass. Doc called him the Johnny Unitas of SOG. He was that good.

Doc took out the LAW rocket launcher, extended the tube to thirty-five-inches, flipped open the plastic sight, and turned to Rocker and said, "OK, Johnny U, let's see what you got."

Rocker aimed and pulled the trigger. The grenade spiraled like a looping pass and dropped into the open window of the truck. When the truck exploded, Doc fired, and the second truck blew into a hundred pieces. The air turned into a collage of human and non-human body parts, splattered blood, and rice. Then all hell broke loose. The hatchet teams opened up, and the fire fight had begun. Rocker threw another pass through a narrow margin between the limbs of two trees. The grenade landed in the back of a truck, and the truck must have been full of ammunition because it exploded in a huge burst of flame.

Doc fired the second rocket launcher. The second rocket was five feet off the target and went through the canvas back of the truck he was aiming at and exploded harmlessly in the jungle. Doc threw the launcher away and shouted, "Fuckin' toy-makers." He grabbed the Swedish K that was hanging from his shoulder and ordered the teams to attack. They ran out of the jungle and onto the road tossing hand grenades into the waiting vehicles and firing at anything that moved. From the middle of the road, using a wreaked truck for cover, Rocker launched his last four grenades at two trucks that had managed to get themselves stuck crossways of the road. Both trucks exploded, and the wreckage of the burning trucks blocked the road completely. Another truck attempted to turn around and flipped over, and as the NVA solders spilled out of the trucks, Happy fired at them unmercifully. Doc shot the driver of one of the trucks when he tried to escape.

"Let's go! Let's go!" he heard Rocker shout.

The team continued to move down the road dropping hand grenades into the backs of trucks and firing almost aimlessly as they tried to create a wall of fire around themselves, but Sleepy got hit in the leg and fell to the ground. Doc ran to his side. He could see that the bullet had gone completely through his left thigh. It had torn a nice piece of flesh off, but it didn't look like it had hit an artery.

Doc quickly dressed the wound, and when he tried to help Sleepy up, Sleepy said, "I'm okay, Doc," and he stood up on his own.

Doc looked at his watch, and then he climbed up onto one of the wrecked trucks to get a better look at the battlefield. The wreckage of trucks and their cargo was strewn all over the road. There were fires everywhere, and the NVA were working frantically to clear the road and remove the cargo to a safe place in anticipation of an air strike. They weren't stupid. They knew the score. They knew the SOG units were only the tip of the spear.

Doc looked at his watch again. Time was running out. They were losing the advantage of surprise and the fear and the confusion that they had created. He shouted at Rocker, "It's time to get the fuck out of here!" He frantically pointed at his watch.

Rocker looked at his watch; he looked at Sleepy; and then he looked at the NVA closing in. "All right, let's move out. Give the word, Doc."

Doc got on the phone and ordered the other units to move out, and then he and his team quickly moved through the jungle. The idea was to get as far away from the enemy as possible and then let the jungle envelop them. They needed to get separation between themselves and the enemy and the target zone, but they only got fifty yards when a burst of machine gun fire spun Happy around. He was hit with another burst of fire before he went down. Doc and the rest of the team took cover. They were facing heavy small arms fire, but they couldn't call for help. Doc saw that both Happy and the radio were dead.

Rocker motioned for the team to pull back. They would try to slip to the left. When they pulled back, however, they were hit by gunfire from the rear. They tried to slip to the right, but they encountered more gunfire. They were surrounded.

Rocker knelt down next to Doc and said, "It's almost dark. I think we can slip by them then, but we have to do it before 0900. If we're here when Puff arrives, we'll have to walk through fuckin' hell to get out of here."

Doc nodded in agreement. Puff the Magic Dragon was a converted C-130 cargo ship. Outwardly, it looked big, slow, and harmless, but the AC-130 carried fourteen men, 7000 pounds of armor plate, several tons of ammunition, two 40mm automatic cannons, two 7.62mm and two 20 mm Gatling guns, a flare launcher, a 1.5 million candle power searchlight, and infrared sensors that reacted to radiated heat from truck engines, campfires, and even collections of human bodies. Doc had seen Puff's work before. Puffs maximized their effect by executing a pylon turn. In a pylon turn, the wings of the plane remained at the same angle to a point on the ground as if it were tied to the spot. Guns mounted on the side, perpendicular to the fuselage fired at the same point through-out the turn. Slowly they would walk the spot up and down the target line destroying and killing everything within the circle of fire. Puff was a monster.

Doc's team dug in and waited. The NVA seemed satisfied with keeping them pinned down. Maybe they thought that the Americans would call off the air strike if they knew their own men were still trapped in the firing zone. Maybe they thought they could trap the other units if they tried to rescue Doc's team, but Doc was certain that the Cobra and Cougar teams were gone. The Hammer team was stranded, surrounded, and on the menu.

When darkness came, they moved out. They were each on their own now. There was no way that they could keep track of one another in the dark. It was decided that if they got through the enemy lines, they would meet at the elephant graveyard, and from there, they would walk home together.

Doc moved out very slowly feeling his way each step, each inch. His hands and feet were like antennas feeling every contour. He moved through the foliage without making a sound, feeling the ground for the smallest twig that could give him away. He listened. He couldn't hear anything, but he could smell the enemy. It was the smell of rice and rice farts and rice sweat and sleeping in the same clothes for days on end. The smell was getting closer and closer. Soon, he could smell them all around him. Then he stopped dead. He heard a man breathing. He couldn't be more than five feet away from him.

A flare went off.

For a moment, everything lit up in the gray blue light. Doc shot the NVA soldier to his right at point blank range. To his left he saw Rocker, and ahead of Rocker and to his right were Grumpy and Sleepy. The NVA were all around them, and everyone was firing in every direction. It was bedlam. Their team moved to form a circle. Back to back they stood firing at the enemy. The darkness enveloped them again and then the only light was the tracers acting like strobe lights turning everyone into flickering images of death. Doc saw Grumpy get shot. He saw the agony of pain and fear on his face before he was swallowed up by the dark. Then the lights went on again, but this time it wasn't a flare.

The Dragon had arrived, and the rain of fire began. Doc estimated that Puff was working its way up the target line from the end of the road. It was about a couple of hundred yards away and getting closer and closer. It was almost like daylight now. He could see the fear on the faces of the NVA soldiers around him. They knew what was happening too. Everyone started running. They were all running for their lives, away from the highway. It was like a forest fire where predators and prey run together.

When the Dragon caught up to them, they were trapped in a blaze of light like they were on stage. Bullets and cannon fire rained down churning the earth up like water in a storm. Doc saw Rocker get torn to pieces, his body cut up into ground beef. Doc tried to reach out for him but only got a piece of meat. Then Doc saw a tree uprooted by cannon fire flip up into the air. It landed on top of him, and he was tangled in the branches. He tried to get loose, but then he realized that the trunk of the tree was giving him some protection against the bullets that were reducing the tree to saw-dust, so he remained still as the Dragon moved on, and it got dark again except for the fires that the Dragon left in its wake.

Most of the fires were on the highway where the focus of the attack had been, but there were fires here and there in the jungle causing what was left of the jungle to flicker like a black and white movie that revealed a blood red graveyard. In the flickering light of the burning trees and the burning trucks, Doc saw that everyone around him was dead, and the jungle became one beast with millions of teeth, eyes, fangs, and leaves like giant hands dragging him into its consuming nightmare. He heard the mashing and grinding of teeth, the sound of life eating life, the screams in the night. He watched a tiger with flaming eyes drag the body of a North Vietnamese soldier into the maw of the jungle, and he could even feel his own body devouring itself.

He was afraid to move. Petrified, he waited until sunrise to untangled himself from the branches of the fallen tree, and now that he could see where he was going, he was ready to move out. It was then that he heard the sequence of explosions. They were coming closer and closer and growing louder and louder, a giant drum beating out the rhythms of death. It became so loud that his ear drums popped, and he could only feel the earth trembling under his feet.

The B-52s were here! He had forgotten about the B fuckin 52s.

Doc fell to his knees. He couldn't take it anymore. He was crying and praying to Jesus to save him when in a flash of light, he saw Jesus Christ pointing to his heart. Doc was weightless, flying through the air. The whole world seemed to be upside down when it landed on him, and everything went dark again.

When Doc woke up, he realized that he had been buried alive. He clawed at the dirt and stone and bone, struggling for air until he finally saw some light. He clawed frantically, crying and kicking like a newborn baby coming out of his mother's womb. Finally, he was free. He stood up gasping for air, and all around him the earth looked like a moonscape, huge craters everywhere, and everything pulverized to dust.

Doc realized that like Lazarus he had raised from the dead, and before him, amidst the desolation and the horror, he saw the light that is Jesus. At that moment Jesus spoke to him, and the Reverend marveled at the infinitely profound simplicity of it all. With a single word Jesus had revealed the ultimate truth behind the mysteries and given us the key to the Gates of Heaven. Jesus was showing him the way out of all of this, and the way was quite simple to follow. Wherever we find love, we find Jesus, and wherever we find Jesus, we find love. There it was, with that single word, Jesus had led us to the core of the universe, and all the labyrinth of lies and confusion disappeared. It was so clear to Doc now. Every father is a Joseph, every mother is a Mary, and every son is a Jesus. We are all the children of God, and love is the eternal light that will bring us all together.

Following the light, Doc walked away from the moonscape and back into the jungle. He walked on for hours and hours. He collapsed and then woke up again and continued to walk never taking his eye off the light, the path ahead of him. He walked through rain and blistering heat. All around him he heard the biting and the chewing, bones between teeth, the sound of flesh being ground into pulp and swallowed with delight, but he continued to walk through the darkness unafraid, following the light of his new mission, repeating to himself over and over again, "Even though I walk through the valley of the shadow of death, I will fear no evil, for you are with me, my shepherd and my rod."

At one point in his journey, he passed through a clearing in the jungle where he could see the heavens and the stars, and he knew that he was seeing his mind, and it came to him that each and every one of us possesses the universe inside of us in its entirety, much like each cell in our bodies carries within it the whole of our DNA. We, each of us, are a fragment of a star long gone, but if we follow the path of Jesus and the path of absolute and eternal love, we will evolve far beyond the human condition, and we will become Gods who will give birth to a new sun.

Five days later, Doc stumbled into a village on the South Vietnamese side of the border. He was nearly dead, and the villagers turned him over to a South Vietnamese Marine unit that was passing through their village. The commander looked at the emblem sewn to Doc's shirt sleeve. It was an emblem of a skull with blood dripping from its mouth. The commander recognized it as the SOG insignia, so he called in a helicopter that flew Doc to a SOG base where he was treated for exposure and shock.

Two weeks later, Doc was standing at attention in front of

Colonel Farley who was sitting at his desk. The Colonel was looking over a report describing the battle fought by Doc's unit and the two hatchet teams on the Ho Chi Minh Trail.

The Colonel put the report down. "You're a hero, son. You blew the hell out of that convoy and left them dead in the water. The Dragon and the B-52s did the rest."

"I was only doing my duty, sir."

"What you did, son, was far beyond the call of duty. It was downright heroic."

Colonel Farley shook his head in frustration and said, "It's just a shame that no one can know what you boys did in Laos. Under normal conditions, I would be recommending you for a Congressional Medal of Honor, and I would be recommending Rocker for one to be awarded posthumously, but..." The Colonel smiled weakly. "You don't exist."

"No sir."

"Well then, sergeant, are you ready to go back to work?"

"No sir, I feel I have a new mission now, sir. I would like to be transferred to the chaplain's office. I want to help my comrades see the light as I have seen it. I want them to know that there is salvation in Jesus."

"Yes, I know. Major Lewis talked to me about your wishes."

The Colonel stared at Doc. For a moment his face expressed

sadness, but then he said, "When does your tour of duty end, son?"

"Two months, six days," Doc looked at his watch, "four hours and thirty-two seconds, sir, but I plan to re-up."

"Well, let's see how you feel two months from now. I'll transfer you to the chaplain's office. When it comes time for you to reenlist, we'll talk this over again."

Doc was dismissed, and he was transferred to the chaplain's office two days later. At the chaplain's office he was put in charge of caring for the dead. He put his heart and soul into the job. So many of the dead young men were not whole, and it was a full-time job sorting out their parts. Often the parts were all mixed up with someone else's parts. In one instance, some poor boy had the wrong head. He knew it was the wrong head because the boy's body was black, and his head was white.

Doc, who was now called, The Reverend, had to sort through all the body bags. Finally, he found the poor boy's head, but then he had to go look for the poor white boy's body. He found that too. Often, he had to go to the site of the battle and look for parts. He felt that it was the least he could do for the families at home, and he kind of thought that maybe the Vietnamese were right. Maybe if a man was not buried whole, he would never join the spirit world of his ancestors, and he would never go home. He thought of Rocker out there somewhere in Laos. He had been reduced to dust, and now he was being reduced to millions and millions of particles and atoms spinning around in space. Somewhere in that sub-particle world, Rocker was a part of the universe. The Reverend prayed for Rocker. He prayed for the Dwarfs. He prayed that the good Lord in his mercy would gather them up and deliver them intact to their ancestors. When Doc's tour of duty ended, the Army denied his request to reenlist, and he was discharged and sent home.

When the Reverend came home, he tried to figure out what was going on in America, what this youth rebellion was all about. He participated in the teach-ins and sit-ins. He went to the happenings and the love-ins. When he saw the kids burn the flag, he was appalled by the act. It was childish, but it was far more childish and tragic to beat and shoot your own children for demonstrating against the war.

The kids were right. That war should never have been fought. He agreed with the old Buddhist monk who he watched burn himself to death in protest. We fought on the wrong side. We never should have backed the landlords. Now in America, the horror behind the illusions was seeping through. There would be no affirmation of our way of life in victory, nor would we cleanse ourselves of the enemy's blood by knowing that we fought in a righteous war. America, like him, was falling apart.

The only hope he saw for America was with the children of the

60s. In their innocence they were a powerful life force filling in the fissures and fault lines of American politics and cultural life with the promise of a new era of love and the rebirth of American democracy. To the Reverend, they were the quantum force within the spirit of the human mystery creating a world of infinite possibilities with love at its core. Civil rights, women's rights, the care of Mother Nature, the belief in one another and in political and economic democracy were just a few words for the same word - love.

The Reverend went to Washington D.C. to protest the Vietnam War. Washington that day was an impressionistic painting, a patchwork of colors that turned into sailboats playing on the Potomac River. The mirror-like-surface of the river reflected the perfectly blue sky, tree lined parks, and magnolias in full bloom, a beautiful setting for the Imperial style of Rome, the columns, the architraves, the pediments, and the marble men.

That day, amid all the Masonic Magic, one million Americans stood as one, and for a moment the Reverend understood what was meant by "We the People" because at that moment, he felt what it would be like to be of one heart, one mind, and one vision. We were we, a vision of what we could be, but then it was gone, destroyed by everything that was wrong about us.

The Reverend went home to his parent's house and locked himself in his room for days on end. To his mother he was a major inconvenience and an embarrassment. To his father he was a thoughtless son who should have died in Vietnam a hero rather than come home a mental cripple.

One night he was eating dinner with his parents. The dining room was furnished in Danish modern, very tasteful and understated, a lot of expensive wood and muted colors. His mother had cooked a French dish from a recipe in *Food and Wine Magazine*. She had her best china and silverware out on the table. The Reverend wondered what the occasion was.

"How do you like the meal, Willie?" his mother asked.

"Very good, Mom, I like fish."

His father, who was picking at his food, looked up from his plate and said, "When are you going back to school, son?"

"I don't want to go back to school."

"Why not?"

"I don't believe in the power of reason anymore, Dad. It's a false God."

"Oh yes, I forgot. You believe in Jesus."

His father looked like he was trying to control his temper. His voice remained controlled, "Then why don't you take the job with the United Nations as an interpreter. At least you will be working."

"I can't do that, Dad."

"Why not?"

351

"I'd go mad listening to people from all over the world talk nonsense in twenty different languages."

"What do you want to do then?"

"I don't know. I feel kind of lost, Dad."

The Reverend's father sighed and said in a resigned voice, "Jimmy, your mother and I have been talking, and we feel it would be best for you if you went off on your own. Then maybe you could find what the hell it is that you want to do with your life. To the point, it's too painful for us to watch you waste your life away, and we would like you to leave our home and go find somewhere else to live. We'll help you with your rent, etcetera until you get on your feet."

The Reverend was deeply hurt. He was being throwing out of his home. He looked to his mother for support, but she merely said, "I think it's for the best, son. If you would only go for psychiatric counseling, we might reconsider."

"Oh, Mom, I need to find a way to serve God, I don't need a psychiatrist. All a psychiatrist will do is try to convince me to sit comfortably on a pile of shit and call it normal."

His father slammed down his fork, "I'm so tired of your excuses, and you talking like a fool with all this religious rubbish. I never thought a son of mine could be so stupid. I'll be glad when you're gone. At least then I will get some work done. There's been no peace around here since you came home."

The Reverend had tears in his eyes when he said, "It seems to me that you're a bigger fool than me. You hide behind your childish paradigms because you're afraid to know the truth. What a joke you are. There is a mystery to the human spirit that you can't rationalize or explain. Thank God for that. If you want evidence for this, all you need to do is look at this so-called family, and you will see a prime example of the abject failure of your so-called social sciences and your belief that we can rationalize human behavior. We're all mad around here, and why? Because what is missing here is something that you can't quantify and, therefore, in your vain and narcissistic mind, does not exist – love."

The Reverend stood up from the table. He stood tall and erect as if he were at attention and said, "You're a coward, sir, both intellectually and spiritually."

His father turned red and shouted, "Get out of my house, you ingrate!"

The Reverend turned away and went upstairs to his room. He threw some of his things in a rucksack and left the house. He didn't know where to go. He only had three dollars in his pocket, but he knew that he could go to the VFW post, and they would probably take him in, at least for a night. When he got to the post, someone introduced him to Bob Sumner, the Commandant. Bob bought him one drink and then another and another. When the Reverend told Bob his story and explained to him that he had nowhere to go and that he was homeless, Bob offered him a job cleaning up the place, appointed him post chaplain, bought him another drink, got him drunk, and led him to a couch in the back room. He passed out, and fifteen years later, he was still at the post, and he was crying.

The Reverend wiped the tears from his eyes and looked around to see if anyone was watching him. He realized that he was in Dewitt Park, and what he thought was a tombstone wasn't a tombstone at all. It was a memorial to the men who died in the Vietnam War. He had to get out of here. He wasn't dead.

He walked to the corner where there was a public telephone booth, and he called Bob, who was at the VFW. When Bob came to the phone, the Reverend said, "You have to come get me."

"Where are you?" Bob asked.

"I'm at Dewitt Park. Where the hell were you? You were supposed to pick me up."

"I got held up."

"Well, you got to come and get me. I'm lost."

"Where did you say you were?"

"Dewitt Park."

Bob laughed and said, "What an asshole. I should leave you there."

"No, Bob, please, in the name of God, help me. I can't go on."

"All right, I'll be there in fifteen minutes."

"Thank you and God bless you my son."

"Fuck you and your god. And no more paint. The fumes are fucking up your brain." Bob hung up.

Chapter Nine

The Reverend waited near the entranceway to Dewitt Park for Bob Sumner to pick him up. Even the buildings around him looked like tombs, tombs with windows, stories upon stories of dead lives.

Bob pulled up to the curb and parked his car. The Reverend was about to get in when Bob said, "What the hell are you doing? The church is across the street." Bob pointed to St. John's Episcopal Church.

"Jesus, why didn't you tell me?"

Bob locked the car, "What for, you'd get lost crossing the street."

The Reverend knew that Bob was right. He wouldn't have made it. He never should have left the bunker alone. It was a mistake. Now nothing would ever be the same.

The Reverend could see that Bob was in a foul mood, so he tried to make conversation. "So, what's happening with the Van Gorder murder case?"

"I got him."

"Who was it?"

"Some stupid scum bag, black, just like I said."

"Well, I guess it just goes to show you that nobody can be wrong all the time."

When they got to the intersection, the light was red. St. John's Church with its needle point spire was across the street. The Reverend stood at the curb and waited.

"Go." Bob said.

The Reverend looked at him in horror, "The light is red."

"I know. Go."

"How can you tell me to do this? You're a cop. You're supposed to uphold the law."

"I resigned today. Now get your ass moving."

Fearfully, the Reverend crossed the street. When he reached the other side, he realized what Bob had said. "What do you mean, you resigned?"

Bob walked up the church stairs. "I don't want to talk about it."

They entered the church, and the Reverend saw Daisy's coffin just below the church altar in the center aisle. The light poured through the stained-glass windows like it did in the elephant grave-yard. In the front pews the Reverend saw Timmy sitting on one side of Charlie, and his daughter with her husband and two chil-dren were sitting on the other side of him. Timmy and Charlie's daughter were both hugging Charlie and resting their heads on his shoulders. Daisy's death had brought them all together and that vision brought tears to the Reverend's eyes. He was pleased to see that quite a few people were at the service, friends from work and church and many VFW members who loved Daisy and were here to support Charlie. The priest stood in front of Daisy's coffin with Christ on the Cross in the background. In his eulogy, the priest said that Daisy was a wonderful woman who brought love and tenderness to her family. She was a woman who sacrificed her own happiness for others and yet never lost her love of life.

Looking at Charlie and his family, the Reverend was touched by their love of each other, and how Daisy and Charlie had made the love of one another and their family the centerpiece of their life. To the Reverend they were everyday heroes with humble expectations and a quiet strength and courage that transcended anything the Reverend had ever done. The Reverend was ashamed of himself. He was a coward who was hiding and afraid to come out and face his responsibilities. He spent more time drinking than caring for the souls of his brothers and sisters. He had lost his way, and what had once been the bright radiant light of Jesus and a vision of redemption for us all was now just a dim light ahead on a very lonely road that was getting darker and darker.

"Oh, God, help me. Give me the strength and courage and the vision to see the way," he prayed. The Reverend continued to pray asking God to give him the strength and courage to follow the path of love. When the service was over Bob drove him to the cemetery, and at the cemetery Bob and the Reverend stood behind Charlie to give him support, but he didn't seem to need it. Charlie handled his grief bravely. He even managed to smile from time to time and be courteous and kind to everyone who approached him, and when Daisy was in the ground, he went about the business of thanking everyone individually for coming to the funeral. It was as if he was comforting others for his loss. Even Charlie's daughter was kindly and affectionate. She told her father that he was welcome to move in with them. The Reverend marveled at how death brought people together in a conspiracy of the living. They were all so happy to be alive.

After the burial Bob and the Reverend took Charlie in hand. Being alcoholics, they knew what Charlie needed. He needed a drink, so they put him in Bob's car and drove him to the VFW. When they arrived, the women had already put food out for the mourners. The Reverend went to one of the tables and dished out some food for Charlie, and then he went behind the bar to help with the serving of drinks to the many mourners that were pouring into the post. He was happy to be behind the bar. He didn't want to play chaplain tonight.

Later the country western band arrived, and the bar and dance floor filled up with the regular Friday night crowd. At one point the band was playing a sad song by Tony Arata, and the vocalist was singing about how "He was glad he didn't know the way things would turn out, the way it all would go. Our lives are better left to chance. I could have missed the pain, but I'd have missed the last dance"

The Reverend could see tears well up in Charlie's eyes, so he walked out from behind the bar and went to the bandstand. When the song was over, he motioned to the band leader to come over to where he was standing. "Listen, Pete," the Reverend said, "We have a guy here tonight who just buried his wife, and so do you think you could skip the tear jerkers tonight. You know what I mean, songs like 'sometimes there's heartache and teardrops will fall.' Shit like that."

Pete nodded and said, "Sure, Reverend."

"Thanks."

The Reverend went back to the bar, and the next song he heard was upbeat. He checked out Charlie. He was playing shuffleboard with Dan, Melinda, and Jake Peters. Bob, however, was sullen and sitting at the end of the bar sucking down doubles. Every time the Reverend tried to talk to Bob, Bob ignored him and stared angrily at the crowd.

Fuck 'em, the Reverend thought, I've given myself up enough

today. Its time I wallowed in my own problems. The Reverend was looking for someone to relieve him at the bar when he heard a commotion at the entranceway to the VFW, and he saw what seemed to be a retinue of people entering the post that included photographers, TV camera men, and the mayor himself. Amid the retinue was Pat Buchanan who was running for President of the United States.

Buchanan was one of the Olympian Gods of TV and Washington, and the membership was awed by his presence. It seemed like he had just walked out of the TV into their lives. He radiated with the reflective light of the millions upon millions of TV viewers who had given themselves up to the image a man who had become the lode stone of the mass mind and the conservative right.

When Pat Buchanan reached the stage, he took the microphone in hand and said, "I'm Pat Buchanan, and I'm running for President."

The membership broke out into a vigorous applause that went on and on. They knew who Pat Buchanan was. He was one of them.

"I thought it was important to come here tonight to make it clear what I stand for. I stand for you, the forgotten majority of working-class Americans and the men who have fought for our country and have done their duty.

"Fact, over 85% of all the wealth in this country is owned by 20% of the population.

"Fact, over 85% of all incomes earned and all increases in income and wealth have gone to the top 20% of the population, and the rest of you, the American people, are two pay checks away from bankruptcy.

"Fact, since the 1970s the American middle class had steadily shrunk, and you are now working more hours for less pay than you did twenty years ago, and you are doing this without any hope of a pension and a secure retirement.

"Fact, today, in America, we have the lowest level of economic mobility of any developed country in the world, and for most of us the American Dream is dead, and more importantly, it is dead for our children, and we are mad as Hell!"

The crowd roared in approval, and someone in the crowd shouted, "You're god damned right we are!"

"The New World Order of the Left has cast aside the old traditional values of Christian capitalism, hard work, and self-reliance, and they have replaced it with socialist policies that encourage dependence on government and weaken capitalism and our Judeo-Christian moral values.

"Today we see the deformed and diseased socialist vision of gay rights, feminism, globalism, and the abandonment of the American nation-state spreading through our government, the media, and academia like a cancerous growth. It has created a propaganda machine that has infected our children and our society with false news, degenerate values, queer studies, and the elimination of the study of Western Civilization because, according to them, it is ethno-centric and race specific. They call this nonsense, multi-culturalism, but it is in fact a concerted effort by the globalist of the New World Order to undermine and weaken the nation-state and bring about the fragmentation and Balkanization of America.

"This poison has not only affected our colleges. Today, in many of our schools our children are being robbed of their conscience. Their minds are being poisoned against their Judeo-Christian heritage, against American heroes, against American history, and against the values of faith, family, and country. Eternal truths that have not changed from the Old Testament to the New Testament have been expelled from our public schools, and our children are being indoctrinated into moral relativism and anti-white propaganda and prejudice.

"On a global scale, we have seen, repeatedly, global institutions like the World Trade Organization, the International Monetary Fund, and the World Bank serve the interests of global corporations and international financial institutions at the expense of the American people and the world community. We have seen the World

Trade Organization usurp our sovereign power as a nation; and, behind closed doors, negate American law as being in hindrance of "free trade," "free trade" being a euphemism for open borders, the exporting of American industries and factories, and the unfair competition of slave and child labor with American labor.

"Yes, we are capitalist, but we are Christian capitalist, and our capitalism is moored in Judeo-Christian values and ethics. The capitalism of the left is crony/state capitalism, a monstrous mutation of the worse elements of socialism and capitalism, the sort of state capitalism that we see emerging in Russia and China.

"In foreign policy the New World Order of the Left is reenacting every folly that brought the great powers of Russia, Germany, and Japan to ruin. From assertions of global hegemony, to imperial overreach, to trumpeting new crusades, and starting wars over weapons of destruction that do not exist, we are reenacting the kind of policies and commitments that produced the greatest disasters of the 20th century. As a matter of fact, imperial intervention creates terror. Sanctions create terror. Minding our own business and pursuing an America first foreign policy does not. If I am elected, I will promise you this.

Number one, we will not fight wars to protect global corporate interests. Under my administration, your sons and daughters will no die to make the world safe for McDonald. This I promise."

The listeners burst into applause.

"Number two, we will pursue an America First foreign policy. Number three, we are going to reindustrialize America and pursue a fair-trade policy, not a free trade policy. When necessary we will institute tariffs to protect American labor and industry from slave and child labor and unfair trade practices. We will punish corporations that believe they can abandon the country that built them, subsidized them, and built the infrastructure and educational system that supported them. We will treat them for what they are, traitors."

Cheers from the crowd and shouts of "America First."

"Number four, we will put an end to open borders by putting a 10-year moratorium on legal immigration. We will expel all illegal immigrants with some humanitarian exceptions. We will end all welfare benefits to illegal aliens except for emergency services. We will crack down on businesses that knowingly and chronically employ illegal aliens. We will legislate a federal law that denies automatic citizenship to "anchor babies" born to illegal aliens. We will eliminate dual citizenship and deport all aliens convicted of a felony and every gang member who is not a citizen. And, finally, we will build a 2000-mile double line security fence between the United States and Mexico."

Cheers and chants of "Build that Wall."

"The goal of our border policy is to get our sovereignty back and protect our workers and that includes Hispanic and African American workers that aspire to ascend into the middle, upper middle, and upper class, into the tech industries and into the higher end jobs and careers. We don't care about gender, ethnicity, or race. This is what the Democrats are all about when they try to divide us through identity and special interest politics. What we care about is securing the rights and freedoms of all Americans and that includes white Americans.

"I don't know if you noticed it or not, but the Democrats are waging a war against white America. We hear repeatedly about dead white men and the soon-to-be-dead white majority in America. It is about time that we reminded everyone who refers to dead white men with such contempt that it was dead white men who created this country and made it great. It was dead white men that created the vision of America as the Promised Land. It was dead white men who pioneered this country, forged its factories and industries, and created the means by which we enjoy the comforts, the freedoms, and the opportunities that we have today. It was white men who created the richest country in the world and the greatest empire the world has ever seen."

Buchanan pauses for the applause to subside, "We have always been at the frontier of Western Civilization leading the way through one wilderness after another into the future, and we have been at the frontier of race and gender relations. There is no other country in the world that has advanced race and gender relations and the rights and freedoms of minorities and women the way we have anywhere else in the world. We have a long ways to go on our way to a more perfect union, but to reject the legacy passed on from one generation to another, to spit in the face of the men who fought for us and died for us and not recognize the bounty that we have inherited, dishonors us all and is the call for revolution."

The audience exploded into applause and cheers then chants, "America First, Build the Wall, White People Matter Too." The Reverend wanted to shout out, "Say Hail," but he restrained himself.

When the chants died down, Pat Buchanan said, "I'm told by my aids that we have to fly to Buffalo tonight so that I can be at a rally there tomorrow, but we do have a few minutes for questions."

Bill Becker raised his hand, and when he was acknowledged by Buchanan, he asked, "What are your views on abortion and gay rights?"

"A society that accepts the killing of a third of its babies as women's 'emancipation,' a society that considers homosexual marriages to be social progress, that hands out contraceptives to 13-year old girls in junior high, that society ought to be seeking out a

367

confessional, better yet, an exorcist, or, in other terms, that society is sick and needs its head examined because that society is imploding upon itself and is eating and killing its own children.

"In fact, if you threw into this witch's brew of abortion and homosexuality the fact that population growth is exploding in the Third World whereas white American and European population are declining, what we are seeing is the Death of the West because history has proven when a nation's population dies, the civilization dies along with it. No nation has ever survived without an ethnic majority and a vibrant cultural core. I believe that if this massive immigrant into our country and the birth rates as projected continue, young Americans will spend their golden years in a Third World America, a nation reduced to a conglomeration of people with nothing in common except the scrapes of a once great civilization to fight over."

There was a silence that enveloped the room. It was the silence of wordless fear, loss of hope, and confusion over what was happening to them. They wanted a target, something to aim at, and Buchanan was giving it to them.

Buchanan acknowledged Ray Yublonski who asked, "Mr. Buchanan, what is your position on affirmative action?"

"Affirmative action is reverse discrimination. We must put an end to the Welfare State and reestablish equal treatment under the law for everyone including white working-class America. Untold trillions have been spent since the 60s on welfare, food stamps, rent supplements, Section 8 housing, Pell grants, student loans, legal services, Medicaid, Earned Income Tax Credits, and poverty programs designed to bring the African American community into the mainstream, and where are we today?

"Claims and accusations of racism and demands for more continue at an accelerated rate, and the corporate welfare state and liberal media cater to all the claims and demands, whether they are true or not or just and fair. They do this to keep the African American community dependent on the Democratic Party, and for African Americans, it's a sucker's game. African Americans need to break the chains that bind them to the Democratic Party and join with us to reindustrialize America and create once again a thriving national economy with borders and good paying jobs for everyone. Otherwise, if they continue to pursue and embrace identity politics and the villainization of white America, then this debate is not about equality and fairness, this is about power and war by other means where we have turned the electoral process into a battle field between irreconcilable armies of voters. This is a dark road I pray we do not go down, otherwise..."

Bob raised his hand and he was acknowledged by Buchanan. Bob had a smile on his face. He was ready to fill in the blanks. "Mr.

Buchanan, where do you stand on our right as citizens to bear arms? Do you support the NRA?"

"Yes, I believe that the stipulation in the Constitution that we as citizens have the right to bear arms is not about hunting and not about personal home security. It is about what Thomas Jefferson believed, it is about the right of the American people to defend themselves against a government that threatens their rights and liberties.

"One of the ways tyrants and kings and dictators stay in power is that they keep guns out of the hands of the people. We may have been peasants at one time, defenseless against the king's armored men, but we are not peasants now, and we have the right as free citizens to bear arms in defense of the American republic."

The audience broke out in applause, and when they quieted down, Brad Gilbert raised his hand and was recognized by Buchanan, "Mr. Buchanan, you have in previous speeches and tonight alluded to our right as American citizens to revolt against our own government if it threats our rights and freedoms. I know I feel threatened. I know that many of the people I know, good people, feel threatened. I agree with what you have said that the very meaning of America is being threatened by what you call The New World Order and that Wall Street and Washington have sold us out. My question is what I think many of us are wondering. Is the time now?"

Buchanan paused for a moment. The room was perfectly silent in anticipation of the answer, "Your concerns are real. We are on the verge of a war about what is right or wrong and what is worth fighting and dying for, but I don't think the time is now. We are not sufficiently organized, and I am hopeful that we can take back our country peacefully.

"But, if this country continues to allow itself to be swallowed up by open border immigration, multi-culturalism, and the globalists who have taken control of our government, our economy, the media, and our schools, … And, if that time comes when we feel we have no recourse because we are faced with a fake democracy and a hopelessly corrupted and decadent government in which we have no voice,…And, as you say, 'the very meaning of America is at stake,… Yes, I do see a time in the not so far future where a leader will emerge who will call on us to bear arms in the defense of the American Republic and March on Washington. God forbid, I hope we never come to that, but we must be prepared and eternally vigilant in the defense of our freedoms."

The audience gave Buchanan a continued ovation and shouts of "Give Them Hell, Pat."

When Buchanan finally made it through the crowd and exited the VFW, the night continued as it had before. It was as if a storm had just passed and life went on as usual, except, at the end of the night, everyone joined hands and sang along with the band. Some of them lit matches and others held their Bic lighters over their head, and they sang,

If tomorrow all the things were gone
I'd worked for all my life,
And I had to start again
With just my children and my wife.
I'd thank my lucky stars to be livin' here today,
Cause the flag still stands for freedom
And they can't take that away
And I'm proud to be an American
Where at least I know I'm free.
And I won't forget the men who died,
Who gave that right to me.
And I'd gladly stand up next to you and defend her still today.
'Cause there ain't no doubt I love this land,
God bless the USA.

After the song the band packed up, and the Reverend swept everyone out of the VFW except for Bob and Charlie. Charlie was sitting at the bar, and Bob was behind the bar cashing out the registers. They were both very drunk.

When the Reverend sat down next to Charlie, Charlie asked the Reverend, "What do you think about Buchanan? Are you going to vote for him?"

The Reverend paused for a moment to consider the question and then said, "Charlie, you ever seen those photo-art portraits where the person's face is half-light and half-darkness? Well, that is Pat Buchanan to me. On the light side, he seems brilliant. I agree with his economic analysis of America today and that in the so-called New World Order of global capitalism, the vast majority of Americans end up being screwed. I'm against globalism in the form it is taking today. This is not the global village. It is much as he describes it, parasitic. I also believe, as he does, that we need to reindustrialize America and impose protective tariffs when necessary to protect key and strategic industries and American workers again unfair trade practices and child and slave labor.

"I love this country, and I see myself as a patriot. In that sense you could say that I am a nationalist, and I think, if we embrace our better selves, our best days are ahead of us, but when Buchanan starts talking about how we can cure the body politic of the ills that plague us and threaten our very existence, that is when I feel Buchanan goes over to the dark side, and I feel like he has taken me back to the Dark Ages where blood suckers were prescribed as a cure for everything.

"He believes, that genetically, African Americans are intellectually inferior, and he cites culturally biased IQ tests and scientists like Herrstein and Shockley whose studies have been denounced as "scientific racism." He believes that women are inferior and

373

constitutionally unable to compete with men in the fiercely competitive world of capitalism and remain women. He attacks the corporate state and corporate global feudalism as an aberration of traditional capitalism. He says that traditional capitalism is rooted in Judeo-Christian ethics and morals. It seems to me that Judeo-Christian Capitalism is an oxymoron, and you would be more likely to see a camel walk through the eye of a needle than you would find anything Christian about the history of capitalism in America. Good God, the man believes that Jesus Christ, the God of Love, is punishing gay people with the plague of AIDS as divine retribution for their crimes against nature. He claims to be a Catholic, but one wonders if he has ever read the New Testament. He claims to love his country, but there is no love in his message, only bitterness and hate.

"Basically, the man is a fascist and a white supremacist that has lowered the bar for who is white and who is not. Back in the 20s and 30s when eugenics was fashionable it was Anglo-Saxon and the Germanic races that were superior in America, but now he has included all of Europe, like Wops and Polacks and even Micks like him who by their own assessment were considered the Niggers of Europe.

"Worse yet, he is anti-democratic, and he warns us against idolizing and romanticizing democracy as a process, and he even suggested tonight that under certain circumstances like in Ancient Rome and Nazi Germany, a dictator or an imperial president may need to be elected by the people or rise up through force of arms to save our country in its time of crisis. This is stone cold fascism."

Bob, while he was cashing out the registers, was listening to Charlie and the Reverend, and he was getting more and more annoyed as he listened to the Reverend go on and on about Pat Buchanan. When he was done working, Bob poured himself another drink and came around the bar and sat next to Charlie and the Reverend and said, "You two are such pussies. America has never been a democracy. It's a republic, and it's not even that anymore. America is what all you hypercritical bleeding-heart liberals refuse to admit it is because you would have to admit that you are all a bunch of losers.

"America from its very beginning has been about winners and loser, competition, and the survival of the fittest. That hard and demanding tradition has made us the greatest empire the world has ever seen and the richest country in the world. That was the America that made us great, but that is not the America today. The New World Order as Buchanan calls it is turning losers into winners and winners into losers; it is turning men into women and women into men, and black into white and white into black.

"Buchanan is right," Bob snapped. "White males in this country are being attacked on all fronts, and if we don't fight back, we will end up losers. Let me put it to you two morons in another way so that you might understand the facts of life minus all the bullshit and myths about democracy and equality. There are only fuckers and fuckies in this world. The fuckies are not really looking for "justice" or "equality" or "freedom." These feel-good words are the psychological weapons mothers, women, and women-like-men use to disarm us. Make no mistake. What the fuckies really want is to become the fuckers."

"You're wrong, Bob," Charlie said. "That is not what I fought for."

"Jesus, Charlie," the Reverend said, "don't tell Bob he's wrong. Bob is never wrong. Isn't that right, Bob?"

"Fuck you, Reverend. At least I have the courage to stand up for what I believe. I'm not a coward like you hiding down here afraid to go out. Look at you. At one time you were one of the most highly skilled killers in the American army, a true warrior. Christ, you deserved a Silver Star more than I did, but now look at you. Out of displaced guilt, you talk like a fuckin woman."

"Wait a minute, Bob," the Reverend said. I'm not the one who gets off fucking the people below him in the ass while he gets off at the same time taking it in the ass from his superiors. What do you porkers call it, the chain of command with the biggest porker on top? Come on, admit it, you're a sadomasochistic prick, and the only reason you won't take it in the ass from the Chief is because you're a prejudiced little whore."

Bob stood up. He was furious. He jabbed his finger into the Reverend's chest and said, "I'm not carrying you anymore, you little fagot. I want you out of here tomorrow, and I don't care what happens to you. You're fired!"

It looked like Bob was about to punch the Reverend when Charlie grabbed Bob's arm and said, "Hold it, Bob. There's no call for this."

Bob pulled his arm away, "Fuck you too, you dumb son-of-a-bitch. You're as big a loser as he is. Who's going to support you now that your wife is dead? Maybe you can move in with your daughter or, better yet, you can move in with that retarded son of yours, and then you both can be on welfare and live happily ever after at the taxpayers' expense."

"Don't you call my son retarded!"

"He's a fuckin' retard, and they should have put him away the day he was born. There are too many handicapped people in this country. Pretty soon, they're going to put a god-damned wheelchair up on the American flag."

Charlie flashed back to when Dick was murdered, beaten to death in the hobo camp. He saw him curled up like he was in his mother's womb, his head bashed in. Charlie was red with rage when he said, "You know, Bob, I've always wondered who the people were who were causing so much pain and suffering for so many people. I knew it wasn't women or blacks or poor people. But now I know. It's people like you, Bob. You're a cold, mean-minded man, and you're no damned good." Charlie paused for a moment, and then said, "And I'm going to do something that I should have done a long time ago." Charlie walked away and stormed out the door.

The Reverend went behind the bar, opened the cooler and pulled out another bottle of beer for himself and then poured Bob another shot of whiskey. "Jesus, Bob, why did you say those things to him? What's wrong with you? We were only kidding around. He's..."

The reverend saw Charlie come through the door. He saw the shotgun. Bob saw it too and reached for his police revolver that was in his side holster. They both shot at the same time. The shotgun blast blew Bob off his stool, and Charlie was knocked on his back and was sprawled out on the floor.

The Reverend rushed out from behind the bar. He first checked Bob and then knelt next to Charlie. They were both dead, shot in the heart. In the background all four TVs were signing off amidst pictures of the American flag superimposed over soldiers marching. There were pictures of America the Beautiful, the Lincoln Memorial, and Mount Rushmore. The national anthem played in the background, and when it was all done, all that the Reverend could hear was white noise as he raised his arms and hands in supplication and cried out, "Oh God in Heaven, what have we done to deserve this?"

Epilogue

T hat was then, and this is now. From the news on the cell phones, the Reverend and Leah learned that the fighting at the Capitol Building and the National Mall had spread to other parts of the Capital, and the fighting had become so fierce between the President's followers and the counter-demonstrators that the President had declared martial law, suspended Congress, and called in the Army to quell the fighting. At some point in the confrontation, the Army turned its guns on the counterdemonstrators and fired on them, and that turned out to be the go-ahead for the President's supporters to fire at will. Now the battle has begun in earnest.

There were conflicting views in the news media as to what happened to initiate the Army's response or who initiated the fighting. Some news sources claimed that black clad anarchists, who were a part of the counterdemonstration, started the fire fight by throwing Molotov cocktails at the tanks. They also reported that there was small arms fire coming from the crowd of demonstrators. To support their statement, they showed a video of a soldier being shot, other soldiers taking cover, and a tank ablaze. Other news sources reported that agent provocateurs had initiated the violence to justify the Army opening fire, and that was the plan along. Whoever or what started it, the pictures and videos on the Internet portrayed it for what is was, a bloodbath, and the battle still raged.

The sound of the battle echoed through the cemetery, and the Reverend heard all the madness that had mutated from war to war, the war cries, the ghosts of swords clashing, war horses charging, volley upon volley of musket fire, machine guns spraying death in broad strokes of red, fighter planes and bombers raining down destruction, fire everywhere, tank threads crushing all before them, buildings crumbling, everyday hopes and dreams crushed into dust amidst the terror. Men were crying out for their mothers, their wives, their lovers, their God, anyone in their final moment before they died on the battlefield alone. It was all coming together in this final moment of madness where we have become a joke, a caricature of all that is wrong with us, a reflection of a demented President who is pregnant with his own self-image, giving birth to the death of the American Republic.

"So, this is it?" the Reverend shouted at his two friends. "After centuries of fighting wars and battles in defense of this country, after all the lives sacrificed, we end up fighting and killing each other? For what? The Boss? Millions of men died in the Second

World War, and now we embrace fascism? The Reverend shook his head in despair. We are at the dead-end of the Labyrinth. The Minotaur is here."

Leah squeezed his hand and said, "It's time to go, Papa Bear."

Leah and the Reverend were now married. The got married soon after the Reverend left the VFW and joined the International Red Cross as a first responder and paramedic. Because of his language skills, combat experience, and medical training the Red Cross sent him all over the world wherever there was a crisis or a violent flare up that involved casualties and killing.

Leah joined him on his missions, and she taught the little ones wherever they went. She also provided backup for him as a paramedic and first responder when she felt he was in real danger. Quite simply, they loved each other; but, more important, they liked each other. They liked being with each other and doing things together. They had two children, Caleb, who was named after the Reverend's grandfather; and Tisha, who was named after Leah's mother. Caleb was working on a master's in environmental studies and public administration, and Tisha was in her first year of medical school. Leah realized that they could die here today, but they had been called to duty, and so they entered the valley of darkness where the battle raged.

As they approached the Capitol Building and the National Mall, the Reverend remembered when he came here to demonstrate for peace during the Vietnam war, and he marveled at the magic of the Masonic temple-makers who designed Washington. It was a beautiful summer day, and the Washington Monument pierced the sky, a sacred mass of masonry that thrusted upwards into a needle point to mark the spot where America became an astral gateway to the stars, the navel of freedom. The Capitol Building with its columns and wings and majestic dome hid the mysteries of the universe in its stone from the masses so that it could play on their subconscious and conjure up images of divine magnificence and power. I upon I, individual pillars working together in harmony and balance carried the burden of time, defying gravity as they rose, symbolic of each generation, tier upon tier, time curving in upon itself into a dome, a globe, a point where a simple heartbeat can hold up the universe.

He remembered what he felt then, when we were we, when we were of one heart, one mind, one people. We should have listened to the children. Leah is right. They're closer to God.

Looking at Washington DC now, however, it was painfully obvious that the Masonic spell has been broken. The Capitol Building had been hit by cannon fire and many of the columns had collapsed and the dome was sagging. There were fires everywhere, trees were ablaze, cars were overturned, windows shattered by gun fire, and the dead and wounded were strewn everywhere.

There was a lull in the battle. Everyone seemed stunned by what had just happened, and it was at this moment that the Reverend and Leah, wearing their Red Cross helmets and arm bands walked between the two opposing forces weaving their way through the dead and dying and the wounded. Wherever they found someone who was wounded, they cared for them; wherever they found someone dying, they comforted them; and wherever they found someone dead, they planted a small American flag. The message was this, that no matter which side this person fought on, they were all Americans who died here.

For the first time since he rose from the dead in Vietnam, the Reverend felt like he was once again walking in the footsteps of Jesus. He looked at Leah, and she was radiant, and he felt like he was on the path to eternity. It was as if he didn't have a body anymore, that in-between each atom in his body was an infinite amount of space, and he was a constellation of stars all leading to Bethlehem.

No one fired on them. The rage on both sides had been spent, and now everyone was looking at the aftermath of what they had done, and there was shame in the air. Many from both sides began to come out to help Leah and the Reverend including doctors, nurses, and medics from the Army's ranks. Large numbers of the combatants were withdrawing from the horror that they created.

One young man, who was a veteran and had taken up the President's call to march on Washington, was fatally injured. The Reverend and Leah were kneeling beside him in a way that was reminiscent of Christmas and the manger scene of Joseph and Mary knelling beside the newborn Jesus, but this young man, that was barely more than a child, was dying.

The young man looked up at the Reverend and Leah and asked, "Did we win?"

The Reverend shook his head sadly and said, "No one won here today, son, but you played your role well and bravely in a tragedy. Rest in peace."

The End

www.ingramcontent.com/pod-product-compliance
Lightning Source LLC
Chambersburg PA
CBHW060150260626
47160CB00001B/199